He would make life so difficult for Gordy, the cop would have no time to investigate…

The man walked to his pickup, lowered the tailgate, and signaled for the dogs to jump in. They did and continued panting nervously in anticipation. Teddy closed the gate and climbed into the cab behind the wheel.

"Okay, fellas," he said through the cab rear window. "Let's go and have some fun."

He drove slowly over to Gordy Powell's place, and by the time he pulled into the woods by the pond it was nearly midnight. He turned the headlights off and inched the truck into the brush as far as he could without leaving an obvious trail. He got out and used his flashlight to check the ground for tire tracks.

Everything was dry enough not to leave any marks.

From inside the house, the two dogs, Romulus and Remus, began to bark. The man heard them pounding against the front door, frantically trying to get out. He'd tend to them later.

He quietly lowered the tailgate and walked to the fence that opened into the barn compound. He carried a large pair of bolt cutters. There, he cut off the padlock on the gate and put it in his pocket. He swung the gate open, curled his tongue, and let out a brief whistle. A moment later the Rottweilers trotted nervously by his side. He walked them to the barn and pulled back the sliding bolt on the door. He opened it, and gestured them to go inside. "Enjoy," he whispered, as they disappeared into the barn.

The man closed the door, sat down on an overturned feed trough and waited. The sounds coming from the barn were chilling, as the two dogs ripped and tore their way through all the flesh they could sink their teeth into.

It all happened so long ago. Does a murderer still stalk the small Connecticut village? Is he watching? Is he still killing?

Local policeman, Gordy Powell, who lives on a small farm with an attached pond, is rarely put in harm's way: traffic stops, car thefts, burglaries, an occasional runaway, domestic squabbles, etc. All that changes one horrible winter night in 1997, when a state senator's daughter and grandchildren drown after their car spins out of control on the icy road and plunges into Gordy's pond. When the pond is drained in an effort to straighten the road, a 1938 Chrysler is found on the muddy bottom, a bullet hole through the head of the skeleton in the front seat, and a sixty-year-old murder mystery unfolds.

Is the killer still alive and living in town? Has he killed again and never been caught? Gordy must use his best investigative skills to solve the crime and capture the killer—except that the killer is also after him, wreaking havoc in Gordy's life…

KUDOS for *The Shoreline Murder(s)*

In *The Shoreline Murder(s)* by William H. Smith, Gordy Powell is dismayed to find that a car has gone out of control and slid into his pond, killing a mother and two little girls. But he is even more shocked when the pond is drained to straighten the road, and there is car on the bottom with a murder victim from sixty years ago. As a local cop, Gordy knows how hard it is to solve a cold case, but this seems to be one that no one cares about. So Gordy decides to investigate it himself with the help of the victim's granddaughter. But as they dig for the truth, they both become targets in the killer's sights. With a complex mystery, fast-paced action, and plenty of surprises, this is one that mystery fans should love. ~ *Taylor Jones, The Review Team of Taylor Jones & Regan Murphy*

The Shoreline Murder(s) by William H. Smith is the story of a local cop who seeks justice for a sixty-year-old murder when the powers that be don't seem to care. When Gordy Powell discovers that a car has gone into his frozen pond, killing a woman and her two daughters, he has no idea that this is just the first of the horrors in store for him. When the pond is drained the following summer so the road can be straightened, a car is discovered on the bottom. The car has a body in it, one with a bullet hole in his head. Even though the murdered man was thought to have disappeared some sixty years ago, now that it is clear that he was murdered, the local authorities don't seem to be interested in solving the case. So Gordy and the victim's granddaughter, Emily, decide to investigate on their own time. Little do they know that some people will do a lot more than commit murder to keep their dark secrets buried. Intense and compelling, switching between the present and the past, *The Shoreline Murder(s)* will keep on the edge of your seat from beginning to end. *~ Regan Murphy, The Review Team of Taylor Jones & Regan Murphy*

ACKNOWLEDGMENTS

Bryan, Donna, Lee, Joyce, and Nick.

THE SHORELINE MURDER(S)

William H. Smith

A Black Opal Books Publication

DEDICATION

Walter Eastman

PART I

Nod Road

CHAPTER 1

Winter, 1997:

Crystalline sheaths of ice formed on tree branches as darkness, wind, and sleet rapidly overwhelmed the evening. The road ahead was furrowed with tracks left by passing vehicles, and icy ridges crisscrossed the treacherous surface. Now and then, cone-shaped beams from headlights revealed shadows of a million bits of falling sleet and snow.

Annie Martin pulled herself close to the steering wheel, hoping this would somehow make it easier to see into the night. The windshield wipers were clogged with slush. Each pass left soupy smears across her view. In the back seat of the Ford Explorer, Annie's two little girls were sound asleep.

Damn, she thought, *this would be so much easier with four-wheel drive.*

She headed west on Nod Road, having just exited Interstate 95. There were another five or six miles to home, where she and the girls would be safe and warm in their own beds. The notion encouraged a little pressure from her foot on the accelerator, resulting in the rear tires spinning on the slippery surface. She quickly eased off the pedal and gripped the wheel even tighter.

"Whew, be careful," she whispered.

Nod Road ran straight for about a mile then bent sharply right and crossed a small bridge. Annie knew the road well and anticipated the familiar course as it meandered through the Connecticut countryside.

She approached the tiny bridge and noticed the glow of on-coming headlights rounding the curve ahead. Light zigzagged left, then right. Now she made out the shape of a car, a light colored car, sliding across the centerline of the road. The headlights lit up a path to her right, and then cut a swath of light over the frozen pond that lay on the north side of the bridge.

No room on the left, she thought.

No room on the right.

God, no room!

Instinctively, Annie pulsed the brakes and aimed for a path between the on-coming car and the guardrail on her right. The Explorer slid right and plowed over the shoulder, missing the security of the guardrail by a few inches. As the Explorer skated away, the approaching car swerved, regained its traction and disappeared into the swirling blackness beyond. Annie felt the pressure of her body against the seat restraint as the SUV tumbled down the embankment onto the surface of the pond. The big Ford struck the ice, spun in a perfect circle, and came to rest about forty feet from a culvert that went under the bridge. A few seconds went by, and Annie's mind raced over what had just happened.

"Goddamn, we're on the pond!" she wailed. "Emma, Kristen, wake up. Wake up!"

The two girls, Emma who was eight, and Kristen, six, were already awake and wide-eyed from jolts received coming off the road.

"What's wrong, Mommy?" Emma shouted. As she spoke, there was a loud crack, like a rifle shot.

Annie knew immediately what was happening, but it was already too late. She felt the Explorer sinking. For a moment, she wasn't sure what to do. If she opened the door, the big car would sink faster; but she thought, maybe the water was only a foot or two deep and they might be able to walk out. Whatever she was going to do, she'd better do it quickly.

"Emma, Kristen, get out of your seat belts and climb up here with me," she shouted. The girls scurried forward and Annie wrapped her arms around them. Trying to be calm, she said, "We'll be okay. We just need to get out of the car."

She looked and saw the water was nearly level with the doorsill. Remarkably, there were only a few inches of water on the floor. The Explorer's headlights were still on, shining into the murky water and ice. Then it occurred to Annie to lower the side window, maybe she could float out and pull the girls through. If she survived the water temperature for a few minutes, she'd get everyone out. She pressed the power window switch.

Nothing!

She clicked the switch back and forth.

Still nothing.

"Shit, shit, shit," she hissed through clenched teeth.

Annie knew her only option was to open the door and let the big car sink. She noticed the water inside was nearly level with the seat. She had been straddling the front console, and she realized she was about to get wet. Next, she pulled at the door handle and discovered the door was locked. She tried the electric door lock button.

No response.

Cold terror gripped Annie's mind at the enormity of what was happening. She then tried to pull on the manual lock plunger. Her hands were cold and wet and she had difficulty getting a grip on the slippery shaft. After several tries, she got a firm hold, and the plunger lifted. She felt a sense of relief for a moment, but as she looked through the window, she realized the water had risen to four inches above the sill.

Annie grabbed them both and hugged them close to her. Trying to be calm, she said, "We'll be okay. We just need to get out of the car."

Annie pulled at the door handle and felt reassured at hearing the mechanism click. She pushed against the door.

Nothing.

"No, no, goddamn it," she wailed.

Water pressure and frozen slush around the door made it impossible for her to push it open. She braced herself against the passenger seat and slammed against the door with all her strength. Water trickled around the bottom of the door seal. Annie pushed harder, but by now, water neared the top of the door and forces holding it were still too great. In desperation, Annie leaned across the center console and lifted the door lock on the other side of the car. Her grip was stronger now, and after a satisfying click, she pushed on the door and again was met with too much resistance.

She was wetter now in nearly freezing water.

The girls were wet too.

And screaming.

CHAPTER 2

Chief of Police Chris Forhey stood on the narrow little bridge at Nod Road. He stared at the hole in the ice just beginning to freeze. It was seven a.m. when Gordon Powell called in the accident at the curve by his pond. Gordon had owned the property for the past eight years and had seen his share of traffic carnage on this stretch of road. Since he'd lived here, he remembered at least five major accidents, claiming four lives. Gordon stood on his front deck with his dogs, looking over the pond, and at a gathering cluster of rescue vehicles.

Chief Forhey turned his gaze from the pond and waved to Gordon. Gordon gestured back and began the trek down two flights of stairs connecting the deck to the ground. His lean body was bundled in a dark blue parka with a fake fur collar. He narrowed his blue eyes into thin slits as protection from the icy wind sweeping across the pond. His blond hair was uncovered and looked un-combed. At thirty-nine, his chiseled features showed some signs of wear and tear. Thin lines radiated from the edges of his eyes and the creases in his forehead spoke of worrisome times.

Gordon was a cop, but he worked for the nearby town of Guilford. He'd lived and worked on the Connecticut shoreline a long time, and most everyone he knew called him Gordy. He picked his way across the ice-covered lawn and driveway to where the chief stood.

"Good morning, Chris," Gordy said, when he was close enough to be heard. "What do you think?" he asked in the same breath.

"Looks like you called it right, Gordy." the chief replied. "Dispatch took a phone message last night from a Mr. Jerry Martin over in Westbrook. He asked about any accidents last night. Seems his wife and two daughters didn't make it home on time. We haven't called him yet with the possibilities here. I figure we'll wait 'til we're sure of what we got. From the way the shoulder ice is chewed up and the pattern of tire tracks leading out on the pond, it looks like we're gonna find something unpleasant. We got two firemen getting into suits right now."

"Yeah, I agree. It wasn't what I expected this morning," Gordy said. "Strange enough, I don't remember hearing anything but wind and sleet all night. I was pretty tired when I got off duty last night so I sacked out early. When I went to the barn this morning, I noticed the hole in the ice. Then I saw ruts in the shoulder and decided to call you guys."

While they stood talking, two men wearing awkward dry suits carried scuba gear down the embankment to the iced-over pond. Three other men wearing yellow parkas, earmuffs, and gloves pulled a small flat-bottom john boat across the ice.

"That will be our ice breaker," Chief Forhey said. "We'll need to keep the ice around the big hole from reforming while our men are in the water."

Several firemen pushed a little boat toward thin ice at the hole while the men in dry suits followed. They launched the john boat and began breaking the ice with axes and garden rakes.

Eric Older and his companion Terry Miller looked like misshapen aliens in their recently acquired dry suits—overstuffed profiles somewhere between the gruesome twins in a Chevy Chase movie and the puffed-up appearance of the Pillsbury Doughboy.

Eric, who was senior to Terry, nodded and displayed a thumps up, signifying he was ready for the descent. Terry responded in kind, indicating he too was ready. Eric tossed a Danforth anchor into the hole and played out a length of rope until it stopped as the weight struck bottom. The rope contained ribbon-like marker flags emblazoned with numbers indicating the number of feet immersed. The rope went to twenty-two feet and stopped.

Eric shuffled back to thicker ice. "Secure the line as a fail safe route to the hole," he instructed one of the nearby firemen. Eric waddled to the edge, turned his back to the icy water, clasped his octopus in one hand, and rolled backward with a splash. Terry quickly followed. The two men regarded one another momentarily before bleeding air from their buoyancy control vests and descending into the murky water, each clinging to the anchored lifeline. The water was a deep amber color. As they descended, the amount of light penetrating the surface was choked away.

Both men carried underwater lanterns tethered to their utility belts and, at fifteen feet, they pressed switches, energizing the bulbs. In the yellow brown glow of artificial light, they began to sweep three hundred and sixty-degree arcs around them.

Visibility was less than three feet. The water temperature was thirty-four degrees. Eric removed a coiled safety line from his belt and attached the end with a large snap shackle to the anchor line. He launched himself toward the bottom, all the while fixing the other end to a ring clipped to his suit. Terry stayed behind and fastened a similar rope to the anchor line. The rules for such dives were very specific, and both men knew the danger of getting lost under the ice.

Once the men were on the bottom, Eric adjusted his buoyancy compensation and made a series of expanding circles around the anchor line until he caught a flash of chrome reflected from his light. He jerked the safety line twice and raised his light to signal Terry who hovered at the main line. Terry signaled a response and dove to meet Eric at the wreck.

The Explorer rested on its left side. All of the windows were closed, sealing the fate of the occupants. The two men pressed their lights against the window glass and peered inside. A young female child clutched the rear view mirror. Her blank, wide-eyed gaze stared back at them, her expression seemed to say, "Here I am, what took you so long?"

Beneath her, clutching yet another child, lay an adult female. Both seemed complacent, with wide dead eyes looking up toward the passenger window, their hair splayed about their heads as if they were caught in a summer breeze.

Eric moved quickly, aware of several cases of cold water drowning that ended with resuscitation and survival. He climbed on the right rear door, braced himself, and pulled open the passenger door. Terry dove inside, grabbed hold of each little girl and pulled them from the wreck.

Eric let go of the door and showed his light toward Terry's tether and followed, lighting the way back to the main safety line. Once there, Eric clasped Terry's BC valve and inflated his vest. Both men began their ascent carrying the two children.

They surfaced in a tumult of hissing, gurgling air, and men in the john boat paddled quickly toward them. As they drew near, they reached over and gently lifted the lifeless forms from the water. Both men dove again leaving a splash of bubbles from their regulators.

"God, this is awful," Gordy said in a low tone.

"Well, it looks like I'm gonna hafta call Mr. Martin back after all," the chief said. He walked to the pond's edge, curled his hands around his mouth, and shouted to the men in the boat. "Ask Eric to get me something on the vehicle."

Once again, a diver surfaced, this time it was Terry Miller. He carried the body of a woman. The men in the boat lifted her like a religious artifact, being careful to protect her from additional injury. One man spoke to the diver, stood up, and shouted to the chief.

"Looks like a Ford Explorer," he called.

"Damn. Damn," the chief muttered as he turned and trudged back to the bridge.

CHAPTER 3

Senator Matt Blanton stood at his window, overlooking the city of Hartford, Connecticut. Even though it was February, his face was unseasonably tanned from his recent visit to Mexico. The contrast of his pure white hair framing his brown skin suggested his work brought him nearer to Hollywood than Washington, DC.

The sky overhead was just clearing, as the ice storm of the night before moved up the coast. Emerging sunlight swept across the Hartford skyline, and Blanton squinted his hazel eyes, shuttering them from the brilliant glare reflecting off the copper building looming before him. He knew he had a busy day ahead and thought he was ready for it.

He wasn't surprised when the interoffice phone chirped. "Yes, what is it?"

"Sir, it's your son-in law," said the woman on the other end. Blanton hesitated a moment, then said, "Okay, put him on. Hello, Jerry."

A strange pause on the other end, then a quaking voice. "Matt, something's happened."

"What's wrong, son?"

"It's Annie—and the girls—" Another long pause.

"Good God, what's wrong with Annie and the girls?"

"There's been an accident," Jerry finally said, with a tremor in his voice.

"Where are they now?" Blanton demanded.

"They're gone, Matt, they're gone."

Silence.

Blood drained from Blanton's face as his body redistributed precious fluid from his extremities to his chest and brain. "Where are you now?"

"I'm here with them, at Yale-New Haven," Jerry answered.

"Can you tell me what happened?"

"Matt, I don't know everything, but they were found this morning at the bottom of a pond off Nod Road in Clinton. The Explorer must have slid off the road and broke through the ice. They—They weren't able to get out. I got a call to come down to the hospital. I knew something was wrong when they didn't get home last night. Jesus! Matt, I called all over the place last night. I tried the local police, and state police. I thought, because of the storm, maybe they stopped at a motel; maybe they were caught with a downed phone service and laid over somewhere safe. At some point, I gave up, figuring I'd hear something in the morning. This can't be real, Matt."

The senator listened, trying to control the sick feeling growing in his stomach. Somehow, he found the strength to interrupt, "Jerry, please, calm down. Give me an hour to get there, I'll see you then."

No answer.

෴

Jerry Martin stood in the hospital corridor, holding the pay phone. His hands were sweaty. His eyes felt tired and gritty while he barely noticed the spasm running amuck on the right side of his face. He spoke through dry, bloodless lips as he fought to control the sobs bubbling under his voice.

The conversation with his father-in-law was over. So much had happened, why was there nothing else to say? Perhaps, it was because his mind was numb. Although he couldn't converse, he didn't want to be alone. The idea of hanging up only amplified his feeling of emptiness. He clung to the headset feeling obligated to say more, do more.

Jerry finally shook his head. "Bye, Matt." Then he placed the receiver on the hook and stared straight ahead.

⌇⌇⌇

Senator Blanton listened for the click of the receiver and hung up his phone. He pressed the intercom button, and a voice responded with, "Yes, sir."

"Thelma, have my car brought out front. I'm driving to New Haven. Cancel all my appointments for today and tomorrow. Something's happened to my daughter. I'll be at Yale- New Haven Hospital. I'll take emergency calls on my cell. Otherwise, please don't disturb me until I know more about what's happened."

⌇⌇⌇

The morning was clear and cold as Senator Blanton and Jerry Martin stood with thirty-five other people on the grounds of Our Lady of Peace Cemetery. They were at the site where Annie Martin was to be buried. Her two little girls, Emma and Kristen, had already been laid to rest.

The tragedy placed a great strain on the public, as well as the close group of family and friends. Certainly, those in attendance, along with almost everyone in the State of

Connecticut, hoped for some kind of closure when Annie was finally buried.

Jerry Martin and the senator stood by the gravesite, dazed by the reality of what had happened. Both were overwhelmed with loss, and both realized there was risk they may never fully recover. As Annie's rosewood casket was lowered into the ground, the sense of relief Blanton hoped for didn't come. Instead, he experienced a spontaneous wave of nausea, nearly causing him to vomit in front of everyone. He held it back, not wanting to attract attention to himself. This was about Annie, not him.

When the funeral ended, the senator didn't feel like returning to his son-in-law's home and the inevitable reception of friends and other relatives. His despair was so great that he just wanted to be alone.

He drove to Nod Road and parked by the curve overlooking the pond. He sat on the ground and stared at the ice-covered water. Then his mind raced through a series of "what ifs," alternate possibilities, any of which could have changed the outcome of the tragedy. As these scenarios played in his head, he permitted himself to imagine the last terrifying moments confronting Annie and the girls. In his mind, Blanton recreated the scene, visualizing the struggle of his three precious darlings.

He stood there alone, no longer a powerful figure. He was only a man, perhaps less than a man. Maybe more like an empty, tired shell of a man. In the back of his mind, the melody of "Amazing Grace" echoed through his mind and tears flooded his eyes as the lyrics whispered "save a wretch like me." He shivered with the notion and inhaled a long hollow breath of winter air.

Senator Blanton's cloak of despair was so heavy that he barely noticed the figure of another man standing in the bony trees across the pond. The man seemed very old and wore a plaid hunting jacket with the collar raised and pulled close to his face. He glared at the frozen surface for a few minutes then turned his gaze toward the senator. Matt Blanton noted the old man's stare and wondered why he was there.

The two men regarded each other for a moment. Then the old man thrust his hands into his pockets, turned, and shuffled into the woods. Two large dogs emerged from nearby trees, stopped at the frozen water's edge, then they turned and followed the old man's trail.

The senator thought the man odd. Something about the stranger seemed out of place, perhaps even sinister. Then a shiver swept through Blanton, and he wondered if it was because of the cold air or the figures disappearing into the brush. He nearly called out, thinking there was something missing in this tragedy and perhaps the old man held some secret, but he kept silent, thinking the idea was just a foolish notion.

When the man and dogs were finally out of sight, Senator Blanton got into his car and headed toward his home in Simsbury. He drove slowly, hoping the visit to the pond would represent a kind of catharsis, somehow reducing his awful feeling of despair. He only felt worse.

When he arrived home, he stayed in and alone for the next three days, scavenging from the refrigerator and cupboards for nourishment. He let the answering machine take whatever calls came through on his private line. On the morning of the fourth day, he called his numbers into his desk phone and waited patiently as the connection went through.

"Harlan Flanders, please," the senator requested into the set.

"May I say who's calling?"

"Tell him it's Senator Matt Blanton"

A moment later Harlan Flanders picked up. "Good morning, Senator. what can I do for you?"

"Harlan, I'm sure you know about my interest in Nod Road?"

"Yes, sir, I do. My condolences, Matt. It was an awful tragedy."

"Well, I want to fix the goddamn thing."

"How do you mean, 'fix'?

"I want to change the shape of the road and get rid of the curve at the pond. Maybe even get rid of the goddamn pond."

"Well, sir, it's a great idea, but it will take a lot of money. There's a considerable number of people who own land along the road, and it'll take some doing to convince them that changing the road is good for them."

"That's why I'm talking to you, Harlan, I want you to set the stage in your town for what needs to be done."

"I'll see what I can do, sir."

"Good, I've got some influence with the governor, and I'm meeting him this week to discuss the matter. Don't worry about the money. The most difficult thing will be convincing the people affected. Do an assessment of what'll be necessary to bring those people on board. Get it done by the end of the month. Then we'll talk again and lay out some kind of plan. Don't take forever. Do you understand?"

ೕೕ

The senator had been persuasive, and he didn't leave much room for Harlan to wiggle, so at this point, he simply said yes and hoped the whole deal didn't turn into some kind of political nightmare. *Besides,* Harlan thought, *if there is money available, maybe the town will benefit.*

Harlan Flanders was the perfect man in a perfect place, one of those New England hybrids. Most every town had one or two like him, clever people, somehow learning their way around local politics and the idiosyncratic twists and turns of town government.

Harlan's father was a local retired chief of police. His late mother was a caring shadow of a woman in his distant past. She died in an auto accident when he was only five and the impact of her life lay in scattered fragments of his memory. Over the years, he reconstructed his relationship with her, combining old photographs with the creative glue of his imagination. He resented her death, feeling he was somehow cheated of some entitlement. Strangely enough, she seemed at fault for not being there when he needed her.

The experience of his childhood left him with the creation of an odd and complex relationship with his mother, reinforcing his need to be both independent and tolerant to ordinary disappointments with women. Maybe this component of his background explained why he avoided long-lasting associations with women in general. Whatever the reason, he was content to live alone. Besides, being a bachelor provided him infinite, albeit short lived, variety with many women.

As a young man, he watched the way his father manipulated the world around him. His father tried tirelessly to encourage him into law enforcement.

"I'm not interested, Dad," he always responded to Teddy's suggestions. "I've seen too much of the violence you accept as routine in your life."

Somehow, Harlan resisted the pressure to go into police work and ultimately stumbled into early success with real estate.

Harlan's business prospered until 1987, when increasing construction costs struck a major blow to the development of real estate. In self-defense, Harlan ran for the position of selectman and won. Although, he had opposition, the other candidate suddenly resigned shortly before the vote. He cited personal reasons and quietly fell into obscurity. After Harlan took office, his real estate business bumped along, breaking even while he prospered in town government.

Wittingly or unwittingly, Harlan owed some of his achievement to his father. Despite conflicts arising from his disinterest in police work, his father seemed to always be there, helping in the background, perhaps, a little too much.

Harlan Flanders pulled his Toyota SUV off Nod Road and into Gordy Powell's driveway. It was seven p.m., and since he had called Gordy to ask for the visit, he didn't want to be late. He parked, got out, and climbed the stairs to the front door. Gordy's dogs heard him pull in and were barking somewhere in the house.

The dogs had Gordy checking at the window, and he was already by the door when Harlan got there. Before the bell rang, he opened the door. Harlan stood there, a big man with a thick mop of white hair long enough so the observer sensed he didn't have a job interview in his immediate future. Beneath his bristling eyebrows lay a pair of dark eyes that seemed to absorb everything around. He smiled, his large boyish face beaming with a confidence that revealed a lifestyle good for him.

"How you doin, Harlan?" Gordy asked as he led him to a living room chair. "Please, sit down."

"Thanks Gordy."

"Can I get you some coffee?"

"Sure, that would be good."

Gordy went to the kitchen, and a few minutes later, brought out two mugs, some milk and sugar, and placed them on the coffee table.

"So tell me what's going on with Nod Road?" Gordy asked as he sat across from Harlan.

"Well it's like this, Gordy, the county, state, and I believe a small piece of the federal government wants to straighten the curve right here at your place. It looks like Senator Blanton has gone all out to do something about the loss of his daughter and grandkids. He's on a mission and we need your help. We'd like you to get on the bandwagon and help us sort out the new property configurations."

"Look, Harlan, it's my home, and I'm not sure I agree with the idea of straightening the road and cutting up everybody's property—"

Harlan was quick to interrupt. "Damn it, Gordy, it's not going to change things that much. Keep in mind the town can acquire the land by Eminent Domain and you won't have much to say about it. Taking that route requires more time and aggravation. On the other hand, if we can work together, the end result will be better for everyone. What I'm proposing is to compensate you for any land taken and invite your participation in the planning process."

ↄ〜ↄ〜

Gordy Powell wasn't naive. In the back of his mind, he thought what seemed like a noble project could also serve as a contractor's dream, and either reality was most likely just a nuisance. Not only were they proposing to straighten the curve, but they also wanted to widen the road. This almost certainly meant lopping off sizable chunks of frontage for everyone along the way.

In addition, there was some talk of permanently filling the pond and rerouting the entire marsh currently draining into Long Island Sound. It was too much for Gordy. He sensed the final compromise would end with straightening the curve. If he were to participate, he might be in a better position to salvage the pond. He also knew when there was state and federal money available, some folks in town saw it as a significant opportunity. It always happened that way.

CHAPTER 4

August, 1998:

On a hot morning in August, the sun rose above the trees to find a construction crew working on Nod Road. Surveyors had started in April to lay out most of the proposed changes. Although widening the road was an important part of the project, the curve at the pond was the driving force for all work scheduled. On this day, the crew was about to finish temporary draining of the infamous pond.

At the north end of the property, a coffer dam was constructed and a series of connecting ditches were carved with the use of a backhoe. The ditches went in a southeasterly direction around the pond and into a temporary culvert. The culvert emptied into the marsh, which eventually found its way into Long Island Sound.

The original idea was to complete this portion of the project during August and September when the water table was at its lowest. The pond drained naturally for the past several days, and yesterday the crew began using high volume pumps to finish the job. As the water level decreased farther, a work crew stood by with portable pumps to remove water from the deep contours that were lower than the customary drainage pitch. Once they straightened the road, a new culvert and bridge were to be constructed. Fill was scheduled to arrive, and a new roadbed would be completed.

Gordy Powell stood on his deck and watched the activity below. His dogs, Romulus and Remus, had been restless for days, barking almost constantly at the crews and the noise. *At least*, he thought, *I'll get some idea of what the bottom of the pond really looks like.* He knew he had a lot of work to do once they allowed the pond to re-fill. Over the years, he had carefully stocked it with an ecological blend of fish and plants. He'd have to start from scratch to restore it. Because he was a cop on the Guilford force, and because a lot of the project was done with state money, the state assured him access to its fisheries, and they would restock the pond with an ample supply of assorted game fish.

As the water drained, the expanding muddy beach left a murky oversized puddle at the deepest end of the pond. Based on soundings Gordy had taken when it was full, he knew the depth covered a substantial range. The northern end averaged seven to eight feet, while the southern portion near the bridge was twenty to twenty-five feet. Water in the pond had never been crystal clear; usually it was amber with some turbidity. Today, with all the pumping going on, the remaining water looked muddy and opaque.

At the north end, Gordy saw a number of brown catfish flapping around in the drained areas. A few appeared quite large and Gordy thought about picking them up for the frying pan. Along the muddy shore, ducks and geese ambled back and forth, restlessly trying to figure out what was happening. Down at the south end, there were still six to eight feet of water left.

Sometime later, Gordy made his way toward the deep end and watched as it drained rapidly with the help of several large pumps. Oddly enough, emerging at the water's surface was the roof of what appeared to be an old car. Gordy watched with interest as more and more of the old wreck materialized.

"I'll be damned," he said aloud.

Gordy's gaze went from the car to several of the workers who also noticed the old car coming into view. He watched as they stopped working just to watch. Then one of them shouted to the others and everyone stopped what they were doing. Soon he saw them converging at the bridge to look down at the car.

"So what kinda car is it?" one man asked.

"I can't be sure," another man answered. "But, I think it's an old Chrysler."

"Maybe middle to late thirties," said another.

Gordy hadn't planned on walking in the bottom of the pond and now he realized he'd need some boots to get a closer view of the mysterious car. He trudged back to the barn, found his knee-high boots, and got ready for a serious encounter with this new surprise. Then he returned to the deep end. At first, he tested the muck gingerly with one foot, trying to find out how far he'd sink into the bottom mud. As he applied more weight, he went down about four or five inches and found a firm bed of clay supporting him.

Slowly, to avoid sliding, Gordy walked to the old car. As he drew nearer, he noticed all the window glass was still intact and blanketed with a thick layer of pond slime. The roof had sagged but it was still in one piece. A mixture of mud and slime sealed the doors. Gordy suspected the inside was still full of water, because the car's bottom still lay buried nearly to the top of the rotten tires. There didn't appear to be any place for the water to go.

The men on the bridge still watched, making wise cracks.

One guy shouted down, "Hey, I'll give you three hundred bucks for it, if you drive it over to my place."

Gordy looked up and countered, "You better give me thirty thousand bucks if I drive this thing to your place."

The rest of the crew chuckled as they broke up and returned to work. Gordy figured on draining the wreck before having it hauled away. He trudged back to the barn to find a sledgehammer.

A few minutes later, he was back at the car. He walked a full circle around it, trying to assess just what kind of condition it was in when it entered the pond. When did it end up in the pond and how? He'd lived here for eight years and had no idea it was there. He supposed someone could have dumped it while he owned the place, but the idea seemed very unlikely. As Gordy contemplated the story of the old car, he decided he was ready to drain it. He walked around to the driver's side window, raised the sledge over his shoulder, and smashed it sideways into the glass.

The breaking window made a noise like a heavily laden jar striking the floor. A thud followed by a liquid sound of syrupy brown water. Gordy quickly sidestepped to avoid the foul smelling liquid that nearly splashed over him. Water flowed over the doorsill but refused to drain any farther.

"Ah shit," he muttered. He peered inside but couldn't see very much. "Oh, well."

He sighed as he slogged to the other side of the wreck. Once again he raised the hammer and then struck the passenger side window.

This time the noise sounded a little more like breaking glass.

As Gordy stood there, he noticed the water inside finally beginning to drain. He watched the murky liquid recede, inch by inch. Inside, the windshield was green with some form of algae, while everything else had a thick layer of brown slime over it. As more water drained, remnants of the front seat became obvious, coil springs, bits of cloth, and some framework.

Gordy peered through to the driver's side. Behind the slime covered steering wheel there was a dark clump of debris covered by what resembled a piece of leather-like clothing. Visible under the pile was a pale yellow object that looked like a length of bone. Gordy bent down, and stuck his head inside the car.

It sure looks like bone, he thought. He took the sledgehammer by the head and poked the handle at the debris in the driver's seat. As he probed, he uncovered more bone.

"What the hell do we have here?" he muttered. Then he decided he'd better get back to the driver's side and figure this out. Once there, he poked again and found the pile was indeed leather, appearing to be some kind of coat or jacket.

Underneath the leather garment were the remains of a human being. The skull, still attached to the backbone, lay nestled in a slimy, black puddle between the ribs and was cocked to the right.

A neat round black hole dotted the temple.

CHAPTER 5

The county coroner arrived about an hour later. His name was Doctor Merle Steiner and he pulled his green state-owned van into Gordy's driveway. He was a chubby man in his late fifties, with pure white hair hanging in a curly mass over his collar. He knew he needed a haircut, but he really didn't care how he looked anymore. Sitting beside him in the van were two younger men, both dressed in EMT uniforms. One fellow, a big man, was Hartley Schiff. The other, a skinny man, was Arnie Ferris. Both had special skills, and Doc Steiner usually brought them along whenever he was called to a traffic fatality.

Hartley was good with emergency tools, like jaws-of-life and metal-cutting chainsaws. Arnie's specialty was cameras. He was very good at taking pictures and did the job with extraordinary enthusiasm. Hartley got out first and went around to the driver's side. He opened the door for Doc Steiner.

Gordy had been sitting on the stairs of his front deck when the van turned into the driveway. He stood up and walked over.

"How are you doing, Doc?" Gordy asked as he reached out his hand in greeting.

"I was doin' okay, until I got this lousy phone call a

while ago," the doctor replied. "What in God's name is going on out here?"

"I really don't know any more about it than you do at this point," Gordy said. "I'll be real interested to hear what you've got to say after you take a look. By the way, Doc, did you remember to bring your boots? You're gonna need them."

"Yeah, yeah, they're in the van."

A few minutes later, Chief Forhey joined the group and all five men slogged their way down to the old wreck. By now, the car was drying, and most of the remaining water had drained out.

Hartley carried a metal-cutting chainsaw and Arnie Ferris carried a big Nikon camera.

Doc Steiner signaled Arnie to go ahead, and he began taking pictures with the digital camera, inside and outside the car. These pictures were in addition to several rolls of traditional film already taken by Chief Forhey's detectives.

The Clinton Police Department was budgeted for three detectives, and two of the three were at the scene. They stood some distance away, out of the mud. A half-hour went by while Arnie snapped off his shots.

"Okay, Hartley, it's your turn," Doc said. "Let's get those doors off, so's I can get a looksee at what's in there."

Hartley responded with, "Sure thing, Doc." He attacked the driver's side door.

Soon, the door lay in mud near the left front fender. Doc Steiner signaled Hartley to use his saw on the right side door, and it too dropped. Steiner pulled on a pair of latex gloves, reached in and poked at the bones in the front seat.

"Hartley, get out your pad and take some notes," he said without looking back.

Hartley placed the chain saw on the hood and pulled out a pad and pen from his back pocket.

"Okay, Doc."

Steiner continued, "By the shape of the crown of the forehead and taper of the chin, the subject is likely male. There is a probable medium caliber entrance wound at the left temple, and a large exit wound on the right side. Can't tell much more until we get the remains out and reconstructed. Wait a minute, there is something on the floor of the passenger side. It looks like a leather bag. Like an old purse or a hand bag."

Steiner and the detectives spent the rest of the afternoon removing the victim's remains, along with whatever else they could find as potential evidence. They pried open the glove box and placed the slimy contents in small transparent bags.

Under the hood, they found a manufacturer's plaque and identified the car as a 1938 Chrysler. They removed the leather bag, placed it on a sheet of plastic, and opened it. Indeed, it was a doctor's bag filled with tools of the trade, as they were sixty years ago. Most of the stainless steel implements were in remarkable condition. Also inside were remnants of what appeared to be an appointment book, a gold ring, and a leather wallet containing paper money. Every item was carefully bagged and cataloged. At day's end, the Chrysler was finally dug out and hauled away.

CHAPTER 6

Gordy took the entire day off and followed the events with keen interest. After all, how often do you stumble across a situation like this in your own back yard? He'd noticed a rusted license plate still fixed to the trunk, and he tried to make out what the numbers were. The doctor's bag in the front seat was also a strong clue as to whom the victim might have been.

The next day, he called the Department of Motor Vehicles and asked for a check of 1938 Chryslers registered to doctors that same year. He asked for only those registered to a shoreline address. The DMV told him their records, if any, were quite incomplete for that time frame, but promised to do their best.

Because the county morgue facility was not equipped for this kind of case, Doc Steiner sent the remains to the forensics lab at Yale-New Haven Hospital.

At one o'clock the following afternoon, Gordy found himself there asking to see Dr. Steiner. He displayed his Guilford badge, and they passed him to the old laboratory in the basement.

Fortunately, no one noticed the distinction between his badge and a Clinton PD one.

Doc Steiner was bent over a gurney as Gordy knocked on the windowed door outside the autopsy room. The doc looked up motioned him in with a latex-gloved hand.

"What brings you down here, Gordy?"

"Curiosity, I guess. I can't seem to get this thing out of my mind. Have you figured out who it is yet?"

"No, but it shouldn't take too long. I confirmed the observations I made yesterday. It is a Caucasian male, about forty-plus years, shot once in the head at close range, probably a thirty eight-caliber weapon. The fellow's got good dental work, fine bone structure in his hands, no poorly healed injuries. These conditions suggest he was well off. He could have been a doctor. There was no other indication of trauma. He was probably quite dead when put in the water."

As Gordy got closer, he could see the reconstruction the doc had created on a six-foot, linen-covered tray. In front of him was the skeleton of the man they had removed from the old Chrysler yesterday. The bones were yellow and soft with strands of matter still clinging here and there. The doc had collected a quantity of hair at the scene, and it lay nested on the linen near the skull.

"Gordy, you sure there were no holes in the side windows of the car before you swung that sledge hammer?"

"Of course I'm sure. The car was full of water when the pond was empty. If there were any holes, the water would have drained, don't you think?" Gordy said. "After all, how could I know there was a body inside the damn car?"

"Calm down, Gordy, I was just askin'. I've been trying to figure out where he was when he was shot. It looks like he was shot somewhere else and placed in the car, or someone shot him in the car with the door open or the window down. Either way, it wasn't a good day for our mysterious doctor.

"I got Hartley working with the Clinton cops as they go through the car today. So far, they examined the doors and much of the remaining glass and everything appears to be intact. No entry or exit points. If we can't find the bullet, maybe he was shot somewhere else and placed in the car."

CHAPTER 7

Emily Pierce woke as usual at seven a.m. She pulled on a soft, saffron colored robe and made her way to the bathroom. The first glimpse of her reflection startled her for just a second.

"Jesus," she said softly. At thirty-six, she was still in pretty good shape, but there were some telltale signs of age. Her hair was dark brown and cropped square across the back just below the bottoms of her ears. Her well-shaped eyes were hazel and, when not sleepy as they were now, had a penetrating quality that almost made you feel defensive. She had shed about twenty pounds since she walked out of her marriage with Charlie Pierce.

When she finished dressing, she went out the front door and retrieved her copy of the *New Haven Reporter*. She threw it on the kitchen table and made coffee while toasting an English muffin. She'd been alone for nearly a year and was becoming quite used to it. Charlie had left the shoreline after the divorce and moved to Atlanta. He'd always said that he wanted to live in the south, so now he had his chance. *Just as well,* she thought, after hearing of his plans, at least she didn't have to worry about bumping into him in the grocery store.

While coffee dripped through the filter paper, she opened a can of Tender Meals for Isabel, her cat, her only live-in housemate. Isabel circled the floor, meowing, anticipating her breakfast. Emily finally sat down with her coffee, muffin, and morning paper. When she opened the shoreline section, on the first page was a picture of an old car. The caption read "Drowned Car Gives up Dead Body."

The article said the remains of a human body were discovered in a 1938 Chrysler found at the bottom of a pond in Clinton. Cause of death and the identity of the remains were as yet undetermined. The article went on to say it was thought the car might have been in the pond since 1938.

A chill rippled from the back of Emily's neck all the way to her temples. She knew immediately. The story told by her mother and her grandmother was crystal clear as it raced through her mind. *No one else is going to know,* she thought. With the exception of her Uncle Bert, there might be no one left alive who knew. She paused, not sure what to do, then she picked up the phone book, thumbed through, and finally dialed Yale-New Haven Hospital.

"Hello," she said. "I need to reach Dr. Merle Steiner right away."

Several minutes went by, and the receptionist finally came back. "I'm sorry, but there doesn't seem to be anybody on staff by that name."

Emily felt a sense of urgency. "I believe he's with the county coroner's office."

"Well," the receptionist replied with a hint of sarcasm. "Maybe you'd be better off calling the coroner's office instead of the hospital."

"It's about the body found in Clinton yesterday. The remains were discovered in an old car. The story was in this morning's paper," Emily explained.

"Look, miss, I don't read the paper and I can't tell you

anything about a body or a Doc Steiner. Why doncha just call the coroner's office direct?"

Now Emily was really upset. She hung up the phone with so much force that she nearly broke the receiver. She wasn't sure what to do next. She picked up the phone book, scanned through it, and called the Clinton Police Department.

"Hello, my name is Emily Pierce, and I want to speak to someone about the body found at Nod Road."

"What did you say your name was?" responded the voice on the other end.

"Emily Pierce," she said calmly.

"Please hold, ma'am."

A minute or two later, a man with a deep voice said, "This is Chief of Police Forhey."

"Yes," she said. "My name is Emily Pierce, and I may have some information about the car found in the pond."

"What kind of information?"

"I may know who was in the car."

"Just who do you think it might be, Miss Pierce?"

"I think you may have found my grandfather."

"Emily, can you come down to the station?"

"Yes, I guess I'd better come down. Give me about forty-five minutes," she said.

"That will be just fine, but go easy. There is no terrible rush."

"Yes, I know," she said and hung up the phone. As librarian for the town of Madison, Emily was supposed to open the building at nine a.m., but now she had to get someone else to do it. She picked up the phone once again and dialed Gladys Bower. "Hello, Gladys, I've got a real emergency, and I need you to open up this morning."

"Okay, I can do that," she replied.

"I'll try to call you before lunch and let you know

what's going on. Got to go now, talk to you later, bye."

Emily was anxious as she got into her two-year-old Camry and headed toward Route 95 East. The highway drive took only ten minutes. She took the Clinton exit and made her way toward the police station. Strangely enough, the route brought her past the entrance to Nod Road. She noticed the street sign as she drove by, and somehow resisted the urge to detour.

A young uniformed police officer sat behind a large desk. He looked up and seemed to know who she was before she introduced herself. She went ahead regardless, announced her name, and asked for Chief Forhey. No sooner had she finished, than the burly chief entered the lobby and walked over to her. He extended his hand and introduced himself. Emily replied in kind.

"Come on into my office, Ms. Pierce," he said, as he led the way to his door. Once inside, he gestured for her to sit before he propped himself in a big chair behind his desk. "Tell me what you think you know about the Nod Road situation," he asked in a soothing voice.

Emily had dressed hastily in a cotton dress, and she'd only pushed her hair back with a brush. Suddenly, she felt very self-conscious. She hesitated a moment, thinking this was ridiculous. She didn't feel good, she didn't look good, and maybe her stroke of insight at the news article was silly and inappropriate.

"Well, I'm not sure how to begin," she said. "I've lived on the shoreline all my life. My family's always lived here. So, it's not like I need publicity or anything. When I read the article this morning, I knew you'd found my grandfather. He disappeared over sixty years ago in a Chrysler car. My grandmother told me the story before she died back in 1983. My mother told the story over and over until her death a year ago. My grandfather was Doctor Sam Stemford. For a while he was the only GP between Clinton and Branford. He disappeared without a trace in 1938."

Chief Forhey leaned back and looked at Emily with some intensity for a full minute.

"We did find something in the car that suggests the situation may involve a doctor. We found an old doctor's bag full of medical instruments. Now, that in itself doesn't mean the remains are your grandfather's. But, it does suggest the car may have belonged to your grandfather."

"Where are the remains now?" Emily asked hoarsely. Her mouth was dry despite the August humidity.

"They're at Yale-New Haven."

"Can I see them?" she asked.

"I don't see why not, but it won't be a pretty sight," the chief answered.

"When?" She pressed.

"In a couple of days. The coroner is still trying to reconstruct the body," he replied.

"I want to know what can be done to identify the remains as soon as possible. If it's my grandfather, I'd like to put closure on this thing after all these years. How awful to die in an accident at the peak of his life and never be found," Emily said.

"Well, Ms. Pierce, it may not be all that easy," the chief said. "You see, we don't think it was an accident."

"What do you mean?"

"We think the person in the car was murdered."

CHAPTER 8

Gordy entered the front office at the Clinton police impound. He knew the three detectives on the force, so he didn't expect much trouble learning what might have turned up during the search of the rusted Chrysler. Even in decrepit shape, there were traces of innovative elegance in the old Airflow design. The 1930s were ripe for the display of symbols depicting all things moving. The period marked an era aching to combine the styling of airplanes, motorcars, and architecture into objects for everyday living.

The Chrysler Airflow made its debut at the end of 1937 and represented the epitome of art deco transportation for the still-recovering post-depression-era masses. The original car sparkled with chrome highlights ranging from its massive grill to winged blazes decorating each of the rear fender skirts. The interior was a handsome blend of burled wood veneer on the dashboard garnished by rich fabrics upholstering the seats and door panels.

Perhaps the car was too far ahead of its time or the competition from the plethora of rivals was too great. At any rate, the car saw only two years of production and then it fell into quiet obscurity.

Now one of the few remaining examples of a deeply troubling period in American history lay in the Clinton police impound. The car and its parts filled up two bays in the garage. The chassis rested on cinder blocks, while the two severed doors lay flat on the floor. All the pieces of the side windows that Gordy had smashed with the sledgehammer, were placed on the floor in an attempt at reconstruction. Obviously, they were looking for a bullet hole in the glass or some other part of the car.

Detective Barry Lands was the only one working on the wreck. He was crouched over one of the doors as Gordy approached. Lands, in his mid-forties, was overweight, with thinning sandy-colored hair. He wore a green polo shirt and blue jeans. Hearing Gordy, he glanced up and shook his head.

"How you doin, Barry?" Gordy asked.

"Just peachy, Gordy," Barry replied. "What brings you to the bad side of town?"

Gordy paused for a minute then said, "I was curious about what you guys may have learned about the wreck."

"Forget it, Gordy, this ain't for you. It's our case and we don't need no help."

"Come on, Barry, don't pull that righteous jurisdiction crap with me. I'm not after your job. Since the damn thing was found in my pond, I've got a natural interest, that's all."

"Interest or no interest, there really isn't much I can tell you, Gordy."

"How 'bout I ask a few questions and you simply say yes or no? I'll try to sort out whether or not you've found anything, okay?"

"Look, what can I say? This is a formal police investigation of a homicide. At this point, I can't tell you anything." Barry was almost pleading.

Gordy ignored him. "Barry, just tell me, was the car in gear or neutral? Was the ignition on or off? Do you think the dead guy was driving or just propped up to look like he was driving? Did you find an entry or exit hole in the vehicle? Did you find the bullet?"

"Can't say. Can't say. Can't say. No. And no. Enough already," Barry said. "We are working on the answers, but at this point, I can't tell you anything more than you can read in the newspaper."

"Barry, cut the bullshit, by now you know the answer to every freakin' one of those questions. You may even know answers to questions I haven't even asked, like who was the poor guy sitting in the car when it took a dive into my pond."

Gordy was so busy grilling Barry that he didn't even notice the woman standing behind him. She had no doubt been there for a while, listening to some of the banter between the two men. Gordy finally sensed her presence. He turned around, looked at the woman for a moment, and then broke into a large smile.

"Hello, miss," he mustered the presence of mind to say.

"Hello," she replied. "Is that the Chrysler found in the pond on Nod Road?"

"Yes, ma'am, it sure is," Gordy said before Barry had a chance to answer.

"Are you Emily Pierce?" Barry asked as he walked toward the two of them.

"Yes, I am," she said. "And you must be Detective Lands."

"That's right," he said.

Gordy was beginning to feel left out, so he extended his hand and introduced himself. "Gordon Powell, Special Investigations Unit, Guilford PD," he said, shamelessly inventing the title.

"Actually, the car was found in Gordy's pond," Barry said.

"It sure was, Ms. Pierce—" Gordy replied.

Barry interrupted again. "Chief Forhey called and said you might stop by."

"I'm glad he did. I've already been to look at my grandfather's remains, and now I'd like to see the car."

"But, Miss Pierce, you can't be certain the remains are your grandfather," Barry went on.

"Oh, I think I can be," Emily said. "They found a ring with the body, a wedding ring with the inscription 'To forever love, Mary.' That's my grandmother, Mary Stemford. They're running DNA tests now to confirm, but I know what the results will be, Detective Lands. Have you found anything new about the car?"

"Well, Ms. Pierce we should talk privately," Barry answered, shifting his eyes toward Gordy.

"Okay, I'll wait till you and Mr. Powell finish your business, and then we can talk," she said.

"I believe Mr. Powell and I have finished our business, haven't we, Gordy?"

"I guess we have, Barry. I'll see ya soon," Gordy said. He turned to Emily and extended his hand once more. "It's been a pleasure to meet you, Emily. I've developed a special interest in this case and I would be glad to work with you, if you need some help."

"Maybe," she replied, "after the dust settles."

CHAPTER 9

Gordy had been in the Guilford Police Department for six years. During that time, he was union president and had received several commendations for action in the line of duty, but he was still only a patrol officer. For one reason or another, he avoided the additional responsibilities of promotion and special assignments.

Maybe times were changing. Since the discovery of the old Chrysler, Gordy was unable to get a good night's sleep. He became absorbed with the need to find out what really happened at Nod Road.

When Gordy finished at the Clinton impound, he went directly to the house. Even if he couldn't sleep well, he knew he had to get some rest, because he was scheduled to work the night shift for the up-coming week. A series of unplanned absences in the department had reached his level of seniority, and he was needed to cover nights for one week in the next four.

Gordy didn't like the shift very much, because nights were usually feast or famine—nothing to do but try to keep from dozing off, or too much to do, dodging bullets or chasing perps on the highway at a hundred miles an hour. Duty called and he was resigned to his one-week assignment.

He reported in at eleven forty-five p.m., went through the duty log with the dispatcher, and found that it had been a pretty boring second shift, with not much local activity. After the review, he picked up his car from Officer Tommy Maybret. Tommy greeted him with a nasal "Hi," and complained about a head cold that had plagued him all afternoon. The complaint caused Gordy to grimace at the prospect of taking over a car that had become a Petri dish for Maybret's infection. Despite his annoyance, he exchanged a few courtesies and climbed into the car. He drove toward his territory, the southwest part of town. This section included Route 1, down to Branford, and north to the Durham line. Not much happened on the East End of the territory, but the stretch of road going toward Branford was always unpredictable.

At twelve-fifteen a.m., he pulled into the Southside Computer Center and began his usual checks of locks and windows. Everything was fine. He exited the driveway and headed south on US 1. He stopped at three other businesses, did his rounds, and posted the results in his log. He checked his watch. The luminous hands pointed to one forty as he pulled into the front lot of Shoreline BMW.

As Gordy spun the steering wheel to the right, he sprayed a bright arc of light across the property with the cruiser's hi-beams. The light passed parked cars in front and panned across the main building. The new cars were in a fenced area in the back lot. He pulled the cruiser near the main showroom door and parked with his hi-beams lighting most of the front of the building. He got out of the cruiser, tried the door, and determined it was locked securely.

Gordy returned to his vehicle and noticed the left door on a 325i convertible in the front row was slightly ajar. He thought, *Damn, what do I do with this? Some bozo probably left the lot after a test drive and forgot to lock the door.*

He had limited choices—one was to close the door, verify it was locked, and write a subsequent report. He could pretend he didn't see it. Or, get real cautious and suppose someone had broken into the car after closing. If someone had done that, they might still be on the property.

Gordy released the strap on his service pistol. He walked slowly to the parked car. The door was unlatched. He decided to close and lock it and write the damn report. When he finished, he started to walk back to the cruiser. He noticed the large gate to the "new car" paddock was not wrapped with the usual length of chain.

He decided he needed a closer look. As he approached the gate, he saw the familiar chain was off and lying in the dim light on the ground about twenty feet away. Gordy drew his Smith & Wesson, nine millimeter-semi automatic, turned around, and started back to the cruiser.

Damn, he thought, *I need back up.* He straddled the front seat and reached for the car radio microphone. As he did, he heard an engine start. A brand new BMW 528 squealed from position behind the fence. It barreled toward the unlatched gate.

Gordy crouched behind the cruiser's opened door and tried to juggle his gun in one hand and the mike in the other. He yelled "Police," as the BMW sped through the gate. It headed straight for Gordy's opened door. He didn't have time to call or even think. His reflexes took control. He leaped across the large front seat. He banged his head on the passenger door, as the BMW struck the cruiser's left door and smashed it into the frame. The speeding car grazed the cruiser's rear fender and sped toward Route 1.

"Shit."

Gordy managed to get behind the wheel. The cruiser's door was hopelessly buckled. There was no way to keep it closed. He clicked his seat belt in place, jammed the shift lever into drive, and spun the big Ford Crown Victoria around in hot pursuit.

Once he was on Route 1, Gordy fished the mike off the floor and yelled into it, "This is car four, Gordy Powell. Officer needs help, in pursuit of black BMW Five-Twenty-Eight. Perps dangerous! Heading south on Route One, at pole marker two-oh-five."

While he talked, a hole appeared in the windshield and he heard the whine of a bullet rush though the interior and strike the back seat with a thump.

"Ah, shit!"

Gordy continued the chase toward the Branford town line. He figured dispatch would call Branford PD and advise them they were heading in that direction. He looked at the speedometer and noted he was doing eighty-five. He wasn't gaining on the BMW. The fleeing car was still pulling away.

The Guilford Police Department was quite small. There were only four patrol cars on night shift. They had a lot of territory to cover. It was unlikely anyone would be joining Gordy before the BMW crossed the Branford line.

Gordy drove with his head low. Once again, he squeezed the button on the mike. "Dispatch, advise Branford PD, the perps are headed in their direction. Also, shots are fired, I'm still in pursuit."

Dispatch relayed the message. Two Branford cruisers converged on Route 1 and headed north. Gordy wondered if the BMW driver would continue to stay on local roads or try to swing onto Route 95. If he did, he entered jurisdiction of the state police. Gordy would have to break off the chase. In the meantime, dispatch came back and gave him permission to maintain pursuit over the Branford town line.

"Thanks a bunch," Gordy muttered.

As the BMW approached the town line, the driver saw two Branford cruisers parked in a V-shape with all lights flashing. The speeding car spun into a right-hand turn, hurdled the curb, and made it to Rire Hill Road without crossing into Branford.

"Ah shit," Gordy said again. "Officer requests assistance," he called into the mike. "Ask the Branford guys to give me a hand."

"Will advise," came the reply.

A minute later, the dispatcher came back, "Gordy, you're on your own, Branford claims no crime committed on its side of the line.

"Great, really great, how far away is some assistance?"

"Officer Peterson is on Route One, about two miles north of Rire Hill Road, estimate closing on your twenty in three to five minutes."

"You know this guy is shooting?" Gordy yelled once again.

"We have that," dispatch replied.

Gordy heard a metallic clink come from the engine compartment. A spray of steam bellowed over the hood. This reduced Gordy's visibility considerably, but he didn't slow down. "Dispatch? How about the state troopers?" Gordy asked in desperation.

"Have them on the line. They're on the way," dispatch confirmed.

Gordy knew he had to keep up the pressure. He hoped whoever was driving the BMW made a mistake before he did. Both cars were doing over ninety miles an hour. Gordy saw on-coming headlights and familiar flashing lights emerging over a rise in the road ahead. He could occasionally see through the veil of steam wafting over the hood. *Great, it looks like we may be able to hold them off at the pass.* The local resident state trooper headed right at them from the opposite direction.

Dispatch came back, "Trooper Ray Marrow has you in sight and is preparing to block the way with his vehicle."

"Do it quick, this guy is nuts," Gordy yelled into the mike.

There is pasture to the left, woods to the right. If the BMW were going to break from the road, it will surely go left, Gordy thought. That was exactly what happened. The luxury car spun into a left-hand skid, went over the shoulder, through a barbed wire fence, and hurdled into the pasture. Gordy slowed and took the same route through the fence and followed suit. The state trooper pulled in next. Officer Bill Peterson soon fell in behind as they raced across the moonlit, hilly pasture.

This Connecticut field was typical, with borders of rocks and shrubs laid out in straight lines separating sections of pasture. The BMW sped along until it came to the first such border in its path. The driver picked a spot with little brush, floored the accelerator, and attempted to careen through. The car bumped and lurched over the ground, making terrible grinding sounds as the car's bottom struck rock and stump, but kept going.

The BMW emerged on the other side of the border and like a launched rocket hurtled into the air. Suddenly there was no pasture in front, only a seven-foot drop to the farm's cow pond. The car's brake lights flashed bright red as the car flew for several seconds completing a graceful, predictable arch and landing with a large moonlit splash. The big six-cylinder motor, roaring with high speed revs, gulped a fatal dose of pond water and seized up immediately.

Gordy drove through on the same path, and slowed to

a stop as the trunk of the BMW disappeared below his line of sight. Then he eased his car over the rise and surveyed the scene below. Trooper Marrow and Officer Peterson pulled in behind, got out, and trotted to the edge of the cow pond, leaving their cruisers' headlights fixed on the scene. The BMW stood immersed to the door handles, its headlights still shining into the water. Reflected light all around showed all three occupants still inside, shaking their heads in either bewilderment or physical shock.

The rest was easy. The three cops aimed their weapons at the car. Gordy ordered the occupants to show their hands and leave the vehicle. Slowly the car doors opened. Three men staggered into waist deep water. Gordy told them to keep their hands raised and walk toward him. They did and were cuffed. Gordy patted them down and ordered them into the back of Bill Peterson's cruiser. He rode in the passenger side as they headed to the station with Trooper Marrow following closely behind.

CHAPTER 10

Emily arrived at the library at seven-fifty a.m. as usual. *Just another Tuesday morning,* she thought. She unlocked the front door, and went inside. The building officially opened at nine o'clock, but she always went in an hour or so early. Behind the offices was a small kitchen where she made coffee and kept fresh milk.

Yesterday she had received confirmation she was a close enough match to DNA taken from the molars of the Nod Road remains to be a genetic granddaughter. Not that she had any doubt, but at least no one could dispute her notion of direct lineage. What surprised her was the feeling of despair that swept over her when the test result was confirmed. She had stayed awake most of the night, thinking about her grandfather, trying to imagine what he was like, and what happened in 1938.

During the course of last night, she made up her mind to visit her Great Uncle Bert and listen to what he remembered about her grandfather and the circumstances surrounding his disappearance. He recently turned eighty, and he lived in a managed care facility in Branford. The last time she visited him was the week before Christmas last year. Although his mind was clear, he was confined to his wheelchair. It was nearly ten months later now and she wasn't sure what to expect, but she decided to drive to the home when she left the library at day's end. She also decided to make a list of everything she already knew about her grandfather.

✁✁✁

The Branford Golden Maturity Center sat on a small knoll overlooking Long Island Sound. The facility was located just north of the Thimble Islands and the property afforded an excellent view of them. The main building was an older construction, with Victorian dormers and weathered cedar shakes for siding. The rooms on the inside opened to the inner courtyard. Uncle Bert was in the south wing and could access the courtyard through a set of aluminum and glass sliders. He had been a resident at the center for the past two years, and he was always glad to see an unscheduled visitor.

Emily stood outside the open door and knocked on the wall. Uncle Bert sat in his wheelchair watching Jeopardy on television. With the TV noise and Uncle Bert's poor hearing, he didn't respond. She entered the room and called, "Uncle Bert."

Bert looked up in surprise, and then his face broke into a huge smile. He was a thin man with white skin and countless freckles. His head was nearly bald and wisps of stringy red hair hung over his ears. His blue eyes welled up with fluid as he recognized his visitor. "Oh, my goodness, Emily, what a surprise."

"Hello, Uncle Bert." She bent over and wrapped him in a big hug. "How have you been?"

"Please sit down, dear." He motioned to a chair by the bed.

"Thank you," she said, as she sat down.

"You know how it is when you get old. If somebody asks how you are, it might take an hour or so to run through just how you really are. So, I try to avoid talking about it as much as possible. For the most part, I'm doing okay. The really important thing is how you are, and what brings you here?"

"I had been just fine up until a few weeks ago. Have you been reading the newspaper?"

"No, not very often?"

"Okay, have you heard about the old car pulled out of a pond in Clinton?"

Uncle Bert's cheerful expression suddenly turned pale, and he turned his face toward the courtyard sliders. "No, I haven't dear," he said with a voice that sounded far away.

She noticed his change, but decided to wait before asking anything. "They found the remains of Sam Stemford in an old car that's been under water since 1938. That's my grandfather and your brother-in-law. They've finally found his body after all these years."

Uncle Bert seemed to rally, and he turned to her, "Well, Emily, that is quite a surprise. How can you be sure it's your grandfather?"

"I'm quite sure. They found his wedding ring with an inscription from grandmother, and they have done preliminary DNA tests to confirm a paternal match to me. But there's more you need to know, Uncle Bert," she went on. "The police told me Sam was shot in the head before ending up in the pond." She paused for a moment to let the remark sink in. "I want to get as much info on Doctor Sam as possible, and I need your help."

Emily reached into her purse and took out a small pocket sized tape recorder. She placed it on the bedside table and pressed the record button.

"Well, dear, I don't know that I can help you very much, it was all such a very long time ago," the old man said with a touch of sadness in his voice. "Doctor Sam Stemford was quite a scurrilous fellow."

"How do you mean scurrilous?"

"I don't know, I guess I just didn't like him very much."

Emily thought for a minute and decided to take a different tack. "Let's start with some specifics that you might remember. For example, do you know when he graduated from medical school? I remember mother telling me that he went to Yale, but she had no idea when."

Uncle Bert scratched his temple. "I'm not sure I can tell you…let me figure this out for a minute. I believe he was forty-nine years old when he disappeared. He must have graduated around the time of the Great War, probably 1917 or 1918. I know he wanted to join the army but the war ended too soon. After graduation, he did an internship at Yale-New Haven and then went to work for a small practice in East Haven. A few years later, he met my father, your great-grandfather, Doctor Lawrence Moorefield.

"Father was a good man and, at that time, his was the only practice between Madison and Branford. I believe it was the year after the stock market crash. Father persuaded Sam to move out here and join his practice. I know father was having trouble with his emphysema and needed help. Sam possessed a kind of charm that gave him an advantage whenever anyone was dealing with him. I remember he was a great proponent of vaccination as a method of disease control, and not everyone was in favor at the time. Even Father had serious reservations on the subject. They often argued about the idea of vaccination.

"Back then, I suspect there was more risk with inoculations than there is today, so Father did have some useful facts to argue against the wide-spread use. Perhaps he was old fashioned, but he found it inconsistent to infect someone with a disease in order to protect them from the disease. I believe Sam wrote some sort of paper on the subject when he was at Yale. At any rate, he came to work for Father in 1930. Four years later, he married my sister Mary." As he spoke, his voice seemed to slow; either the strain of conversation or the content was weighing heavily on him.

Emily asked, "Tell me about their relationship. What were they like as a couple?"

Uncle Bert let out a great sigh and stretched his arms. Through the glass sliders, Emily noticed shadows spreading across the shrubs and flowers. She realized the old gentleman was tired and she probably wouldn't learn much more today.

Uncle Bert went on, his voice slow, giving the impression of choosing his words carefully. "Mary was very quiet and shy. Since Father's practice was in the house, Sam saw Mary almost every day. At first there didn't seem to be much interest between them with Sam being so much older, but a year later they began to spend time together. Another year passed and they announced they were going to marry. Dear, I'm feeling very tired and running out of things to remember. Perhaps we can talk some more about this some other time."

Emily agreed it was enough for now. Then she thought of one more urgent question. "Just one more thing, Uncle Bert, can you tell me the date Sam disappeared?"

"Why yes, dear, I remember it clearly, it was September 14, 1938. It was a week or two before the terrible hurricane. Teddy Flanders was in charge of the case, despite his tender age. I didn't like him much, either."

"Thank you, Uncle Bert," she said and then quickly asked "Would you mind terribly if I dropped by next week and perhaps we can talk some more?"

"No, dear, not at all. That will give me some time to find my thinking cap and try to have more information for you."

"Thanks Uncle Bert. We'll try again next week. Get some rest now and I'll talk to you later," she said as she picked up the little tape recorder and tucked it into her purse.

As Emily drove home from the center, she made up her mind to call Gordy Powell and see if he was still interested in the case. There was so much she didn't know, and she was obsessed with finding it. Uncle Bert seemed to tire so easily. She pulled into her driveway, locked up the Camry, and walked toward the house.

Twilight had stolen the colors from the day, leaving dark gray shadows in the path ahead. She walked briskly, toward the front porch. Suddenly, she heard something rustle and huff in the thick bushes that wrapped around the house. The noise startled her and she slowed her pace.

Her mind raced through the possibilities. Then she turned around and returned to the Camry. She retrieved a flashlight from the glove box and once again headed for the door. This time she projected a circle of white light at the overgrown ornamental bushes and stepped briskly to the door. She fumbled with the key and finally unlocked it. Once inside, she locked the door behind her. She was shaking.

Emily hadn't experienced real fear in a long time. She convinced herself the noise was probably a dog or some other animal, but still, she was surprised with her reaction. Was it the noise or simply the surprise? Was it because of the murder of her grandfather?

A chilling revelation swept through her mind as she realized why she was so frightened.

Suppose her grandfather's killer was still alive.

And lived nearby.
And was watching.

❧❧❧

Two blocks away, a man whistled. Two large Rottweilers emerged from the darkness. He extended his hand and dispensed crunchy treats to both the animals.

"Good dogs," he whispered as he patted the side of his truck. Both animals leaped into the pickup bed. The man climbed into the cab and drove away.

CHAPTER 11

Gordy was glad to be back on day shift. The excitement of last week was enough to last him the rest of his career. Although his sergeant recommended him for a commendation, he knew he was lucky to be alive and uninjured.

"We're still trying to determine who actually fired the shots that damaged your car," the investigators said. "So far, we've confirmed who was driving the BMW, but the other two men wouldn't admit to the shooting. Both men tested negative for gunshot residue, and it's possible the shooter wiped himself clean while he was in the cow pond, but the ballistics report is worrisome. It took two days to recover a gun from the pond. By that time, prints were undetectable. But it wasn't even the same caliber gun that shot up your car."

All three men were from New York City and specialized in hitting upscale car dealerships in Connecticut and New Jersey.

The police learned there were actually four men in the theft ring, and they ran stolen cars regularly into the city for either chopping or resale.

"The fourth man was parked nearby when you made your rounds," the head investigator said, "and simply drove away when the altercation started. We're pretty sure he wasn't the shooter, either. We have his name and have issued a warrant to the tri-state area."

Gordy didn't think much of the mystery. Instead, he enjoyed the relative peace and quiet of his regular day shift. He arrived home on Tuesday and finished his regular chores. He considered himself a gentleman farmer and maintained a small collection of livestock. His two dogs, Romulus and Remus, were rescues from the local shelter. They had the run of a fenced in acre behind his house. His three cats, Dolly, Rocky, and Izzy lived in the house. Counted among the barn animals were a horse, a donkey, two goats, two pigs, and a number of ducks, geese, and chickens. The first task he faced when he arrived home every day was the care and feeding of the menagerie.

After Gordy finished his chores, he walked to the front of his property to inspect the progress of the roadwork. To his delight, the entire fill was put in place and the new culvert installed.

Nod Road had to be severed for four days while the curve was straightened, and preparations for the new bridge were being made. This meant Gordy was forced to enter his driveway from the west. All his neighbors on the east side of the pond had to enter their property from the east end of the road. Things were finishing up and hopefully they could open the coffer dam next week and refill the pond.

The dry pond bed was crazed with mud cracks like the patina on an old piece of china. Residents in the area had experienced nearly a week of terrible odors as the pond bottom slowly evaporated and the residual organic material decomposed.

While Gordy rummaged through the construction area, he noticed fresh diggings around the depression that once held the old Chrysler. A large number of new shovel holes were scattered here and there. Gordy figured the

Clinton PD had come back to the site and searched for something, maybe a piece of the car, a bullet, or even a gun.

It was getting dark now and he decided to go back to the house. As he climbed the front door stairs, he heard the phone ring inside. He hurried through the door and picked up just before the answering machine intercepted.

"Hello, Mr. Gordy Powell please," said a woman's voice on the other end.

"Speaking," Gordy answered, hoping it wasn't a tele-marketer trying to peddle something.

"Mr. Powell, my name's Emily Pierce. We met at the Clinton impound a week or so ago. How have you been?"

Gordy tried responding in a cool, professional voice, but his heart was pumping hard. "Yes, Ms. Pierce," he answered. "I'm fine. What can I do for you?"

"I've been wondering if we can meet and discuss the death of my grandfather. Sort of compare notes, if you don't mind?"

Gordy didn't hesitate. "Yeah, I think that's a great idea. I've been poking around and I've discovered a few pieces of info that might be worthwhile. When do you want to meet?"

"How about seven o'clock tomorrow, here at my place," she said.

"Okay, where's your place?"

She rattled off instructions and, when she finished, she hung up with a polite "Goodbye."

CHAPTER 12

Gordy arrived at the home of Emily Pierce a little earlier than expected. He felt guilty and hoped he didn't interrupt her dinner. He'd rushed through his regular routine at Nod Road so quickly, he was surprised with his lack of timing. He pressed the doorbell and waited on the porch.

Emily opened the door and welcomed him in. "Hello, Mr. Powell, or should I call you Officer Powell."

"Just call me Gordy," he replied as he followed her into the living room.

The house was an older Dutch colonial with a gambrel roof and wrap-around porch. The place was sorely in need of repair. Outside paint was weathered and peeling. Overgrown shrubs around the front porch poked their branches through the railings. Alongside the house was a detached garage with hinged wooden doors that sagged toward the center. Inside, light poured into the entry hall through port light windows on either side of the door. A rather old glass chandelier hung in the center of the foyer and Queen Anne furniture graced the entrance and the living room. By any standard, the place had character, but somehow it didn't fit the lifestyle of a 90s woman.

"Nice place you've got here, Ms. Pierce."

"Thank you, it was my mother's. She died a year ago

in September. I've been living here for nearly two years. By the way, please call me Emily. Would you like some coffee?"

"Sure, that would be nice."

She brought out a tray with two mugs wafting steam, alongside a creamer and sugar bowl.

"Well, let's get down to business," she said as she sat down in a wingback chair across from Gordy. "You said you were interested in finding out what happened to the man in the car. If you meant what you said, I'd like your help. Frankly, I don't think the Clinton Police are going to make much progress working with a sixty-year-old murder case. And I don't accept that. I want to know everything's being done to find out what happened."

"I feel the same way," Gordy said. "I've not been able to forget the image of the remains in the car. Usually things like that don't bother me, but this one does."

As Gordy talked, he found himself studying her large hazel eyes and at the same time, thinking he wanted to know more about her.

Emily went on, "What I've been doing is making a list of all the information that's available. If you're interested, I'd like to form a team to access whatever resources we might need to put some kind of closure on my grandfather's death. There's so much to be done. There may be records that can help. There may be people we can interview who might have some threads of information. I'm not exactly sure how to proceed, but I'd feel a lot better if I were working as hard, maybe harder, than the local PD. For example, I met with my Great Uncle Bert yesterday, at his nursing home in Branford, and we talked for a while. He wasn't even aware Sam Stemford's body had been found. He seemed so sad when I told him, but at the same time, he told me he didn't like Sam very much when he was alive. That kind of surprised me."

"It does seem a little strange," Gordy said. "At any rate, you're right about gathering information, Emily. There must have been some kind of paperwork filed when your grandmother reported your grandfather's disappearance. We'll need to try and find those records, see if anyone's alive who may have been involved with working on them, and we'll need to confirm the date of his disappearance. It could provide an approximate date of death."

Emily said, "Good. Uncle Bert said Sam disappeared on September 14, 1938. He also said several other revealing things. They may provide clues to Sam's personality. Uncle Bert called him a scurrilous fellow but wouldn't elaborate. He also said Sam had some kind of charm that made him clever in negotiating, and Sam was a fan of inoculating against disease, not necessarily a popular position at the time. I'm sure there is a great deal more he can tell us about Sam's life. Although it may be difficult to draw it out of him. After all, if there's anyone else out there who knew Sam or the Moorefields, we've got to find them."

"How about the newspaper?" Gordy offered. "There may have been some articles written after the disappearance."

"That's a good idea," Emily said. "I know I must go to New Haven, stop at Yale, and check on when he graduated. Uncle Bert thinks Sam wrote a paper on the use of vaccination for disease control. Maybe I can find the paper. In the meantime, let's make a list of things we can do separately so we don't end up stepping all over each other."

CHAPTER 13

The first item on Gordy's list brought him to the Madison Police Department. Chief Terry Deering had lived his entire life on the shoreline. He wasn't a recent import like so many other officials. He was an uncomplicated man, direct in his methods and fair in his regard. He was forty-one and enjoyed his work very much. He was sitting behind a big oak desk when Gordy entered his office. Deering was in full summer uniform, and his large brown eyes opened wide in greeting.

"How're you doin', Gordy?" he said, reaching out his hand without getting up. "What brings you to my neck of the woods?"

"Well, chief, I'm sure you know about the Sam Stemford affair, the old Chrysler found in my pond," Gordy said.

"Yes, I do, but isn't that a Clinton problem?"

"Yes and no, Terry. The fact is his granddaughter is Emily Pierce. She's a very stubborn lady, and she wants to know what happened. She's doing some backup research on the crime, and I'm helping her. We'd like to get into the records of 1938 and see what we can find out about his disappearance. According to Emily, the situation was reported here in Madison, and there should have been reports filed. I'd like to look through the old records and see what I can find."

The chief leaned back in his chair, "I don't mind, but you're a couple of days late. Fact is, Barry Lands from the Clinton PD rummaged through the archives in the town hall cellar a few days ago. I don't know what he found, but I told him to let me know if he took anything. To the best of my knowledge he didn't find much to take. You're welcome to look through the old junk and see what you can find, but you might save yourself some time and just ask Barry if he found anything."

As the chief spoke, Gordy recalled his last conversation with Barry Lands, and he dismissed any hope of the policeman sharing information with him. Gordy explained he'd just as soon check it out himself and advise the chief of any information he found.

A little while later, he was at the Madison Town Hall. The building was original, a three- story colonial painted white with black trim. The front of the structure boasted a large open porch with four Doric columns supporting a slate covered roof.

Gordy entered the front double doors and smiled at the matronly receptionist. He showed his police badge. "I have the chief's permission to look through the old records kept in the cellar."

"I know. He called. Sign the logbook," she said and handed him two keys. She directed him to a door that led downstairs.

The archives, organized in rows of shelves, stood behind a chain link fence that reached from floor to ceiling. In between each row was a series of sixty-watt incandescent bulbs hanging from old, cloth-covered wires. The resulting light was poor, and Gordy smiled to himself as he thought the last time any work was done down here was probably back in the 1930s. Little did he know, at the time, his casual notion was right on the mark. The last time the cellar had any work was in the aftermath of the infamous 1938 hurricane.

The terrible storm ravaged Southern New England, sweeping across Long Island, slamming the Connecticut shoreline and into Rhode Island's Narragansett Bay. Millions of gallons of water pushed up the bay, flooding the entire city of Providence. When the storm was over, six hundred people were dead and over three billion dollars of damage was done.

The cellar of the old town hall was formed of stone and mortar and, on the wall—nearly obscured by an old wooden bookshelf—was a faded yellow line with tiny letters that read, "High Water 1938." The line was a full six feet off the floor. It was a good thing police records of the time were still secured at the old police department building, because almost everything prior to 1938, languishing in the town hall cellar, was lost when the building flooded. The original police building was on higher ground and sustained less damage.

Gordy had used one key to open the door leading downstairs. He took the second key and unlocked the chain link gate that allowed access into the archives. He wished he'd brought a flashlight but decided he could do without. He convinced himself he had better search now, instead of trying to return later. As he entered the enclosure, he saw seven-foot racks with shelves containing hundreds of boxes of papers.

The only thing that would simplify the search was the placement of the beginning racks. They were dated 1938, and there wasn't much dated before then. Gordy had no idea why there weren't many annual records prior to the 1938 hurricane, but he was astonished with the fact that there seemed to be ample information available from March 1938, forward.

Within two hours, he had found a box with PD records dated September 1938. To his delight, he found a missing person report dated September 15, 1938. Mary Stemford filed the report, and it described her husband Doctor Samuel Stemford in careful detail. A yellow photograph was attached with a rusty staple to the back of the report. The paper was frail but the type was still quite legible. At the bottom of the page was a place for the reviewing cop's signature and there, in pale black ink, was the name Theodore Flanders.

Holy shit, Gordy thought. I'll bet that's Harlan's father. Flanders was a rookie cop back then, just out of the academy. He knew Teddy Flanders had been a chief of police somewhere on the shoreline before he retired. At least he was still alive and maybe could remember something about the original investigation.

Also tucked into the same file were several pages of old newspaper clippings and various forms with handwritten notes attached. Gordy pulled a clear plastic bag from his pocket. It was large enough to hold all the paperwork. He carefully inserted everything into the bag, all the while thinking something troubled him. Why didn't Barry Lands find the same stuff? Surely if he did, he would have taken it. Gordy would have never known it existed. Maybe Lands just missed it.

CHAPTER 14

Emily disliked the drive into New Haven. There was usually a traffic snarl starting in East Haven that spread all the way to Bridgeport. It was one of the reasons she valued the shoreline so much. Each of the townships from Branford to Old Lyme was relatively uncongested. Each retained a unique identity, and even though Interstate 95 passed through the area, somehow the shoreline maintained a certain aura of anonymity.

Until recently there wasn't much in the way of shopping malls, little in the way of price-busting warehouses, and still not even a resident television station. The area catered to a few quiet businesses, sleepy older neighborhoods, and several choice marinas that maintained Connecticut's largest sailing fleet. The complexion of the area changed now. With the advent of the Pequot Indian Casino, there were new problems; new challenges; and, on the weekends, new congestion.

Emily's family had been there for three generations and, although all things must change, she could not imagine living anywhere else in the world. She finally arrived at the exit ramp that took her to Yale University.

The venerable institution sat in the middle of downtown New Haven like an old, veiled queen mother shrouded in black shadows, hiding her age in the cold recesses of brick and stone. She lay permanently fixed by the foundations of her buildings. A fortress for wisdom and knowledge assaulted from all sides by the ignorance of the inner city, a curious paradox of our times.

Mozart by day.

A chorus of gunshots at night.

Emily had been there many times and had no trouble finding a parking spot at the main administration building. She knew of several resources that could assist in the search for information about her grandfather. But, because the dates were vague, she decided to visit directly with the dean of Information Services and ask for special help.

Emily had worked with Evelyn Van Denaker on several local projects, and she believed she'd be a willing aid. Emily's experience with large bureaucracies was less than positive, and she was prepared to cope with some frustration as she appealed for special consideration. Certainly, the degree of frustration she encountered depended on whom she dealt with.

She went to the front desk, introduced herself, and asked to see Dean Van Denaker. When asked, she conceded she did not have an appointment but explained she was there on a matter of the utmost importance and she knew the dean personally. She explained who she was and that she and the dean had worked together in the past. She was confident the dean would see her. A few minutes passed and she was invited to proceed to the dean's office.

Evelyn Van Denaker was a plump woman in her early forties. She sat behind a large Chippendale desk and didn't get up as Emily entered.

Van Denaker wore a plain beige dress with a straight neckline. Her hair was cut short and frosted. She looked at Emily through rimless glasses that magnified her steely gray eyes. Her overall appearance gave the impression she was both efficient and perhaps a little lofty.

"What can we do for you, Emily?"

Emily resented people using the royal "we" when referring to themselves. But she needed this woman's help so she was determined to remain extra courteous. "Well, Evelyn, you know the discovery of my grandfather's remains has been in the newspaper."

"Yes, I've been following the story with interest."

"Did you know he graduated from Yale?" Emily asked.

"No, I didn't," the dean answered.

"Well, he did, and I would like to find as much information about him as I can. I need your help. May I look through his school records? I've been told he had some special interest in the field of inoculations and he may have written a paper on the subject while he was here. I'd also like to see the paper. I don't know the exact dates, but I believe he attended Yale during the years of 1916, through 1918. He may have graduated in 1917 or 1918. Because it was so long ago, you could be a tremendous help."

"I'm afraid I'll have to discuss your request with other members of the staff. Give me a few days, and we'll see what we can do," Evelyn said.

Emily felt her tension building and the idea that she may be facing some sort of bureaucratic gauntlet crept into her mind. Suppose Yale feared any references connected to a local murder could be some kind of board or committee decision. Suppose this staid institution refused to help in any way. Emily considered the possibility and decided to take a risk.

In a carefully controlled voice, she said, "Evelyn, this whole situation is terribly sad and even more frustrating. Not only am I dealing with a tragedy, but I have precious little information to know what my grandfather was like, as a man or as a doctor. Given enough time, I can probably find the information I need all by myself. But with your resources, it would be so much easier. Please don't force me to wade through a bureaucratic nightmare. I'll be in your debt if you just turn around to that terminal behind you and pull up any information available regarding Dr. Sam Stemford. I understand your concern and obligation to the university. But, I assure you, I am looking for my own personal reasons. None of what I'm doing is going to the press."

"Emily, I understand your situation, and I will try to help. Please take a seat out in the lobby, give me a few minutes, and I'll try to find out what information's available and just how long it will take to get it out."

CHAPTER 15

Emily always enjoyed driving out and away from New Haven. On the front seat beside her was the thick portfolio of information Dean Van Denaker had given her only moments before. She had been there for four hours.

Emily arrived back at the library and went directly to her office, carrying the package of papers. She sat down at her desk and dialed Gordy Powell's number. As she expected, she was greeted by his answering machine.

"Gordy? It's Emily. I've got the information from Yale. Can we get together tonight and review where we're at? Let me know. I'll be at the library till five and at home from five-thirty on. Bye." She hung up and began looking through the paperwork.

❧

Later in the afternoon, Gordy Powell checked his message machine before he got off duty. He smiled to himself as Emily's message rattled through the receiver. When the recording was over, he called the library and confirmed with Emily that tonight would be fine at his place at five-thirty. He'd fix dinner and she could bring a six pack of diet Coke.

As soon as Gordy got home, he scurried through the house, picking up files and old newspapers. The place was very clean, but untidy. He didn't want Emily to think he was domestically challenged. He'd been more or less alone since his divorce in 1983 and didn't spend a lot of time organizing the household. He'd married a Japanese woman while stationed there during his hitch in the marines.

Gordy brought Son Lea home in 1981, full of high expectations and youthful idealism. After two years of conflict, they divorced and she returned to Japan. As far as he knew, Son Lea never returned to the states. Although that period of his life was painful, he didn't regret his failed attempt at marriage. The situation gave him a healthy respect for relationships and probably contributed to his remaining single for such a long time. Throughout his association with local women, he kept a comfortable distance and avoided the usual traps relationships could spring.

Gordy had a feeling Emily Pierce was different. She seemed self-sufficient and very motivated. These attributes suggested she was fine all by herself. Those characteristics attracted him.

He thought about the way her hazel eyes flashed when she talked about her grandfather. The kind of half smile she displayed, when she heard something she liked, and the shape of her supple body underneath the light cotton dresses she seemed to favor on these hot August days.

Gordy took two steaks from the refrigerator and husked four ears of corn. He had picked two large, plump red tomatoes from his garden the day before and he set them aside for slicing later.

When the doorbell finally rang, his heart started pounding. As she opened the door, he noticed that she was wearing another of the light cotton dresses that he found so pleasing. He swallowed hard and said, "Hi."

"Hello, Gordy."

"Come on in," he urged and reached for the six-pack to relieve her burden. "I've got some steaks and corn, but if you don't mind, I'm running a little late, and I should take care of the animals before we sit down." He put the Cokes in the fridge.

On the sills of three separate windows sat the three ugliest cats Emily had ever seen. They blinked at her amicably from their perches.

"I'd asked for the three cats that had been at the shelter the longest," said Gordy, "And came home with Dolly, Rocky, and Izzy."

"How many animals do you have?" she asked with some hesitation in her voice.

"Oh, just a few, right now," he answered. "It varies, from time to time. Come along. I can introduce you as we go."

Emily followed Gordy down the porch stairs. In the back yard were two of the ugliest dogs she had ever seen. They came up to her and nuzzled her hands. "Same story with Romulus and Remus," Gordy answered her silent question.

He led her to the barn. In a fenced area nearby was a speckled horse standing with one of its legs raised. In the background, a large gray donkey grazed on clumps of pasture grass. As Gordy and Emily drew near, the donkey and horse advanced to the fence. From way behind them came a pair of pitch-black goats, running at full tilt.

Gordy entered the barn and emerged with two large pails of feed. He approached the gated fence and motioned for Emily to follow. He opened the gate, carried the feed pails to three separate troughs, and emptied the two pails evenly into all three. The big appaloosa walked over to Gordy and muzzled his hand. Gordy cupped his free hand over the horse's nose and introduced Emily.

"Ivan this is Emily, and Emily this is Ivan. Forgive me for dispensing with last names, but he has a terrible memory for them," Gordy said, smiling. The donkey was already up to his snout, deep in a trough when Gordy gestured to Emily to come nearer. "This fine fellow is Sammy." He patted the animal's shoulder. The donkey looked up momentarily, as if to say hello, then returned to the feed. Gordy walked over to the goats, and said, "These two guys are Heckle and Jeckle." As he spoke, he patted each of their foreheads.

Emily's face broke into a large grin as she nodded her head. "Please to meetcha, all of ya."

Gordy took a garden hose and filled a big galvanized tub with fresh water. While he was doing this, a rather large number of chickens, ducks, and geese emerged from everywhere and converged on them. Gordy once more went to the barn and this time returned with two coffee cans filled with feed for the newcomers. He threw the feed in a spray, and the feathered critters pecked and pushed their way into a near frenzied state. The cacophony was almost deafening.

"Too many to name," he shouted. "Come on to the barn." He motioned to her to follow.

He closed the gate, secured it, and walked back to the wood frame building. Inside, was a boarded pen that spanned the length of one wall. On the other side of the boards were two little, pink piglets. "Last, but not least, I'd like you to meet Pirate and Penzance," Gordy said, as he reached down and picked up Pirate. The little guy weighed about twenty-five pounds, and he squealed as he was lifted.

"Care to hold him?"

"Will he bite?"

"I don't think so."

Emily reached out and took the little pig and held it close. Gordy looked at her and smiled. She stood in the doorway with the afternoon sunlight behind her. The glow framed her and some light illuminated her cotton dress revealing the shadow of her body inside. She was lovely and he was struck by the image.

He wanted to touch her, but instead he reached to take Pirate from her embrace. Emily moved closer and, as he removed the little pig, his hand grazed the top of her breast. She flinched, and then her eyes softened as she gave up the animal. Gordy smelled the fragrance of her shampoo, and he felt overwhelmed.

There was a moment when they regarded each other in a different way. But the moment passed quickly as Emily tossed her head back. "I'm starved, how about you?"

Gordy nodded in agreement and gently lowered Pirate into the pen. From a wooden basket nearby, Gordy tossed bread, buns, and bagels into the pen and the two little pigs grunted with delight. They tore into the provisions with slovenly greed. Gordy felt the need to explain, so he did.

"I have an agreement with the local Food Mart. Instead of throwing out all of their outdated bread, I haul it away a couple times a week. These little guys love it, and it rounds out their diet. They watched for another minute or two, and Gordy said, "That's it, we're done. Let's go make dinner."

As the man and woman left the barn, long, dark shadows stretched across the landscape while the late August sun fell below the trees. They returned to the house and worked together on fixing dinner. After they'd eaten and cleared the table, Gordy took out his plastic bag of paperwork taken from Madison Town Hall, and Emily laid out her cache of papers obtained from Yale. Neither had time to do much with the papers prior to their meeting.

Emily went first, spreading her papers into discrete piles as she read the contents. The first document was a copy of Sam Stemford's Medical Doctor Degree dated June 2, 1919.

"Well, Uncle Bert was pretty close," Emily said. The second document was about fifteen pages, entitled "Inoculations for a Healthier World (The Great Spanish Influenza of 1918)." The rest were one and two-page grant request queries, all justifying research money to develop vaccines of one sort or another.

There was a two-page request to fund the development of a vaccine for the Spanish Flu disease. There were printouts of various billing receipts for laboratory supplies and an enrollment application. The application fixed his date of birth at June 10, 1891. Emily scratched some numbers on a napkin and concluded Doc Sam was twenty-eight when he graduated from medical school and only forty-three when he disappeared.

Gordy went next. He laid out the original missing person report filed by Mary Stemford. That was indeed a treasure. He pointed out the attached photograph. Emily picked it up tenderly.

"My god," she said. Apart from her grandmother's old wedding picture, she had not seen any other pictures of the doctor. This one was sepia, and was a close up of a thin man with chiseled features. He wore a fedora and a leather jacket. His smile showed a neat row of perfectly spaced teeth and a pronounced dimple on the right side of his face. Emily knew she had the same dimple in the same place.

She noticed his eyes. She couldn't be sure because of the sepia, but the transparent flecks in his eyes looked like the hazel characteristics of her own. No one else in the family carried the color of her eyes, and as a little girl, she thought she was a genetic accident. A great sadness swept over her as she studied the picture.

Gordy saw her tears building up and quickly said, "Look what else I've got here. It's a series of newspaper pages. Here's an article dated September 16, 1938, it's titled 'Shoreline Doctor's Disappearance,' and another one about a fiery truck crash that killed a woman on Horse Hill Road. Here's an old speeding ticket issued to the doctor by, guess who, Teddy Flanders. He's the same cop who filled out the missing person report after the doc disappeared. Looks like he was a pretty busy guy back in those days. Here's an article about an outbreak of a Spanish flu-like disease in March of 1938. It started in New York City and by the end of May it had spread all the way to Rhode Island. They compare the 1938 version to the Spanish flu of 1918. Major difference being very few people died in 1938. It says here, the 1918 epidemic killed nearly five hundred thousand people in the United States.

"So, why is all this stuff stuck in the same file? It seems odd, because I don't see much connection between them. At any rate, someone did a reasonable job of saving information about the period. We'll need to make double copies of everything and return these originals to the archives. I'll need to tell Chief Deering what we've got so he won't have any surprises later. By the way, you know what's really strange? Terry Deering said Barry Lands were there a few days before me. Evidently, he didn't find this material or else he would have taken it. It wasn't that hard to find, although the light was pretty bad."

"So what's next?" Emily asked.

Gordy thought for a minute. "Here's what I think we should do. I'll track down Teddy Flanders, see what he remembers about the original investigation, make copies of the files from the Madison Town Hall, and return all the paperwork. Plan to sit with Uncle Bert one more time and try to get more information from him. You can also stop by the Clinton impound again and see if they have uncovered anything new. They'll probably talk to you easier than they will to me. Besides, I'd rather not be put in a position of withholding information from Barry Lands.

"Ask about whether they found any kind of paperwork in the car. The doc must have kept an appointment book of some sort with him. The Titanic research has spawned some great new techniques for restoring submerged papers. Maybe you can find something there. In the missing person report, Mary listed a couple of stops that were on the doc's house calls the day before. I'll see what I can find out about them. In the meantime, read through the stuff that you've accumulated. We can set up a crime board on an old easel I've got, and we can list information as we find it. It will be important to recreate as much of the seventy-two hours before his disappearance as possible. We'll need to list all the folks involved with his life at that time. And it will give us the first look at our suspects."

"Everybody?"

"Everybody."

"Like my grandmother?" she said with some hesitation.

"Yes, and even Uncle Bert," he said. "Then, as we find more facts, we can begin to apply the notions of motive and opportunity. But the list has to be large enough to stand a chance of including the killer."

"Well. I think it's silly to include my grandmother and Uncle Bert, but if you say so, they can go on the list," she agreed.

CHAPTER 16

Gordy reported early in the morning to make copies of everything he had taken from the Madison Town Hall. He kept the old photograph and hoped to make an enlargement if possible. He sensed that Emily wanted it.

The next morning, while sitting in his cruiser, Gordy called Chief Deering from his cell phone. He explained what he found in the archives, and that he was returning the papers during lunch today. He drove to the old town hall and walked to the front desk.

The same matronly woman was sitting there. She looked up and greeted him with a smile. "Hello, Officer Powell, how are you today," she said cheerfully.

"Good afternoon," he said. "I have made some copies of old documents that were on file, and I want to return the originals."

"That will be fine," she said.

Gordy thought for a moment and then asked, "By the way, do you get many requests to go through the stuff downstairs?"

"Oh, it comes in cycles," she answered. "Sometimes months go by and nobody has any interest, and then there times like this month when everybody and their brother needs to go down there."

"Do you keep a list of people who actually do go downstairs?"

"Yes of course, it's the same book that you signed when you went downstairs a couple of days ago."

"May I look through it?" he asked.

"Sure, you'll have to sign it again anyway."

When Gordy had signed it the first time, he was so intent on getting to the archives, it didn't occur to him to discover who else had been there. *Bad cop*, he thought. His name started the beginning of a page, so he had to turn back to find the others. The book was divided into sections across the top of the page. The section titles were, *NAME, DATE, OCCUPATION, ADDRESS.*

He turned the page and noted five names recorded since the beginning of August. Those names were: Peter Simpson a local contractor, Allen Drew retired merchant, Theodore Flanders, chief of police (retired), Avery Johnson, reporter for the New Haven newspaper, and Barry Lands, detective for the Clinton PD. The name Peter Simpson was familiar right away. It was his company, Simpson Construction, doing the work at Nod Road. Most of the other names were familiar, too, except Allen Drew.

I wonder who he is, Gordy thought. Then he jotted names in his notebook.

"Perhaps you can help me," Gordy asked. "What kind of permission do people need to go downstairs?"

"Well, it depends," she said.

"Depends on what?"

"It depends on who they are," she said.

"How about if it's a fellow like Peter Simpson, what happens?"

"Mr. Simpson is a local contractor; he's had access to the archives for years. He is always doing research on land parcels and the like, and he is completely trustworthy. Mr. Drew has been around for a long time. He used to run a hardware business over in Clinton many years ago. He said he was doing research on his family tree. Mr. Flanders used to be the chief of police in Madison a long time ago. He is well known in town and highly regarded." This woman was a veritable fountain of information and it just kept coming. "Oh, and Mr. Johnson works for the *New Haven Reporter;* he was trying to find information on that body they found in the old car in Clinton."

"Did Avery Johnson have permission from Terry Deering?" Gordy asked.

"Not at first. The day he came in, I told him he must have authorization if he were planning to look into police records. He left and came back the next day with a typed letter giving him permission, so I let him go."

Jesus, Gordy thought. *Terrific security system they've got here. That's a boatload of people in the past three weeks, and who knows whether everyone really did sign in.* Gordy sighed, thanked the woman, and returned the papers to the cellar.

When he finished, he climbed into his cruiser and headed toward Guilford. While he was driving, he had an idea, picked up his cell phone, and dialed the *New Haven Reporter.*

"May I speak to Avery Johnson, please," he asked. "Tell him it's Gordy Powell from the Guilford Police Department. Tell him it's urgent."

A minute later Avery Johnson was on the line. "What's going on?"

"Avery, Gordy Powell here. I'm working with Emily Pierce on the death of her grandfather."

Avery said that he had heard as much. He sounded unimpressed.

"I need to ask you something," Gordy went on. "A

couple of weeks ago you were in the archives at the old Madison Town Hall."

"Yes."

"What were you looking for?" Gordy asked.

"I was trying to find information on Doc Stemford," he replied.

"May I ask what you found?" Gordy went on.

"Sure, you can ask," he replied. "I didn't find anything. I spent three lousy hours in that hole and found nothing at all,"

Mystified, Gordy said, "Thanks. That was what I needed to know."

He pushed the off button as Avery Johnson yelled, "Wait a minute" into the phone.

Now Gordy knew he would have to talk to each person in the logbook and learn when those papers were seen last. It was unlikely both Barry Lands and Avery Johnson missed the files if they were there. Gordy had written down the dates that each of the men had signed in alongside their names on his personal note pad.

CHAPTER 17

That evening after Gordy finished his chores, he called Emily.

"Hello" she said.

"It's Gordy. I've had one hell of a day."

"What's wrong?"

"You know the files I borrowed from Madison? Maybe they weren't there when Barry Lands was looking for them," he said.

"What do you mean?"

"Just what I said. Seems Avery Johnson looked for them the day before and he didn't find anything, either. I doubt that two reasonably motivated people were in there within a few days of one another, looking in the same places that I did, and not find anything. It doesn't make sense, if the files were there. Did you have chance to talk with Barry Lands today?"

"Yes, I did. He said they did find an appointment book, but it was unreadable. They sent it out to a specialized lab to see what they can do with it. He doesn't expect to hear from them for a couple of weeks. We'll just have to wait."

"Did you find out anything else?" he asked.

"No, he was rather closed, seemed a little uptight."

"He probably got a call from Terry Deering telling

him I was returning the 1938 police files," Gordy said. "Emily, I've got some ideas that need discussion. How about spending a couple of days on a sailboat?"

"Maybe, but not a couple of days. That isn't such a good idea. How about one day?" she said.

"How about this Saturday?"

Silence.

Gordy went on, "A buddy has a Catalina Twenty-Seven at the town dock in Clinton. I've got a lot of time on the boat and he's out of town for the next couple of weeks. If we leave early in the morning we can have lunch in Mattituck, and be back before dark."

"Okay, if you are going to supply the boat, I'll supply lunch," she offered.

"Okay, see you Saturday. By the way, bring all your notes," Gordy said, as he hung up. He went through his Rolodex, looked up the home phone number of Harlan Flanders, and dialed the number.

"Hello Harlan, its Gordy Powell. How are you doing?"

"Okay, Gordy, what can I do for you?"

"Sorry to bother you at home, but I need a favor. This may seem a little strange, but I need to speak to your dad. I was hoping you could help." As he spoke, Gordy thought payback was great. After all the pressure that Harlan had put on him to settle the Nod Road affair, he enjoyed requiring something, however small, from Harlan.

"What do you want with my father?" Harlan asked with some concern in his voice.

"Nothing much," Gordy said. "I just want to hear what he may remember about the Stemfords. Evidently he was the cop on the desk when Mary reported Sam missing."

"How do you know that?"

"Found it in some old records over in the Madison archives. All we're doing is trying to reconstruct as much of what went on at the time as possible. I'm sure it won't take much of your dad's time."

"God. Gordy, Teddy's an old man. He's recently turned eighty and has become pretty cantankerous."

"That's okay, I'm up for it. Just arrange some kind of introduction for me so I can fill in the background on this case," Gordy said.

"I'll see what I can do, but keep in mind this is still Clinton police business, "Harlan said. There was a touch of reluctance in his tone.

"Please don't wait too long, Harlan. Emily Pierce is pulling out all stops to get information on her grandfather's murder. I appreciate whatever you can do. I'll talk to you later, goodbye."

Next, Gordy dialed information and asked for the number of Allen Drew. He called and there was no answer. He listed the number on his cell phone and set out to make himself dinner.

CHAPTER 18

At six a.m. Saturday morning Gordy opened the front door for Emily. She was wearing cotton pants with a plaid cotton blouse tied in a knot just above her navel. On her head, she wore a white baseball cap that read Toyota in blue embroidery. She smiled. "So tell me, where did you learn to sail?"

"It's a long story," he answered. "Want some coffee before we go?"

"Sure," she replied.

He emptied the pot into two cups that were already on the table. They sat down and slurped gingerly at the hot brew, staring at each other.

"Do you know much about sailing?" Gordy asked through the veil of steam spiraling from his cup.

"A little," she said. "I'm sort of self-taught on a Sunfish."

"Well, you'll have a good time then; have you ever been to Mattituck Inlet?"

"No, Gordy, I haven't. Where is it?"

"Just across the sound, almost due south of here it's not too difficult to find. With a morning breeze, we should be in by eleven, and if we leave by two, we'll be back by six or so. The tide will be in our favor most of the day. I've checked the weather. It looks like it's going to be a fine day for us, mostly sunny, maybe a chance of some thunderstorms late in the day. Pretty standard for this time of year," he said.

It was six-thirty when they left the house. There was a glow in the morning sky to the east as the sun was about to rise above the horizon. They transferred several bags of groceries from Emily's Camry to Gordy's truck and headed for the town dock. As the couple walked down the ramp connecting the dock to the bulkhead, the Catalina 27 shined among the rest of the small boats tied along the way. The boat was clean and white with blue non-skid decks. She sported blue covers on the sails and companionway. Carefully scripted letters on the transom spelled the name *Raggedy Ann* just above a brightly painted smiling doll face.

They loaded their gear and supplies aboard, and Gordy took a few minutes to explain the various features of the boat. He showed Emily the head and how it worked. He showed her where the life jackets and fire extinguishers were located and gave her basic information on the running and standing rigging. They donned the life jackets. When he was convinced Emily knew her way around, Gordy switched on the bilge blower and started the little Atomic Four engine.

By now, the sun was an orange dome in the eastern horizon and the sky above was pale blue and cloudless. Emily helped untie the dock lines, and Gordy coached her into the boat as he undid the last line and climbed in behind her. He took the wheel, pushed the shift lever forward, and throttled up the engine. The *Raggedy Ann* slid gracefully away from her berth and into Clinton Harbor.

The channel leaving the harbor was formed by the Hammonasset River and ran due east for several hundred yards before taking a buttonhook turn to the right, and then another turn left as it flowed into Long Island Sound.

Once clear of the harbor, Gordy picked up a compass heading for Mattituck Inlet and set the boat on course. He asked Emily to steer the boat while he tended the sails. He raised the mainsail, set the trim, and cleated the main sheet. The big genoa was on roller furling, so all he had to do was unwind the control line and the big headsail blew out full size with only the force of the prevailing breeze. He trimmed it with the port side sheet and cleated it. The wind blew from the southwest at about twelve knots making for an ideal passage. It was one of those rare days on the sound when everything seemed perfect.

Emily lay back in the cockpit. "So what did you want to talk to me about?"

"I think there is more going on than we can easily see. I believe someone else besides the police, you, and me is somehow involved. I think somebody took the old files from the Madison archives and for some reason returned them. That's why Barry Lands and Avery Johnson didn't find anything when they were there."

Emily stared at him for a minute. "That's crazy, but let's assume you're right, the next questions is, who and why? Got any ideas?"

"That's why I wanted to talk to you. I made a list of people who showed up in the logbook at the Town Hall. The procedure for access is far from secure. There's an old doll who is the gatekeeper, and she more or less decides who can go to the basement based on the reason they give her or whether they had reason to go there before. Although she keeps a logbook, who's to say it's always been used? I've made a list of people who have signed in so far in August, but nobody has signed in twice. If someone did take the stuff out, they didn't sign in to return it. So there's at least one flaw in my theory.

How did they take it out without signing in to return it?"

Emily looked out at the open Sound. "Okay, let's say they somehow returned the files and didn't sign in, what did they do with them while they had them? We can both testify they appeared original and more than complete."

They paused for a moment in the conversation. The sound of water rushing by the hull and the motion of the boat drew them from the subject. It was as though a subtle form of hypnosis redirected their attention to the quiet joy of the passage. The wind was modest and the waves were casual, measuring two to three feet in height. In the sky, several small thunderheads reached for the altitude needed to build towering anvil shapes. Time passed while Gordy and Emily mused within the scene around them

Finally Emily broke the spell. "Maybe that's it. Suppose nothing is missing, and information was deliberately added. Just suppose some of what we found was not part of the original file but added to provide more information. Doesn't it suggest someone may be trying to help us?"

"Yes. I suppose so, but this is about as indirect an influence as I can imagine. Whoever it is may be trying to help the local police, and we just ended up as the beneficiaries. They couldn't have known we'd be the first ones to find the files."

"Well, let's assume there is someone out there who has a serious interest in the case. We need to find out who it is," Emily said.

"I've taken copies of everything with us. Let's go over it again, in detail, during lunch," Gordy said.

He secured the wheel, studied the sails for a moment, and then made several adjustments to the sheets. A little while later, he sat next to Emily. "I called Harlan Flanders and asked him to help get me in to see his dad Teddy. He said he'd try to set up something. So, next week,

I'll interview him. At least he's a contemporary to the crime. Maybe he can tell us something new."

"I hope so," Emily said. "By the way, I spoke to Merle Steiner this week. He is now convinced Sam was shot fairly close up, and the bullet path suggests the gun was held nearly level, like someone walked up to the car window and shot him while he was sitting. That goes against his original theory of Sam being shot somewhere else and placed in the car afterward, but I think he's right. They'll eventually find the bullet somewhere in the car. Tomorrow, I'm planning to see Uncle Bert again."

The entrance to Mattituck Inlet could be hard to find by an inexperienced sailor. But Gordy had been there several times and had little trouble picking up the outer marker. His compass course brought them within viewing distance of the buoy. The rest of the passage was a straight line toward the stone jetties that spread open to the sound like the maw of a great beast.

Gordy furled the sails while Emily took the wheel and steered the *Raggedy Ann* into the inlet. A short distance inside, the route bent to the left then to right and proceeded a mile or so, until it ended in a tidal basin that was the perfect anchorage. When they arrived in the basin, Gordy checked his watch. It was eleven-twenty. Not too bad, he thought. He gave Emily brief instructions on anchoring procedure and went forward to complete the task. In a few minutes the hook was set and the boat was secure.

Emily went below and started fixing lunch. Gordy tidied the deck and cockpit, and then went below to see if he could help. She was doing well, so Gordy opened the brief that contained copies of the archive files. He took the material and spread it across the dinette table. He separated the newspaper articles from the more official looking documents.

He picked up the article about the outbreak of flu, which hit the New Haven area in 1938.

"Well, this doesn't look like it belongs in a police file," he said. "I wonder why our friend picked it, to get our attention?"

Emily stopped washing lettuce momentarily. "Probably had something to do with the work Sam was doing. Is there any mention of someone developing some sort of vaccine?"

"Not much, but there is a reference to the fact that several doctors felt this was a less virulent form of the Spanish Flu infecting the country in 1918. A few docs thought it might be a candidate bug for use in developing a flu vaccine. Although, a lot of people showed symptoms, there were only a few severe cases and fewer deaths in 1938. There was a major fear the event might become the epidemic of 1918, but it never happened."

"Let's look at the car wreck again," Emily said. "What was the woman's name?"

Gordy shuffled through the articles, found what he was looking for, and started reading aloud, "'Local woman killed in fiery crash'…here's something. Guess what her name was—Never mind the guess, her name was Molly Drew. How much will you bet she was related to Allen Drew?"

"Gordy, there's a connection. What do you think?"

"I don't know, but it sure goes on my list of questions for Allen, once I get hold of him. Let's take a look at the missing person report again. See who Mary listed as Sam's appointments for that day." Gordy pulled out the copy of the report and read the names aloud, "'Claudia Bishop, Robert Blein, and Samantha Harris.' Those were the only names that he had listed for the day. Not a very aggressive schedule, I'd say."

"Well, those were people he was scheduled to see.

That doesn't mean those were people he actually saw," Emily said.

"Let's hope the lab working on the appointment book can come up with some better results," Gordy said.

Emily finished preparing lunch and carried a tray through the companionway into the cockpit. The tray was overflowing with colorful things to eat. Sliced peaches and papaya surrounded a large bowl of lobster salad. Crackers formed an outer ring and two columns of sliced cheddar cheese were stacked on either side. She asked Gordy to bring two large glasses of ice tea that were still on the galley counter top.

"You have a choice, Officer Powell: you can create your own lobster roll or have the salad straight up. What's your pleasure?"

"My goodness, Emily, I'll have a roll if you please," he said, thinking he wanted to add "in the hay," but resisted the temptation.

They ate with an appetite that could only come from a wonderful morning's sail. When they finished, Emily went forward and removed her cotton blouse. Underneath she wore a tiny bikini top that highlighted her modest breasts. She laid down on the foredeck in an effort to take advantage of the late August sun. Gordy watched her graceful moves from the corner of his eye, and decided he had better use the time productively. He sighed quietly and directed his energy to plotting the compass headings for the return trip.

At two o'clock, Gordy announced it was time to head back. He went about the task of getting the boat ready for the passage home. He checked the sky and noticed an accumulation of clouds had built up during the early afternoon. Nothing too menacing, but he knew it was a good time to leave. The wind had freshened and from the movement displayed in the nearby tree branches, he estimated it was blowing eighteen to twenty-five knots.

He decided to leave the inlet with a reef in the mainsail, and he set about to rig it before they left. He could always shake out the reef if the wind eased on the way back. He explained to Emily what he was doing. She listened with an absolute attention Gordy enjoyed. It gave him a sense of control that was both flattering and a little seductive. When he finished, he started the engine and soon they left the breakwaters of the inlet behind.

Two hours into the return passage, the *Raggedy Ann* was in a broad reach, surging ahead at full speed. The knot log registered six point seven with occasional swings as high as seven point zero. The wind blustered with gusts over twenty-five knots.

Gordy was thankful he had put the reef in the mainsail before they left. The boat worked hard and he ran the genoa loose enough to allow a fisherman's reef at the leech of the sail. Emily's face showed the strain of the constant, sometimes harsh motion, and Gordy tried to think of ways to keep her from getting sick.

"How are you doing?" he shouted over the sound of water breaking along the side of the hull.

"Okay, I think I'll be all right," she replied with some hesitation.

"Come on back and take the wheel while I make some sail adjustments," he said. He knew he had to keep her busy. Reluctantly, she inched back behind the wheel, and Gordy let go. "Steer this course," he instructed, pointing to the binnacle on the wheel post. "Concentrate on this heading."

"I'll try."

The *Raggedy Ann* plunged ahead with occasional spume flying across the foredeck. The boat was grand, and the sea spectacular. In a few minutes, Emily's concentration became so focused, so intense, her effort to control the boat overwhelmed the snake of nausea roiling in her stomach, and she no longer felt sick. She was no longer a passive victim of the sea and wind. Without realizing it, she was transformed. She became a participant in the drama of the passage, a force within the forces and she felt exhilaration.

Emily smiled, gripped the wheel tight with both hands, and shouted, "God, this is great."

Gordy looked at her and saw something new. He saw a woman in passion. The sight was so revealing that for a moment he felt like an intruder.

And then she reached out and grabbed his arm and shouted, "It's fantastic, Gordy."

He moved closer to her and she hugged him with one arm and steered with the other.

Gordy laughed. "You are terrific."

She held him for a while and the *Raggedy Ann* surged ahead.

Soon, Gordy saw the outline of Faulkner's Island to the left and he knew the passage was nearing an end. He picked up the mark from the end of the Clinton breakwater and began his approach to the harbor.

Forty-five minutes later, the *Raggedy Ann* was tied up at the finger dock and Gordy hosed the boat down to remove the salt spray. Emily unloaded the leftovers and stowed them in the truck. When the boat was clean and empty they climbed into the truck and headed home.

"Well, how did you like sailing?" he asked as he drove the pickup.

"It was wonderful," she said with a toss of her wet hair. "Where did you learn to do that?"

"It's a long story," he said, as he shifted gears. "My parents," Gordy continued. "They're the sailors. That's where it began anyway. Seems like we were always on the water when I was a kid. During most summers, we were usually skipping around from anchorage to anchorage, putting in at Green Port or Shelter Island or Newport or Block Island. While most kids were sent to camp, my sister and I spent a lot of time on the boat or in the marinas. Some of the time we spent cooped up below, like when the weather was bad, or we rowed around a strange harbor in a dingy. Anyway, as I think back on it, it was a lot of fun. I guess I picked up just enough to get by. I'm not nearly as good as my dad. I don't sail as passionately as my parents, but I don't have to cope with the expenses they considered normal."

Emily listened intently. "You have a sister?"

"Yes, her name's Lillianne. She lives in Florida near my parents. She's married to an engineer and has three kids. She was a nurse until my niece came along. Then she took a break and it seems like she's taking it easy now."

Emily was quiet for a moment. She seemed reflective, like she was carefully weighing what she was thinking.

"What made you decide to become a cop?" she blurted.

Gordy smiled, as if he knew the question was inevitable.

"Well, when I was in the marines, I was stationed in Japan. I was trained to run a cryogenic plant. That's a machine that makes cold gases like liquid nitrogen, and carbon dioxide. All in all, pretty boring. At any rate, the cold gas business was slow, and at some point I was asked if I would help with some prisoner transports. I helped move a few guys from the brig to various lock-ups around the islands and got to like the duty. Did a lot of traveling, met a lot of people, and picked up some training. Actually got pretty good at it.

"When I was about to be mustered out, I married a Japanese princess, literally, and brought her home. The local police departments were pretty inbred back then, with a lot of the guys related—fathers, sons, cousins, or uncles. That kind of thing. At any rate, I applied to the Guilford PD, they liked my background and they hired me. Eight years later, here we are."

Emily's face took on a serious expression, "What about the danger, the risks associated with what you do? Doesn't it bother you? Didn't it bother your wife? Which brings me to the next question. What happened to your wife?"

"She lasted about two years. Then it was over. She's back in Japan happily married to a Japanese man who works very hard installing computer chips for Samsung. And for the most part, I like my job. I sleep well at night and have few regrets. As for the danger, there's little of it. We're way below the national average in violent crime, about average for white collar crime, and a little ahead in miscellaneous, such as domestic violence and runaways. We have more than a few cold cases involving missing persons, but they aren't a priority, at least not with my department. What about you?" Gordy decided it was his turn, "Why did you decide to become a librarian?"

"My family's lived on the shoreline for a very long time. After high school, I went to University of Connecticut, got a Masters in Library Science and married badly. I didn't really expect to work at all after I got married. Charlie Pierce was a hoot. The whole marriage might have been a hoot if it weren't so damn tragic. He was in sales for Rogers Distributors. He had a territory from the Palisades to Kennebunk Port and went as far west as Watertown, New York. Basically, he sold the hardware stuff you find in the supermarkets. He had a great time, and I didn't. I wanted to have a family back then. I was never sure of what he wanted. After the second year, we found out his sperm count was nonexistent, so that explained a few things. We looked into the possibility of sperm donors, along with some new procedures using in vitro methods. We even talked about adoption. While this was going on, I found out he'd been leaving his soldier-less seminal fluids all over five states. At first, I couldn't believe it. Then I spoke to some of his bimbos and realized I had no idea who he was. We separated, and a year later divorced.

"The position at the library happened along in the middle of the divorce. Just as well. It gave me something I needed at a very difficult time."

CHAPTER 19

When they arrived at Gordy's, they unloaded the truck and brought the remaining food to the kitchen. They went to the barn, fed the animals, and, when they finished, returned to the house.

Once inside, Gordy announced he had a surprise for Emily. He spoke as he began making a pot of decaffeinated coffee. "Remember the idea of starting a crime board? Well, I've begun putting down everything we've got so far, and I wanted to add what we discussed today. We can keep adding as we go along."

After Gordy got the coffee going, he left the room and returned a short time later carrying a large aluminum easel with a flip pad mounted on it. He brought it into the living room, placed it in the middle of the floor, and flipped over the cover page. At the top of the next page was:

The Murder of Doctor Samuel Stemford
DOD: September 15, 1938
COD: Bullet wound to the left temple.
Discovery of body: Bottom of Powell Pond, Nod road, Clinton, CT
Body found in front seat of 1938 Chrysler. Fully decomposed with only bones remaining.

List of items at the crime scene: Doctor's bag with implements.
Gold wedding band
Clothing remnants/leather jacket
Unreadable papers in glove box
Appointment book, unreadable
Wallet with forty dollars cash

The second page had a list of names contemporary to the crime. The list contained:

Dr. Sam Stemford
Mary Stemford
Albert Moorefield

"That's what we had. Now I've got to add Allen and Molly Drew and names of the folks Mary had given as appointments for the day he disappeared," Gordy said.

Emily looked at the list with some intensity. "What about the cop, Teddy Flanders?"

"Jesus, Emily, he's a cop, probably the first cop to work on the case when it happened. I don't think we can put him on the suspect list."

Emily shook her head and rolled her eyes, "You mean it's okay to put my grandmother and uncle on the list, but it's not okay to put a cop's name on the list? Just what do you use for your open-minded, open-investigation criteria? Whatever doesn't violate your unbiased, police-trained sensibilities? Excuse me, but you said we must to try to keep the field large enough to stand a chance of including the murderer. Am I mistaken, or did you really say that?"

Gordy reflected for a minute and thought, *Oops, bad cop.* He tried a little reversal. "You're right, you're absolutely right. We'll include Teddy Flanders on the list." As he made the statement, he took his Magic Marker and spelled out Teddy Flanders just below Albert Moorefield. Right below, he wrote in Allen Drew and Molly Drew. "I guess they belong here, too."

"That's better," Emily said with a sense of victory. "Now I'm ready for coffee."

Gordy was beginning to realize Emily possessed a forceful personality. There was a price for her self-sufficiency and he must accept the price to get close to her. He knew he wanted very much to get close to her.

They spent the remaining hour or so talking about the day's sailing. Then she said it was time to feed her cat, and, with that, she prepared to go home. They agreed to talk again on Wednesday of the coming week, unless some major break-through occurred before then. Finally, Emily said goodnight and left.

When she was gone, Gordy realized the entire encounter was still more professional than he would have liked. Why had she not shown any real interest? Even when she talked about herself, she maintained a considerable distance, and it seemed she wasn't going to be the one to make a first move.

Maybe there were no moves in this situation. Maybe she was no longer interested in men. It was probably just as well. His life was fine and he'd be better off keeping it uncomplicated. Although he rationalized well, he still felt a tinge of disappointment.

CHAPTER 20

On Sunday afternoon, Emily found herself again driving toward the Golden Maturity Center. Once inside, she signed the guest book and took her visitor's pass.

Uncle Bert was sitting in his wheelchair, gazing through the glass slider into the courtyard.

Although it was only afternoon, long shadows of late summer were beginning their trek through the garden. September had just begun, and the weather would soon change. This month signaled the birth of another fall and announced the death of passing summer.

Emily knocked on the half-opened door. With the television off, Uncle Bert had no trouble hearing the knock. He turned and smiled as he recognized his visitor.

"Hello, Emily," he said. "Please come in. How have you been dear?"

"Just fine, Uncle, and how have you been doing?"

"Okay, I guess. I've been thinking a lot about Sam since I saw you last. Will there be a funeral?"

"Oh, I suppose so, someday, but right now the police are holding his remains as evidence. They may not release him for a formal burial for quite some time, but I'll let you know as things change."

"Wouldn't it be ironic if I died and ended up buried

before Sam, even though he died over sixty years ago," Uncle Bert mused.

"What a morbid thought, Uncle, I'm sure you have a lot of years left."

"Well, dear, one thing you learn at my age is everyone dies and very few know when it's going to happen."

The old man seemed more cynical and cryptic than Emily had remembered him. She tried to change the subject and took a box of chocolate turtles from her purse. They were his favorite treat and this box would last him weeks. He smiled, reached over, and removed one from the box. He carefully bit off a corner from the chocolate, caramel, and pecan concoction. Suddenly there was a twinkle in his eyes. She waited a minute, removed her little tape recorder from her purse, placed it on the table, and pressed the record button.

"So were you able to recall more about the relationship between grandmother and Sam?" she asked.

"Oh, a little," he replied as he gingerly chewed on the turtle. There was considerably less tension in his voice now. "They were always very formal around me," he continued. "I was nineteen when they were married, Mary was twenty-four. That made Sam nineteen years older than she. I never did like that idea. Your grandmother didn't seem to have many gentlemen callers while she was single. Perhaps it was because she was a little plain, but she had a generous heart and seemed to care for Sam very much. My personal feeling was that Sam used the marriage as the most direct way to keep the house and practice after Father died.

"Father's will did split assets uniformly between mother, Mary, and me. But Mary inherited the house and office in the event of mother's death. And that's more or less what happened. Father died of emphysema the year after they were married and mother died two years later.

She lived at the house right up to her death.

"After Sam disappeared, your grandmother sold the old place and moved into a smaller house; that's where she lived when your mother was born. Mary was pregnant when Sam disappeared. And, as you know, she never remarried."

Some of what the old man recounted, Emily had heard at one time or another, but this was the first time everything was tied together. The information helped to paint a picture of the times.

"What about their personal relationship? Did they have much conflict?" Emily pressed.

"Oh, dear, you don't think Mary had anything to do with Sam's death, do you?" Uncle Bert asked. His face paled.

"No, not really, but these are questions the police may ask, if and when they come to see you."

"Well, your grandmother was a gentle woman, and she couldn't have harmed anyone," he said.

Emily thought for a moment and tried a different approach. "If you had to guess, who do you think could have killed Sam?"

"I couldn't say, Emily, I don't know of anyone who could have done such a thing," Bert said with certainty.

Emily pressed again, "You mentioned you thought Sam was a scurrilous man. Can you remember what made you say that?"

"Nothing specific, I just thought he was very concerned with himself, perhaps too much. He did work hard. And he seemed to have a need to do great things; but I thought he was too self-centered. Even Mary didn't care for his occasional displays of arrogance.

"There was a time when a serious flu epidemic swept the shoreline, and Sam was determined to find a cure. Imagine, thinking he could find such a cure all by himself. He had one patient in Clinton who was very ill. He collected all kinds of samples from her and sent them for special tests. He was constantly running back and forth to New Haven, doing some kind of lab work. The time he spent with her was unreasonable, and Mary told me she felt isolated.

"I remember thinking Sam paid a price for his passion for medicine. Of course, I didn't interfere. In time, things seemed to settle down, after the epidemic passed. I don't think he ever came up with a cure for the disease, but I know we now get annual flu shots at the center. Maybe his work helped somehow."

"Do you remember the name of the woman, Uncle Bert?"

"No, but she was married to a fellow who worked at the local hardware store in Clinton. As the story went, Sam was there the day he disappeared. As I recall, the Clinton Police tracked him down on his rounds and got him to set the man's leg. Seems he broke it when some barrels toppled over at the store. I believe it was the last stop Sam made before he disappeared. I know Mary was frantic when Sam didn't come home. She went to the police the very next day. She pined for a very long time afterward. The hurricane went through a week or so later and seemed to drain the energy from the police investigation into Sam's disappearance.

"Certainly nothing was learned during the clean-up period. By the time the police got back to the case, perhaps a couple of months had passed. The trail was pretty cold by then with not many clues left to follow. Mary found this very frustrating, but there was little she could do. She was carrying your mother and was having a difficult pregnancy."

"Uncle, do you remember much about the investigation," Emily asked, sensing Bert was beginning to tire.

"No, dear, I never got involved. The only facts I knew were those Mary told to me. I had very little direct contact with the police."

CHAPTER 21

Gordy had tried several times to reach Allen Drew on the telephone, but there was no answer. He decided to drive to the Drew home. He had no trouble finding the address, and a short time later he parked in front of the place. The house was in an older development in Clinton. The outside was a typical Cape Cod style structure with twin dormers on the roof and a small breezeway connecting to a two-car garage. The place was reasonably maintained, with trimmed shrubs in front and sections of green grass surrounding islands of brown spots here and there in the lawn.

The front windows opened to screens and a porch light bulb over the front door still blazed, in spite of the time of day. Gordy walked to the front door and rang the bell. A few minutes later the main door opened with a swish of weather stripping scraping against the floor. An old man with silver hair stood behind the screened outer door. His shoulders were stooped and narrow but he moved sprightly behind the screen.

"Yes, can I help you?"

Gordy introduced himself and told the old man he was looking for Allen Drew. He explained he was working with the relatives of Doctor Sam Stemford and was investigating the discovery of his body.

The old man listened intently, as though he were hard of hearing. When Gordy finished speaking, the man said he was Allen Drew. He opened the screen door and invited Gordy inside. The man led Gordy to the living room and gestured for him to sit in a wooden-armed colonial chair.

Gordy obliged but waited for his host to sit before telling him he saw Allen's name in the sign-in log of the town hall archives. "Can you tell me what you were looking for when you were down there?" Gordy asked.

The old man had pale wrinkled skin with patches of red that looked like a form of psoriasis. The red spots contained flaking crusted layers. Occasionally the man scratched the patches, and bits of white flakes fell to the carpet. "Oh, I was doing research on my family tree. Genealogy, I believe you call it."

Thinking the man was old enough to know Doc Stemford, Gordy asked," Did you happen to know Doctor Sam Stemford?"

"Yes, I knew the man," Allen replied. His brown eyes narrowed behind his glasses.

Gordy felt a touch of excitement as he looked at the crusty old man. He overcame a sudden compulsion to smile. Such a gesture certainly ran against good detective behavior. He reminded himself instead, *This gentleman might end up as a prime suspect in the Stemford investigation.* All the signals learned from Gordy's experience suggested he should proceed with caution.

"As part of the investigation, we are trying to reconstruct as much of his life as possible. Can you help?" Gordy asked.

"As much as I can, but all this goes back sixty years. That's a long time, you know," Allen said.

"Yes, I do." Gordy said. "What can you tell me about Stemford?"

"Only a little, I guess. I didn't like him much. In those days, I worked in my uncle's hardware store. Even broke my leg there. As a matter of fact, I may have been the last patient Stemford ever worked on. Still have a little gimp from the job he did back then."

"Did you know Molly Drew?" Gordy asked.

"Of course I did, she was my wife," he answered.

"We've learned she died in an automobile crash. What can you tell me about the accident?" Gordy asked.

"Dear Molly was burned to death in the crash. It happened a month or so after the 'thirty-eight hurricane. They found her up on Horse Hill Road, or what was left of her, burned to a crisp. Never did believe it was an accident."

"Why do you say that?"

"It just didn't seem right at the time. I loved her very much and it was too soon. She was so full of life. She was a like a child of the forest, loving everything around her. We had a bad year in 1938. First, she got sick with the flu and nearly died, and then she was killed in the truck, seven months later. Doc Stemford treated her when she had the flu. She seemed to have it worse than most other folks that came down with it. I still don't understand how those bugs work. Take me for example. I never caught the flu at all.

"Stemford said he had a theory my skin condition may have somehow protected me. Who knows? I remember he tried to make some kind of vaccine from Molly's blood. While she was sick, he took samples of her blood and other fluids and did tests. He even took blood samples from me. He spent a long time helping her get well. I thought he was being selfish, and at some point I began to resent the time he spent with her. But it's possible he was trying to do good. And after all, she did fully recover."

"Now that Sam has been found, do you have any thoughts on who may have wanted him dead?" Gordy asked.

Allen paused for a moment then replied, "Nope, but I never was comfortable with the way his disappearance was handled. To my recollection, there weren't many reports published except one article right after it. As far as the public was concerned, Stemford simply disappeared. There were rumors he left when his wife announced she was pregnant, but he wasn't that kind of man.

"He had his practice and his ideas for research. It didn't seem likely he just up and left. I always felt there was something wrong with the police investigation. But I believed he would turn up sooner or later, dead or alive."

"Did you know any police at the time?" Gordy asked. "Like a police officer named Theodore Flanders."

"Yes, I knew him. Didn't like him." Allen replied with a solemn tone to his voice. "He went on to become chief of police in Madison." Allen swallowed hard and seemed like he was about to say something else, but didn't. Instead, he asked Gordy if he wanted some coffee or iced tea.

Gordy sensed Allen was holding something back and decided to accept the offer of refreshment to see if the secret came out. "Sure. Ice tea would be great," he said.

Allen added nothing new during the remaining time Gordy spent with him.

Twenty minutes later, Gordy left the house, thinking the old man was still hiding something. He would have to invent a reason for another visit.

As Gordy drove back to Clinton, he reached for his cell phone and dialed Harlan Flanders.

Harlan picked up on the first ring.

"Hello, Harlan, Gordy Powell here."

"Yes Gordy, what can I do for you?"

"How did you make out with your dad, I really need to talk to him."

"Well, he's not been feeling well, and I don't think he'll be ready for a couple of weeks, anyway."

"I would really like to see him before then."

"I'll let you know," Flanders said as he hung up.

✌✍✌

Harlan Flanders pressed on the receiver button just long enough to be sure that the connection to Gordy Powell was broken. He released the button and dialed his father's place. The phone rang four times and the message machine intercepted.

When the greeting was over, Harlan said, "Pick up, Dad, it's me."

Suddenly there was a voice on the other end. "Harlan. That you, boy?"

"Yes, Dad. It's me. Just got another call from Gordy Powell. He still wants to talk to you. I think we should go ahead and set something up. He's becoming a pain in the neck."

"Look, Harlan, this fella's becoming a pain in my rosy red ass. Never mind your neck," Teddy Flanders said. "Don't want to speak to the man. Get it. I don't even want to know the man. Just keep him out of my hair."

Harlan paused for a few seconds. "All he wants to do is ask some questions about the doctor they found in his pond."

"Harlan, whatever happened was a very long time ago. There ain't much I'm going to remember about something that's sixty years old. Tell him I'm still sick. Tell him I'm contagious. Tell him anything you want, but I have no interest in talking to him."

"Dad, he's a very persistent guy, and from what he's

told me, the Clinton PD has some old files from Madison. I'm sure they'll want to talk to you."

"Look, you've got some influence in town, just tell them all to leave me alone," Teddy said.

Harlan listened then said, "Somewhere along the way, you're going to have to talk with somebody. Why don't I schedule an interview with Powell and later with a Clinton detective? Give them a statement, and then if you want, take off to Florida for a couple of months. Let the dust settle and come back home. If you refuse to see everybody, it's going to look fishy as hell. And there isn't anything fishy to be worried about, is there?"

"No," the old man said softly.

"Then, certainly, we don't want to give that impression, do we?"

There was long a pause and finally Teddy said, "Okay, go ahead and set something up. I'll deal with it. Do it at my place. Make it during the day for Powell and late afternoon for the Clinton PD. The worst I can do is make it on their own time. That should keep it short."

"Okay, Dad, I'll go ahead and arrange the times and let you know."

"All right, boy. Talk to you later." With that, Teddy Flanders hung up.

Later in the day, Harlan dialed Gordy Powell's number at home.

After two rings, Gordy picked up.

"Hello, Gordy, its Harlan. I've made arrangements for you to see Teddy. The best he could do is Tuesday at two p.m. Is that okay?"

Gordy thought it over for a minute. He did have some time coming and he figured he would be able to get a half-day off. He answered, "It's kind of inconvenient but I can make it after work. Tell him I'll see him at his place at two o'clock on Tuesday."

Harlan provided some brief directions to Teddy's home, said goodbye, and hung up.

CHAPTER 22

Gun manufacturing in the United State was once centered in the Pioneer Valley. It's the valley created by the Connecticut River as it makes its way through Massachusetts and Connecticut. Every cop and gun enthusiast in America was aware of hallowed names like Colt, Savage Arms, Ruger, and Smith & Wesson, and, oddly enough, all of these brands had production facilities in the region. Because guns were such a huge area tradition, it was no surprise to find an emphasis on professional training situated in the same location.

In today's world, it was hard to ignore the need for special law enforcement teams trained specifically to cope with the over-abundance of hostage situations, campus shootings, and terrorist threats. During the past twenty-five years, situations that were once unimaginable began playing out routinely within the public view. These situations, once found only in densely populated cities and cramped urban centers, had spread throughout the country.

It was just a matter of time until small towns like those in the Shoreline would be compelled to organize and adapt to the threats of a changing world. In the beginning, these towns relied on New Haven for their SWAT teams, but now, the shoreline commissioners finally decided to form their own specialized force using selected individuals from the local police departments.

When all this came about, Gordy Powell of the Guilford PD was among the fine cops selected for training in the newly formed shoreline SWAT team. The training was to take place at the Smith & Wesson facilities in Springfield, Massachusetts. The course required one full week of study and represented the ultimate experience in gun control. When news of the special assignment came, a feeling of "too much to do, and not enough time to do it" overwhelmed Gordy. He was compelled to devise some kind of schedule that satisfied the demands of his job, the Stemford investigation, and his domestic life, which happened to include the care and feeding of many hungry mouths.

When he arrived home that evening, he called Emily. "I've had a kind of good news, bad news day. The chief finally announced our participation in a combined SWAT team for the shoreline towns. Fifteen guys have been identified to go through a very exclusive sniper school at Smith and Wesson in Springfield, Massachusetts. This is first-class SWAT training, and it turns out I'm one of the fifteen chosen.

"That's great news, Gordy. It seems like quite an honor."

"Well, that's the good news. The bad news is I have to get someone to take care of my place for a week while I'm gone. All of us must live on campus during the entire course. I've got to call my vet and see if she can recommend somebody. I'm afraid I won't be of much help on your grandfather's case while I'm gone. You'll be on your own until I get back."

"Don't worry about my grandfather for a week. It's okay. When you've finished, there'll be plenty of time to catch up," Emily said.

"By the way, I've got a meeting with Teddy Flanders this week. At least I can get that done before I go. I'll brief you as soon as it's over. Let me make a few phone calls and I'll talk to you later tonight."

"All right, I'll talk to you later," she said.

When Gordy finished his chores, he returned to the house just in time to catch the phone ringing. It was Emily calling back. "I've got an idea" she said.

"What kind of idea?"

"How about I take care of your place while you're gone."

"Are you sure?" Gordy realized the magnitude of what she was offering.

"Of course I'm sure."

"If you're serious, come on over and I'll run you through what's it like. Shouldn't take much more than an hour a day."

The next day Gordy arranged with his sergeant to have a fellow officer relieve him early so he could keep his appointment with Teddy Flanders. At one-thirty in the afternoon, Gordy parked his cruiser, slid behind the wheel of his truck, and headed toward Teddy Flanders's place in Durham.

Teddy's home was a considerable distance into the country, and Gordy had some trouble finding the little dirt road that connected it to civilization. When he finally found the road, it was nearly too late. He had to turn the wheel sharply right to avoid over-shooting the entrance. The tires of his truck protested, spitting chunks of gravel as they left the security of the black top. He brought his speed to twenty-five miles per hour and checked the rearview mirror in time to see clouds of dust spiraling away.

Just as his instructions had predicted, about a mile down the road, he came to a fork; the left branch continued into the woods. And on the right, the road ran a quarter mile and turned into Teddy Flanders's driveway.

The Flanders' house was an old two story colonial with an open porch covering the entire front of the building. To the right were a large barn and several smaller outbuildings. On the left was a detached two-car garage.

As Gordy approached the front of the house, two large Rottweilers emerged from behind the barn and ran directly at the truck. They barked loudly. Both dogs reached the driver's side door and paced in circles still barking ferociously. Gordy thought it unwise to leave the truck, so he rolled up the window and waited. A few minutes went by and the dogs kept circling and barking.

Finally, Gordy put his forearm on the horn and pushed. The noise was deafening. A minute or so later, a man appeared at the screen door. He shouted to the dogs. They stopped barking, turned from Gordy's truck, and trotted to the porch. Both animals were panting, and long slimy strands of saliva hung from their mouths.

"Lay down," the man said with authority. The dogs stared at the man intensely for a moment and then lowered their rear haunches and spread out on the porch floor, still panting. Finally, the man came through the door, walked over to the stairs, and asked, "You, Gordy Powell?"

Gordy had rolled down his window when the dogs went to the porch, so he heard the man perfectly. "Yeah, that's me," he replied.

"Well, get out of the truck and come on in," the man said.

Gordy left the truck and approached the porch stairs without making any sudden moves. He climbed the steps slowly, allowing ample distance between himself and the two dogs. They momentarily stopped licking themselves to watch Gordy pass by.

The old man held the screen door open and Gordy went inside. As Gordy crossed the threshold, he was nearly overcome by the pungent smells of dog and urine. The odors made the air thick and heavy. It was as though someone had thrown a kennel blanket over Gordy's face. He struggled to keep from gagging as his brain tried to shut down his lungs in defense against the awful stench. In Gordy's experience, it was unusual for a cop's place, even a widowed retired cop's place, to be so dirty and smelly. Usually cops were spit and polish, especially in their homes.

The man seemed unaffected by the mess. He smiled at Gordy, said he was Theodore Flanders, and gestured toward the couch. He didn't offer a handshake, so Gordy went to the couch and sat down. The fabric was thick with matted dog hair and Gordy's face began to itch.

He wasn't sure if it was from the matted hair or some other infestation lurking in the house.

"So what can I do for ya, mister, or should I say, Officer Powell?"

Gordy faked a slight smile. "Just call me Gordy. The reason I wanted to talk to you concerns the Doc Stemford affair. Have you been following the story?"

"Yeah. A little. Seems they found Stemford's body at the bottom of a pond over in Clinton, ain't that right?"

"Yes, sir. Actually, it was my pond he was found in."

Teddy Flanders sat down in a chair directly across from Gordy. He was a robust man, despite his age. He didn't look sick at all. His barrel-shaped chest supported two burly arms covered with black and white hair. His face was almost wrinkle free and round, with deep-set black eyes.

He was nearly bald; a band of closely cropped gray hair circled his head just above his ears. Although he was about eighty, the skin barely sagged under his eyes. He was handsome, despite a day's growth of white stubble on his chin.

Gordy continued the interview. "We found some old records indicating you worked on the original investigation into his disappearance. Since we're trying to piece together the events of the time, I thought you might be able to help."

"Well. I don't know what I can tell you. Stemford vanished sixty years ago, and I sure as hell don't remember a lot of what happened last month, never mind back then."

Gordy ignored the remark and continued, "I couldn't find any follow-up reports on the case. All I found was the original report Mary Stemford filed with you. Was there any follow-up information?"

"I'm sure there was more information, but I don't know where it is. I know I was on and off the case during the next few months. There was a lot of shifting with assignments after the storm of 'thirty-eight. Things were upside-down for quite a while."

"At any rate, Theodore, what can you remember about the case? Did you suspect foul play at the time?"

"All I remember was I couldn't get enough information to suspect anything. We put out an 'all-points bulletin' after the Stemford woman filed the report, and we didn't get any response from a five-state area. I think we even included Massachusetts and Rhode Island. As far as I could figure, the doctor and his car just disappeared. I remember thinking he must have been pretty upset at the prospect of his old lady getting pregnant. I mean he was gonna be in his sixties when the kid was in high school."

"Is there anything else you remember about the case?"

"Nope."

"We also found a record of an old speeding ticket issued by you to Doc Stemford. I thought that was strange.

An area doctor could have had all sorts of reasons for driving fast. It seemed odd you gave him a ticket for it."

"It's like you said, he could have had all sorts of reasons, but he didn't give me one at the time, so I gave him a ticket."

Gordy paused for a moment then asked, "Did you know Allen and Molly Drew?"

Teddy Flanders mouth dropped for a second and his face flushed. Spider web patches of pink appeared on his cheeks. Along with a look of surprise, his black eyes narrowed. "What makes you ask that?"

"Well, I've been talking to Allen Drew, and both his name and your name appeared in the archives log at Madison Town Hall. I was just wondering if you two knew each other."

"Yeah, I met the little guy. Been a long time since I've seen him though. I knew he was still around."

"How did you know him?"

"He broke his leg the day Stemford disappeared. As I recall, he may have been the last person to see Stemford, either him or Molly, that is."

"Then you knew Molly, too?" Gordy asked.

"Not really. Don't think I met her till the Stemford investigation."

"What was she like?"

"Pretty, I guess you could say. Had lots of energy. Seemed like too much of a woman for the guy she was married to. Look there's not much more I can remember and I got things to do," Teddy said.

Gordy wanted to pursue more of what Teddy knew about the Drews, mostly because he seemed to have very strong impressions of them, considering they met during a lame police investigation sixty years ago. He reluctantly decided to drop the Drews and tried to get another question in.

"Just one more thing," he said, "Can you tell me what you were doing in the town hall cellar?"

Teddy Flanders looked surprised for a second or two. "Yes, some personal research, was all."

"Personal research on what?"

"Genealogy. It's all the rage now, doncha know? Now, if that's all, I've got things to do and I'm about done with this interview. It was nice meeting you, Gordy, but if you'll excuse me…"

Gordy realized the meeting was over and there wasn't much he could do about it.

The old man walked to the screen door and held it open. Gordy took the hint and headed for the porch. Both Rottweilers were still lying down as Gordy walked past. They raised their heads, and Gordy noticed they both had unusual yellow eyes. The pair growled softly as he moved by.

"Easy fellas, he's okay," Teddy said, as Gordy went down the steps and continued toward his truck.

On the way to Clinton, Gordy thought about what he had learned about the case. He visualized a list of people he knew were involved and tried to apply the classic elements of a murder to each of them, those elements being, motive, opportunity, and method. He tried to imagine each player with a gun in his or her hand, and with cold-blooded intent, putting a bullet in the head of Doctor Sam Stemford.

He sensed both Allen Drew and Teddy Flanders knew more than they were telling him.

He tried to imagine Mary Stemford, pregnant and in some kind of rage, waiting for Sam to get home after his rounds, shooting him in the car, driving him to Nod Road in the middle of the night, and running the Chrysler into the pond. Hardly likely, he thought. She would have needed lots of help, and then it would become some kind of conspiracy, again, unlikely. Conspiracies were hard to keep secret for a week, never mind sixty years.

Then there was Uncle Bert, who from all accounts, was a gentle man. Was he a methodical killer? If so, for what reason? Not much substance there. What about Allen Drew? What was he hiding? Could he be a cold-blooded killer, and if so, for what reason? Then there was Molly Drew. Was she a killer? If so, where'd she learn about guns and what was her motive to kill the man who nursed her back to health?

And last, what was the story behind this strange retired cop, Teddy Flanders? What was he hiding, and why? Certainly, he had training in the use of firearms, and a 38-caliber revolver was probably the weapon of choice for the police back in 1938, but he was a cop, and the notion of a cop murdering a civilian was not an easy concept for Gordy to accept. Gordy made a mental note to check out the type of gun used by the Madison PD in 1938. This raised the need to find the bullet. He knew he had to see Barry Lands to find out if there was anything new about the bullet.

There was always the possibility a transient murdered the doc or someone entirely missed by the investigation, perhaps by a disgruntled patient. Although Gordy had to consider these possibilities, he doubted their likelihood. A transient would have stripped the doc of his wallet and probably would not have taken the time or risk of putting the car into the pond.

As far as someone else who knew Sam was concerned, who could that be? The number of people in his life was finite and appeared to consist of only patients and family. There wasn't an obvious list of social friends and acquaintances, probably because there weren't any.

Gordy decided to check out the other patients whose names appeared for visits on the doc's last day. When he

arrived home he posted his thoughts on two full pages at
the crime board. Then he fed the animals and called Emily.

PART II

Neighbors

CHAPTER 23

April 15, 1938:

Molly Drew woke up to sunlight streaming through the bedroom window. She raised her head off the pillow just far enough to see the alarm clock on her bedside stand. It was eight o'clock.

"Darn, darn," she said, "late again."

She felt tired, even though she went to bed early last night. As she pulled herself from the covers, she felt a wave of nausea and laid her head back on the pillow. The dizziness passed quickly, and she tried to rise again, this time with better results.

Molly and Allen had moved to the shoreline from Middletown nearly a year ago. And although the Great Depression still had a grip on the nation, there were noticeable improvements in their world showing up every day. A recent newspaper article quoted the US census department as estimating one fifth of American workers were without jobs. It was a fabulous improvement over five years ago when over thirty percent of the workforce was unemployed.

Included in the improvement, at least for the Drews, was an offer from Allen's Uncle Raymond to work at his hardware store in Clinton.

Molly and Allen were married five years and this was the first real job he was able to hold. Molly enjoyed the security of the store and often helped stock the shelves and tag merchandise. Until the aftermath of the Great Depression, it was unusual for a married woman to venture into the work place. This particular morning, she promised Allen she would arrive at eight, and now she knew she wouldn't make it until after nine.

She turned on the radio and let it play while she washed up and brushed her teeth. In the background, Johnny Mercer's latest hit was playing: "Jeepers Creepers, Where'd You Get Those Peepers." She hummed the tune as she dressed for work.

Finally, Molly went to the mirror, brushed her long brown hair, and put on a little makeup. Her blue eyes contained small specks of red pigment. The resulting combination produced a color closer to violet than usual variations of green and blue.

Her cheekbones were set high on her face, reflecting a genetic gift from a distant Native American ancestor. Her skin was olive colored and smooth and provided an appealing resistance to the southern New England sun. She was full-figured with round shoulders and breasts that tucked neatly into a wasp-like waist. Her well-shaped legs tapered into thin ankles and tiny feet. Not only was she lovely to look at, but she moved with athletic grace. She did a turn in front of the glass.

"Not bad, even sick."

Molly donned a blue cardigan with a light spring jacket in preparation for her walk to the store. She had nearly a mile to cover and she allowed herself fifteen minutes to do it. As she stepped outside, the April morning air felt chilly on her face. She sneezed as she closed the door.

"Ouch!"

A pain in her chest. After the first sneeze, she sneezed

again and again. When the sneezing fit finally subsided, she felt a distinct scratchy sensation in the back of her throat and burning under her ribcage.

She walked briskly up the narrow lane to the sidewalk, which paralleled Route 1A. The WPA had recently completed the walkway and a small bronze plaque that specified a commemorative date of March 1938.

When Molly arrived at the store, she signed in on her time card.

"Hi, Allen. Hi, Uncle Raymond." She put on an apron. "I'll stock the shelves in the fishing equipment section," and she headed toward it.

Molly realized she had become an important member of the store and the family. Although, she was paid for her work, she thought her pay was a little less than what she was worth but, all in all, this new stage of her life could have been near perfect were it not for Allen's excessive interest in the business. He seemed to view it as his own, and in her mind, it wasn't his, it belonged to Uncle Raymond.

She complained to Allen, telling him that he was spending too much time in the business, telling him he was neglecting their relationship, but nothing seemed to move him. The more she complained, the more time he spent at the store. There was merchandise to purchase, shelves to stock, and the endless journal entries required to keep track of the various customers' debt to the store. The renewed idea of credit was springing from the ashes of the depression. Molly knew Uncle Raymond loved the idea of revenue and having a mix of loyal customers owing money was better than holding mortgages.

Raymond had enlarged several departments during the past two years and currently offered a wide variety of marine and fishing gear. Since the beginning of the Great Depression, more people attempted to make a living from

Long Island Sound. Even folks who weren't engaged in some form of commercial fishing supplemented their incomes and kitchens with as much bounty from the sound as they could harvest.

Uncle Raymond spent the morning complaining. "It's impossible keeping enough inventory of quahog rakes, fishing poles, buckets, nets, and crab and bait traps these days. The oyster business is booming, and folks around here have a wicked appetite for native lobster. I'd say thirty percent of my customers are on some kind of credit or barter plan, and I sure am tired a'tryng to keep up with their stuff."

The rising demand convinced him it was a good time to hire his nephew. Being family, he knew enough about Allen to feel comfortable with him in his business. Besides the young man was good with numbers and this was a welcome skill. Allen was twenty-five, with a slender build and kinky yellow hair. He was rather plain looking with pink skin and freckles. He did have some kind of skin condition, which exposed patches of crusty red sores on his neck and arms, patches that never seemed to heal. This condition had appeared a couple years ago, and Raymond knew Allen was trying over-the-counter remedies until he earned enough money to pay for professional treatment.

The boy had married reasonably well. Molly was a good-looking young woman and in the back of his mind Raymond was thinking she may be a pretty good worker in the store as well.

Kind of 'two for one, he thought.

The couple seemed to complement each other. She had an outgoing bubbly personality, which anchored well to Allen's more serious view of the world.

Raymond watched Molly carefully during the day, realizing she wasn't her usual self. She was sneezing and coughing. She moved with effort and seemed to lack focus.

It was nearly noon when he went to Allen and asked him to get involved.

CHAPTER 24

By afternoon, Molly was feverish. Her scratchy throat of the morning turned into an excruciating pain. She found it difficult to swallow, and she had trouble keeping her balance.

"There's something wrong, dear," Allen said. But as he watched, her condition worsened. When she fainted onto the feed sacks in the back room, he reacted. "I'll borrow Uncle Raymond's pickup truck and take you home."

When they arrived at the cottage, Molly, though conscious, could barely walk. Allen carried her into the house and put her on the bed. Molly moaned and threw her forearm across her forehead. Beads of perspiration bubbled from her cheeks and red welts erupted on her pale skin. Her moaning turned into unintelligible babbling. Allen felt her face with the back of his hand.

"You're burning up," he said, "What should I do? I need a telephone and we don't have one."

In order to find a phone, Allen would have to go to a neighbor or drive back to the store. Either of these options meant leaving Molly alone. "I can't do that."

Two hours passed, and Molly was still unresponsive and hot. Allen finally decided he had no choice. He wrapped some ice in a facecloth, draped it on her forehead. "I'm going up the street to the Miller's place to phone Doc Stemford. I'll be right back."

She was so delirious he wasn't sure whether she understood him or not, but he knew he had to go. A few minutes later, at Edna and Jim Miller's home, he reached Mary Stemford and told her Molly had suddenly taken sick. He needed help as soon as possible.

∾∾

Doctor Sam Stemford was in his office when Mary took the call from Allen Drew. Mary was only twenty-five but she looked and behaved with the maturity of a much older woman. Her face was round with small pale eyes and a sloping almost nonexistent chin. She tried to screen Sam's calls whenever she could.

"Sam, it's Allen Drew, that fellow from the Clinton Hardware Store. He says his wife Molly has come down with a fever and she's on fire. He says he needs your help as soon as possible. Can you see her?"

"Ask him if he has a thermometer," Sam told her.

"No, he doesn't but he says he has felt fevers before and believes this is very bad."

"You better give me the phone. Hello, Mr. Drew, this is Doctor Stemford. When did Molly first show any symptoms? Oh, that fast, was it? How was she yesterday? You don't know? Look, try to keep her cool with ice, and I'll get over there within the hour. It's probably a touch of the flu that's going round."

Doctor Sam Stemford pulled up in front of the little cottage Allen and Molly Drew were renting. He turned the key off, and the engine of his prized 1938 Chrysler Airflow sputtered to a stop. The car was elegant art deco, sleek and bold, but not an overstatement. The chrome and paint were still as shiny as when he drove it from the showroom floor. He had bought the car four months ear-lier and took pride in keeping it in immaculate condition.

Stemford grabbed his bag from the passenger side of the seat, pulled on the door handle, and pushed it open. He had to cock his head slightly to keep his gray fedora from hitting the doorsill, and then he drew his long legs, one at a time, from the front seat. It took only a few of his lanky strides to get from the car to the front door. He rang the bell and waited.

A moment later, the door flew open and Allen Drew welcomed the doctor. In one motion, he greeted the man, offered to take his jacket, and led him into the bedroom.

"Here she is, Doc. She's still burning up," Allen said, breathless.

While Sam inserted a thermometer into Molly's mouth, he talked to her in a soothing voice, trying to keep her aware so she wouldn't bite down and break the glass. A moment later he removed it, held it to the light, and uttered, "One-oh-four point two. Not good at all."

"What's it mean Doc?" Allen asked.

"It means that we had better cool her down. How much ice do you have?"

CHAPTER 25

Molly Drew was a young and energetic woman. When she felt well, she tried very hard to keep busy. She was a natural romantic and, given the opportunity, she was subject to infatuations. Although she didn't consciously pursue the idea of being with other men, it had happened before, and it recently happened again.

Years ago, while in high school, she realized she was vulnerable to a man's attention and she tried to avoid situations that placed her at risk, but try as she might, something happened and she found herself yielding to a phrase, a look, or a touch. She knew she wasn't looking for a substitute for Allen, and even if she were married to someone else, she would still be as vulnerable. It was in her nature.

The best outcome for this dilemma was that she hoped for discretion. She compensated for her weakness by proclaiming to herself, "The biggest error I can commit is to be caught."

It was because of her love for Allen that she was determined to hide this weakness from him. And strangely enough, she believed she loved, cherished, and obeyed in their relationship, so long as he never knew some of the things she did.

During the month of February, she met a young police officer from a neighboring village. He was a powerfully built man, with black eyes and a head full of thick black hair. His face was round with crisp, boyish features and an easy, confident demeanor. He was just twenty and fresh from the academy. They met while Molly was driving through the nearby town of Madison. Although she and Allen didn't own an automobile, she had learned to drive and, from time to time, ran errands using Uncle Raymond's 1934 pickup truck.

While she was running one of these errands, she was stopped by the young Madison police officer. He pulled her over, "You were driving too fast through the center of town," he claimed.

His stature was impressive as he stood by the truck's open window. Molly sat inside, feeling angry, diminutive, and a little humiliated as she tried to hide her feelings with a bright, almost seductive smile.

"Speeding's a serious offense," he said. "I could write a ticket that'll cost you ten dollars, but you've got such a pretty smile, I think I'll give you a warning this time. Just don't let me catch you doing' it again."

The phrase "pretty smile" quickly drained her of the anger and humiliation of being stopped. She felt more in control, so she answered with fem-fatale look. "That is awfully kind of you."

The next several times she drove through Madison, she looked for him, and if she saw him, she waved and smiled. In time, she found herself choosing when to run her errands so she might catch a glimpse of the young cop while he was on duty.

On one such trip through town, Molly slowed down, trying to find him parked in a side street or on the roadside, but he was nowhere around. In her mind, she had this notion that if they were intended to meet again, fate would somehow take charge and shape a circumstance to bring them together. She enjoyed the random act of flirting and saw no harm in it.

As Molly drove through town, she was a little disappointed with not seeing the cop at any of the usual places. During her tour, she maneuvered the Ford pickup around the town green and headed west on Route 1A.

As Molly left the village, her feeling of disappointment was short-lived, as her rear view mirror revealed a black and white police car pulling behind her and following for a while. About two miles from town, the red light on the patrol car roof began flashing. She slowed down and recognized the smiling face of the young cop in the mirror. She drove another half-mile or so, pulled over, and stopped. He tucked the patrol car behind her truck, got out, and walked to her window.

He looked in at her. "Hi."

The February air was cold and crisp. He wore his jacket collar raised high around his neck. Clouds of warm steam condensed and puffed from his mouth as he spoke, "Is there anything I can help you with?"

She looked at him for a long moment and decided to play along. "Yes, Officer, for a while there, I thought I was lost, but now I think I might find my way, perhaps with your help."

"Well, ma'am, if you will come over to my patrol car, I'll write up some directions that should keep you on track."

She looked at him for another long moment. "Of course, Officer."

She opened the truck door, got out, closed it, and followed the cop back to his car. He asked her to get in, and she went around to the passenger side and did as she was asked. He opened the driver's door and slid in beside her. He picked up a clipboard containing a pad with a pencil on a string. Before he started to write anything, he looked at her face and deeply into her eyes. She didn't turn away. Instead she looked back and they both knew what they were about to do.

"Scrunch down in that seat," he said as he put the car into first gear and released the clutch. "Try to keep your head below the dashboard," he said as they drove away.

He drove the patrol car to an old fire road and went two or three miles into the woods. When he stopped, he left the motor running and the heater on.

He said, "Okay, you can put your head up now. Do you know how much trouble I'd be in if anybody saw us coming out here?"

"Probably as much as I'd be in," she answered. "You know I'm married."

"Yeah, I know. I also know you're working part time over at the Clinton Hardware store."

One remark led to another, and soon the conversation shifted from talk to touch. Touch ignited sparks which flourished into fire. Unbridled passion ruled the encounter. They coupled, nearly tearing each other's clothes.

When they had finished, they sat in the patrol car with the windows steamed and the motor still running. He lit a cigarette and passed it to her. Molly took a deep drag and realized how much of a rush the whole episode had been. She felt satisfied. The first sense of sexual satisfaction she could remember with a man. There was numbness between her thighs that she had rarely experienced, and clarity of mind so calming it nearly frightened her.

They talked for a moment or two, and then he drove her back to the truck.

As she got out of the car, the cop smiled. "I want to see you again."

She looked at him thoughtfully. "This could get very complicated, but we'll see." Then she pulled her coat tight around her and trudged toward the truck.

Now that the rush was over, and she was thinking more clearly, she realized she had better tidy up. On the way back to the store, she stopped at the first gas station and used the bathroom.

After the first encounter, Molly and the cop met regularly, sometimes as often as twice a week. Since he was still new on the police force, he was usually assigned to a second shift, which required a three o'clock afternoon start. This provided them daytime opportunities to meet on a regular basis. Sometimes Molly walked to the harbor, or bicycled to a park, where she met him with little risk of being seen. Sometimes, when she kept her head below the dashboard, she discovered new activities to keep herself occupied. Their relationship was very physical, and Molly relished the attention.

The cop was young, single, and passionate. Because he was a cop, she felt safe with their secret. But as time passed, she found herself having to rationalize her marriage to him. He began with small insulting remarks about Allen. Remarks, which seemed innocent at first, changed, and took on an angry tone. Gradually, the policeman seemed more and more annoyed with her husband, and Molly found herself uncomfortable with justifying the way she felt about Allen. She didn't want to leave her marriage. Certainly, Allen had done nothing wrong and, in her own way, she did love him. This new aspect of her extramarital relationship began to trouble her.

CHAPTER 26

August, 1938:

The affair between Molly Drew and Teddy Flanders flourished through February, March, and much of April. The relationship remained hot until she became ill during a notable flu epidemic that swept through the region. The illness struck her suddenly and more severely than most people it affected. She became so debilitated she required constant daily care during the first two weeks of the infection. Doc Stemford worked closely with Allen Drew to establish a care routine that probably saved her life.

By the end of the third week, Molly was almost fully recovered. While she was sick, Doc Stemford was concerned that the current flu strain may have the deadly potential of the Spanish Flu of 1918. Because of his fear, he began taking fluid samples from Molly in hope of using the materials for the development of a vaccine.

One morning while sitting at the kitchen table with Allen Drew, Stemford wanted to talk. He had been in and out the Drew household so often he felt he needed say something about what had been on his mind during all those visits.

He also wanted Allen to listen, perhaps understand

where he was coming from and what he hoped to achieve beyond Molly's recovery.

He sat there holding a cup of hot coffee and said, "When I was in med school, I read a great deal about the practice of vaccinations. I guess it was then that I became convinced that people could be protected against severe infections by the use of proper inoculation techniques. I also believe there's a connection between those pathogens involved in travesties like the Spanish Flu Epidemic of 1918 and other large population illnesses."

Allen listened attentively, seemingly trying to understand why the doctor was so intense during his care of Molly.

"But you know," Stemford said, "even though there's lots of evidence showing the benefits of inoculations as far back as five hundred years ago, there's always been great reluctance to refine and scientifically understand the process. Back in 1712, there were published results on vaccinations and its impact on smallpox. But for whatever reason, much of the information was ignored until later in the century. By then, thousands of people had died, perhaps needlessly.

There was a huge small pox epidemic in Boston around 1720. The whole town refused to accept the idea of vaccination. People died by the hundreds as the pox swept over the entire Charles River basin. Mortality ran at fifty percent, with the very young and very old struck particularly hard.

"There's so little being done and there seems to be so much that could be done. I've no idea why we're plagued with these diseases, but I believe there's a way to understand and protect against them. It's my theory that much of the resistance to sicknesses like the flu, the pox, and other scourges lies within the human body itself."

Allen seemed thoughtful as he asked, "Do you think

this flu that's going around now will be as bad as that business in 1918?"

"That's hard to say, but I've got serum samples from Molly and, now that she's recovering, I'll get post flu samples and try to do some isolation and identification work, at least for her blood type. Then we'll see where we go next."

♋♋

Allen Drew tried to understand the good doctor's explanation, but then he shrugged his shoulders and said, "However your work turns out, please know how grateful I am for all you've done for Molly and me. I thought for sure she was going to burn up from the fever. Then the terrible cough that followed seemed like she might die from pneumonia."

By the beginning of the fourth week of recovery, Molly felt much better and became restless and bored from being cooped up in the cottage. Doc Stemford was concerned about her weakened immune system and wanted to avoid the threat of more pneumonia, so he insisted she remain in quarantine.

Doc Stemford had become a powerful influence in Molly's life during the past several weeks, and she reluctantly agreed to the isolation. However, the situation continued to aggravate her boredom.

In this environment, Molly began to fantasize about what the good doctor would be like as a lover. She knew she was an attractive woman and, if she were determined, she believed he'd find her impossible to resist. And so, during his morning visit of the fourth week of her recovery, Molly became a different kind of patient.

Dr. Stemford arrived at seven-thirty that morning. He unlocked the door using a key given to him by Allen

Drew. Knowing Allen was already at the hardware store, Stemford went to the kitchen, opened the hot water faucet at the sink, and scrubbed his hands vigorously. While he scrubbed, he called out, "Molly, are you awake?"

"Yes, Doctor Stemford."

"How's your temperature this morning?" he asked, while still scrubbing.

"I think I'm fine."

"Please go ahead and shake out the thermometer. I'll be finished in a minute and we can pick up where we left off yesterday," he said.

"Okay."

A few minutes passed and Stemford entered the bedroom. Molly lay in the bed with a thermometer perched in her lips like the end of a lollypop. There was something different about her this morning. Something he'd never noticed before. She sat propped up by double pillows behind her back. She had just showered and willowy puffs of steam still clung to the ceiling like miniature clouds in a summer sky.

She'd dried her hair and it appeared soft and flowing as it cascaded over her shoulders. During the past few weeks, her hair was usually matted, slick with sweat, scented with body odor, camphor, and alcohol. Today she looked clean, not just clean, but a healthy, glowing kind of clean that in itself was more telling than the numbers on the thermometer.

She smiled, careful not lose the glass tube between her lips. Her nightgown was different too. Not the boyish pajamas she'd been wearing. The white gown was nearly sheer with lace sprinkled like flowers in a garden all around the deeply plummeting bodice.

Before this morning, her skin was pale and clammy to the touch. Today, the color of her skin was rich and her cheeks were aglow as though she had just experienced a secret sexual pleasure. Even the room smelled different, the fragrance of lilacs bursting from a porcelain vase wafted in the air, and Sam realized Molly was feeling much better.

"I guess you've made a complete recovery," he said.

"It's about time, don' cha think?"

He reached over and removed the thermometer. He read it aloud, "'Ninety-eight point six.' Perfect temperature."

He placed his hand on her forehead and tried to maintain his professional distance as she rolled her shoulder to allow one of the straps of her gown to slide away, revealing most of her right breast. Then he realized she had more on her mind than her recent illness.

"Molly, you don't understand, as your doctor I can't become involved?" he said defensively. "It simply can't happen."

"Look, Sam," she said, "I'm not looking for some kind of enduring relationship. Please, try to understand the way I'm built. I'm totally grateful for what you've done. And I care for you and your skill as a doctor. I want you. Even if only one time. I need to express myself with you, for you. No strings or obligations implied. This is no threat to your marriage or your practice."

Molly rolled her other shoulder and the gown slipped lower exposing both her breasts.

Doctor Sam Stemford wasn't even sure why he placed his hand on her cheek, but he did. Maybe it was intended to soften a further effort at rejection or maybe it was his desire to continue the liaison, but in that touch there was no denying the chemistry between them.

Molly ran her hand over Stemford's trousers. Soon, they coupled in as many ways as could be imagined by the pair.

When they had finished the fragrance of lilacs in the

room was displaced with the fresh-mowed-grass scent of sex.

As Stemford prepared to leave, he swallowed hard and announced that she had recovered and any future medical visits would be at her discretion. Making no promises or indications of a continued liaison, he felt guilty over succumbing to the situation and his inkling of regret was like a seed planted in fertile earth. He sensed this feeling would either grow or subside with the passage of time. Since the act was over, there was little to do but wait for his own sensibilities to reveal an appropriate course of behavior.

During the next several weeks, Stemford reassessed the encounter with Molly Drew and became more determined to make sure there was never a repeat of the event. A few weeks later, they met at the Drew cottage and Stemford expressed profound guilt.

As they sat at the kitchen table he told Molly, "It will never happen again. My marriage is of primary importance in my life and I'll do everything possible to avoid placing it in jeopardy."

Molly listened carefully. She was disappointed. "I understand. I enjoyed the encounter, but in spite of that, I will make no demands on you."

As time passed, Molly contemplated Doctor Stemford's remarks regarding his life, beliefs, and expectations. His intimacy with her was, by itself, a powerful experience. From her perspective, he was a thoughtful man with rich and enduring values, which seemed to tower over her behavior. She found it ironic that the results of a spontaneous sexual encounter left her with a feeling of vicarious guilt given, as a gift, from a reluctant partner.

The experience with Sam eroded the pleasure Molly got from her relationship with Teddy Flanders, and soon she realized it caused more pressure than gratification. She finally decided the affair must end.

As she thought about ending the affair, she realized that Allen really needed both her and her fidelity, and she concluded she'd better focus on her marriage before it became trivialized by her behavior.

By the end of July, she was weary of the stress of Teddy's expectations, and she set out to close off the relationship. She began by rehearsing what she was going to say to Teddy Flanders over and over in her head. When she felt the script was ready, she chose the time and place to present it.

Molly tried to be convincing when she told Teddy it was over. "Teddy, I've been thinking we need to figure out where this is going," she said, trying to keep her tone as nonchalant as possible.

"Why does it have to be going anywhere?" Teddy said.

"That's the point," she said. "It's not going anywhere."

"It's not going anywhere, if you don't let it," Teddy said. "If you'd recognize the mistake you made when you hooked up with that crumby little clerk in the first place, the answer would be pretty clear. Get rid of your past life and get ready for a new life, a new life with me. We're the real thing."

"Teddy, you make it sound so simple. But Allen isn't like you say he is." He's a good man, trying to get through a lifetime just like everybody else."

෫ඉ෫ඉ

Teddy looked into Molly's eyes. He tried to figure out what she was thinking. Was this an attempt at getting some kind of commitment from him, or was this really designed to put him on the defensive and run some new course?

The problem, in his mind, was he didn't recognize or accept rejection. They'd been through too much together. Besides, he believed whatever different was going on had something to do with Sam Stemford. Ever since her illness, she'd not been quite the same toward Teddy.

As the relationship waned, Teddy became more obsessed than ever with Molly. He didn't understand why she changed as completely as she did. He couldn't accept that she'd give up the power and passion of being together. He couldn't believe Molly really had changed that much, or that fast. In the back of his mind, he believed Doc Stemford was at the heart of his unhappy situation.

Teddy's obsession challenged him with ideas as to how he might confirm his suspicions. Whenever possible, he followed and observed the doctor during his daily activities. When he wasn't stalking Sam Stemford, he stalked Molly. He found himself behaving like a bad divorce detective, with himself as his only client.

It was early in his shift when Teddy heard a call on his car radio from the Clinton Police Headquarters requesting information on the whereabouts of Doc Stemford.

"Officer Flanders, Officer Flanders," the dispatcher droned through the receiver.

Teddy picked up the mike. "Flanders here," he responded, "What's going on?"

"We've got a situation," the dispatcher advised.

"What kind of situation?"

"One of the fellas over at the Clinton hardware store's gotta broken bone. We can't find Doc Stemford nowhere. We've got every department from Old Saybrook to Branford on the lookout. If you see his car, let me know. Dispatch over and out."

A little while later, Teddy's radio lit up again. "Officer Flanders, Officer Flanders, calling car four. Teddy, are you there?"

"This is car four, Dispatch. What've you got?"

"The search for Stemford's over. We found him here in Madison, and he's on his way. Over and out."

CHAPTER 27

Teddy paid close attention to the radio conversations. He wasn't entirely sure what had happened at the Clinton Hardware store, but he decided to cruise by the Drew place just to see if what happened involved them. After dark, he drove his patrol car East on Route 1 and parked in the woods behind the Drew cottage. He left the car, removed his hat, and threw it on the front seat.

As he neared the house, Teddy recognized Doc Stemford's black Chrysler parked in front. He crouched in the shadows and slowly made his way to a bedroom window. He raised himself enough to look in and discovered he could see into the room through a space between the curtain and window frame. As he watched, Allen Drew lay on the bed, his leg wrapped in a wooden splint. He seemed asleep.

Teddy crept from window to window trying to see who was in the house and what was happening inside. Finally, he paused at a large window facing the front living room. It was open halfway, leaving only a drawn shade and screen between him and the interior. He heard Molly's voice, quiet and soft on the other side of the wall.

"Sam, will he be all right?"

"I think he'll be just fine. It looks like a simple fracture and the splint will hold everything in place till tomorrow. I'll be back in the morning and make a plaster cast for the leg. I've given him a strong sedative for tonight. He'll be out for quite a while. He may not wake until I get back."

An observer might speculate on the motive for the potency of the sedative. Was it Allen Drew's pain from the injury or something else? Was latent desire in the picture or was it just happenstance? It was doubtful either Stemford or Molly could have answered the question if asked. Nonetheless, they were alone together, intentionally or not. There was no turning back, at least in Molly's mind.

There was silence for a moment and then Molly spoke. "Sam, I've missed you."

"I sensed as much. We both know we shouldn't be alone together," he said.

"A situation like this makes it so hard," she said. "Sam, I ache for your touch. It's been too long."

As Molly spoke, Teddy listened, his heart pounding like explosions in his chest. He felt his temples pulsating as his body flushed a stew of hormones into his blood stream. Molly was speaking the way she used to speak to him.

But there was something else in her voice, something missing from his experience with her. There was a tone, expressing emotion so deep he was enraged at hearing it. Teddy's mind raced from terrible thought to terrible thought.

"I could rip through the screen, tear down the shade, and kill both of them from the window," he whispered. "I could wait and nail the doc when he comes out the door, or break through the front door and shoot them where they sit."

All of those options, however satisfying they might

sound, left Teddy with little hope of escape. Even in the darkness, the sound of gunshots and the revved up exit of an out-of-town patrol car left little in the way of anonymity. He would surely be caught, and prosecuted.

So he crouched there and listened. He heard Molly sigh and mutter in a husky voice, "Oh, Sam."

Then there was a kind of silence, and all he heard was the sound of rustling fabric and the clatter of an unfastened belt buckle. Teddy left the window, went around to the rear of the house, and tried the door. It was unlocked. He carefully opened it just enough to squeeze his bulk through and stealthily moved toward the living room. There, he stood in the unlighted kitchen and saw into the dimly lit living room.

Molly was nearly naked, sitting on the floor. Sam's trouser belt was undone.

Teddy felt a rage he'd never experienced. He wanted to kill them so badly he bit into his lower lip. The metallic taste of his own blood made him even angrier. He stayed until he couldn't watch any longer, fearing his rage would better his reason. Then he silently backed out the door and closed it behind him.

He was sweating when he reached the patrol car. He started the engine and quietly coasted away from the cottage. He checked the time. It was eight forty-five. He called in.

"Car four to dispatch," he said into the mike.

There was a blast of static and then white noise as the return carrier wave burst off the car's antenna. "Go ahead, car four," was the response.

"I've had some trouble with the radio. The light's been out for the past twenty minutes. I think it's okay now. If you couldn't get me, it should be fixed now," Teddy lied, but he needed to know if there were any calls for him while he was at the Drew house.

"Car four, it's been a quiet night so far. Do you need to come in for repairs?"

"No, I think I've got it fixed now. I should be able to finish out the shift. Thanks for the check-in. This is car four standing by."

"You take care, Teddy, Madison dispatch over and out."

CHAPTER 28

Teddy knew Sam used Nod Road on his drive back to Madison. The policeman parked in woods near the pond where Nod Road began. He sat there, hidden in the brush, and waited for Stemford's black Chrysler. He knew Clinton and the other neighboring villages were so small in population they relied on a local state trooper to occasionally patrol major roads on off-shifts. There was so much territory to cover, Teddy believed there was no risk of encountering another police officer, so he sat, stewing in his rage, and waited.

Teddy still wasn't sure what he would do next. The security and seclusion of this place in the brush helped calm him, allowing a temporary reprieve from the rage he felt when he left the Drew cottage. As he waited, he thought back to when he was a boy and had stalked these woods, hunting, trapping, and sometimes just raising hell.

He remembered the first deer he shot a long time ago. He was just nine years old, tall, and strong for his age. The year was 1929, the year of the fateful crash of the American stock market.

Teddy totally startled himself and the deer early that summer morning. He carried his father's twenty-two caliber lever action rifle. He had entered the woods with the idea of plinking whatever targets he could find. And suddenly he found himself face to face with a young doe. He was quick to realize the opportunity. He shouldered the rifle and tried to fire. But he moved too fast and forgot to release the safety on the gun.

The deer, spooked by the boy's sudden action, spun away and leaped toward the brush. Teddy fumbled for the safety and managed to release it. This time he pulled the trigger and the rifle fired.

Teddy knew right away that he had a hit the deer. The animal broke stride, faltered, then recovered and tried to regain its pace. It seemed to require time for the animal's brain to reconnect with the act of running. Perhaps it was the pain of the bullet's path that caused the distraction. Teddy knew his twenty-two was too small a bore for larger game so he fired again. *Plenty might be an adequate substitute for bigger,* he thought. This was a better strike because the animal shuddered and dropped to her knees. Blood splattered from her nose indicating damage to the lungs. Despite the injury, she seemed able to process enough air to get to her feet and keep on running. A third bullet hit her in the hindquarter forcing her to lope along on three good legs.

Teddy chased her for twenty minutes, shooting her every time he was able to get close enough to assure a hit. He finally forced her down to the pond where she stood in the shallows up to her forelocks in water. She panted as red foam oozed from her mouth and nostrils. Her head lowered, she seemed to know she was beaten and no longer had the will or energy to flee.

Teddy studied her from twenty feet away trying to decide where to shoot her next. The water beneath her ran red. In all, Teddy shot the animal nine times that morning, once for each year of his age. Finally, she dropped on her forelocks and Teddy went close to her. He cocked his head and looked carefully into her glassy eyes. She was losing consciousness and events around her were slowing down.

Teddy drew his hunting knife from his belt and slashed the blade firmly across her throat. The remaining blood pumped from her body, pouring over his arms and into the pond. Then, she slowly crumpled into the water and died.

Teddy stood bathed in the warm red liquid and the process seemed like a corrupt baptismal ritual. He crouched low in the pink water, still breathing heavy, and realized he'd never experienced such a rush. He learned shooting large animals with a small caliber rifle could be a real treat, and with a little practice, he might be able to make the chase and inevitable kill last for hours.

The memory of his first deer brought his mind even farther back to the months before the deer, when the town of Clinton had decided to excavate the sandy mound that became the pond at Nod Road.

In 1928, the town was growing rapidly because of the prosperity of the period. Little did the population know, in less than a year, the world would face the beginning of the longest and most severe financial crises in the history of modern civilization.

Connecticut pretty much paralleled the rest of the country in many ways. In the shoreline, for example, the unprecedented growth of the early 1920s pressured local selectmen to pass a referendum approving money to quarry the land parcel north of Nod Road.

As quarry work progressed, the town removed large quantities of indigenous sand and used it in various construction projects. The soil found its way into concrete sidewalks, bridges, and building foundations throughout the shoreline community.

Teddy remembered the final days at the quarry site, as work crews carved the trough that became the pond at

Nod Road. The hole was one hundred yards long and thirty-five yards across. In less than a year's time, what was once a sandy mound became a large earthen pit, tapering from twelve feet below ground level to thirty feet deep as it neared the roadside.

The pit was steep and dry until the work crews struck a large underground spring. In a matter of days, the sand quarry was flooded into a teardrop shaped pond abutting Nod Road. As the water level increased, the town engineer was asked to design a suitable drainage culvert, because they feared water pressure from the spring would overflow the road and perhaps even wash it away.

CHAPTER 29

Teddy was eight years old when the pond was created, and he knew the bottom contours well. As he thought about the pond's origin, he finally decided what to do about Doc Stemford. The plan he needed unfolded in his head, replete with detail, and the clarity pleased him.

At nine-thirty, a pair of headlights sprayed shafts of light around the corner and turned onto Nod Road. Teddy opened his eyes wide to determine the make of the vehicle. As it rolled in front of him, he recognized Sam Stemford's Chrysler. He pulled out behind it, and followed for a moment before flashing the red light on the patrol car roof. He flashed it twice and Sam pulled over near the pond on Nod Road.

Teddy got out and walked to the car. As he drew closer, he saw the doctor roll down his window. Teddy carried his thirty eight-caliber service revolver behind his back. He had stopped the doctor a month before in Madison just to harass him, and he knew that when he was close enough, the Doc would recognize him.

In the meantime, Sam shuffled around in the front seat trying to get his wallet out of his pocket. He was still shuffling when Teddy approached the Chrysler. Teddy's heart raced as he walked up to the driver's side of the car, pointed the gun, and fired a single shot into the head of Doctor Samuel Stemford. The impact of the bullet threw the doctor's head violently to the right and blood sprayed over the top of the front seat.

"How's that feel? You son-of-a-bitch."

Although Sam's mind was shattered, his chest heaved in fruitless attempts to suck in more air. His lungs worked hard, as if an infusion of oxygen could repair the broken connections in his head. He made rasping sounds as the life drained from his body. A moment or two later, Sam sat slumped in the seat with his empty eyes staring straight ahead.

"All right Doc, it's time to take a bath. It's a shame to waste such a beautiful car, but it'll make a swell coffin," Teddy muttered, still wide eyed from the adrenaline pumping through his body.

There was a four-foot drop to the surface of the pond below the bridge. While Teddy had been sitting in the patrol car, he thought out the details of what he was to do. And now, the action he was about to take was clear in his mind.

Nod Road was so rural after ten p.m., there was seldom, if ever, any traffic. In spite of this, Teddy knew that he must work quickly. The time was now ten-fifteen, and so far, no one else had driven down Nod Road. All he needed was another five or six minutes. He removed his holster, his shirt, trousers, and boots and placed them in the patrol car that was still parked in the brush. In the darkness, he walked back to the Chrysler and slid into the driver's side, pushing Sam's crumpled body to the center of the seat.

Teddy took his uniform tie and fixed a double half hitch around the outside door handle of the Chrysler. He pulled the other end through the door jam and grasped it firmly with his left hand. He was concerned that the door might slam closed when it landed in the water. If that happened, it would be difficult for him to escape.

He also knew that if the car were to become a proper tomb, he had to make sure it was sealed securely by the time it reached the bottom. This meant that the windows and doors must be closed while the car sank. Before starting the engine, he rolled up the driver's side window.

Teddy backed the car and pulled across the center of the road facing the pond. He put the transmission into first gear and eased out the clutch. Nod Road was a small country lane and there were no guardrails to hinder the inevitable clash between objects from the path above and the water below.

The Chrysler careened over the shoulder and plunged toward the pond. Teddy had played out this scene in his mind. The real experience was a tremendous rush that went well beyond his expectations. For a moment, the event seemed dreamlike and passage of time slowed. Teddy had braced himself as the hurtling mass splashed into the water.

Just as he had planned, his tie prevented the car door from slamming closed on impact, but the unlatched door created another problem. Even though the Chrysler landed upright, it began to fill rapidly on the left side. This caused it to develop a list that threatened to roll it over. Teddy tumbled out of the car. He nearly panicked when he realized that Sam's body was falling out behind him. Sam's body pressed hard against Teddy. Blood from his massive head wound smeared over the policeman's face.

Suddenly Teddy found himself embroiled in a fight for survival against a dead man.

While he struggled, he kept his wits and managed to get the door closed enough to hold Sam's body inside. With the left door partially latched, water flow decreased on that side and the car slowly began to right as it continued to sink into the murky water. With his lungs bursting, Teddy let go of the tie and pushed as hard as he could against the door. He rejoiced when he heard the satisfying click of the door latch. The force of the water pressure had helped him to seal the car.

A few moments later all that remained at the scene were a few bubbles billowing to the surface. Teddy gasped for air as he swam for the embankment. Exhausted, he staggered out of the chilly water and collapsed on the ground. He lay there for a few minutes trying to catch his breath. Finally, he forced himself to make his way back to the patrol car. He moved cautiously through the brush, when suddenly the glow of headlights rounded the curve by the pond. In the darkness, a car drove by without a hint of seeing anything.

Teddy was nearly naked, crouched low in the brush as the car sped away into the night. He thought that was too close for comfort. But luck was with him tonight, and he felt like he could get away with anything. He returned to the patrol car, removed his wet underwear, and dressed in his uniform. He slid in behind the wheel, started the motor, and drove back to the Madison Police Headquarters.

CHAPTER 30

A few days later, Teddy Flanders got a call from Molly Drew. "Teddy, I need to see you," she said.

Teddy was flattered, thinking that the woman had finally come to her senses. Maybe Stemford's disappearance was having the right effect. "Sure, baby, sure. When and where?"

"Hammonasset Reserve. How about we meet there? On your next day off, I can bike over from the store during the afternoon. Is that okay?" she asked.

"Good choice, Molly," Teddy agreed. "By the way, I've got tomorrow off."

"Okay, that's it then, tomorrow at three o'clock. Teddy, this isn't anything other than I need to talk to you. Nothing else, right?"

"I got it baby. I need to talk to you, too."

The next day Molly dressed in a pair of loose trousers and, as the clock drew near, she readied herself for the trip to the dunes. Before she climbed on the bike, she clipped the right pant cuff in place to keep it out of the chain.

The September morning was overcast by low, gray clouds that obscured the sun as Molly peddled down the dirt road that connected the beach to Route 1. On her left, lay vast stretches of marsh crisscrossed with dozens of trench-like rills that eventually drained into Long Island Sound.

In the distance behind her, a windsock belonging to the tiny Griswald Airport fluttered in the light breeze that blew in from the water. Hammonasset Beach began in the flood plain of the Hammonasset River and spanned the nearly three miles west until it abutted the Madison town line. She could see the dunes of the beach over the top of the bulrushes that surrounded her. She had nearly another mile to go to reach the place where she was to meet Teddy Flanders.

As she drew near, Teddy pulled in from the other direction and parked his 1932 Ford coupe on the sand. He turned off the motor and got out of the car. He wore street clothes with a light jacket and a baseball cap. He stood there, framed by the gray sky and pale yellow sand, and smiled.

"It's about time," he said as she laid the bicycle down on the ground. "I've missed you."

Molly's face seemed sad as she walked to where he stood. "Teddy, what do you know about Sam Stemford's disappearance?"

"Only that Mary Stemford came into headquarters a couple of days ago and reported him missing," he replied.

"Are you sure that's all you know about it?"

"Come on, Molly, what are you trying to say? Why would I have anything to do with Sam Stemford?" He reached out and tried to put his arm around her, and she pulled away. "What's wrong with you?" he asked. "It's been a long time and I thought you called because you wanted to be with me."

"No, I don't want to be with you. I thought you understood after our last talk. The relationship is over. The only reason I wanted to see you was to ask about the disappearance of Sam Stemford. I had a feeling something was wrong, and I thought maybe you could help."

"All of a sudden, you've got some kind of a soft spot for this missing doctor. Who are you trying to kid? You stopped screwing me and started screwing him."

Molly looked at Teddy for a long moment. "So that's it," she said, knowingly.

All of a sudden, repressed, unspoken thoughts that had been ricocheting inside her head took shape. In a flash of insight, she visualized Teddy Flanders doing the unthinkable. She saw him committing murder. She knew him well and she felt afraid. "You did something to him, didn't you?" she said. Her violet eyes narrowed as she hurtled the accusation.

"Don't be silly, Molly. Of course I didn't do anything to him. He's just missing. I'm sure he'll show up in a few days. He'll come home to his wife and practice. Come on, don't be sore. Let's go for a walk and just be together a few minutes."

She knew he wanted to find a way to get her to lay with him. He was insatiable and he would try to find a way to be intimate with her, but she was frightened now and she realized she had to get away from him. "Look Teddy, I've got to get back, I just wanted to know what was going on with Sam Stemford, and I guess you've told me all there is to know. If you don't mind, I've got to leave now."

Teddy was disappointed in both her attitude and with himself for what he may have inadvertently disclosed to her. Since she didn't respond favorably to the idea of their past association, he found himself deliberately using intimidation in order to keep her there. He knew it was a mistake, but he was reaching for a feeling of power in a situation where he was no longer in control. She was so determined to leave, he believed he had little to lose if he tried harder. "Molly, whatever you think about me, you've got to know I've cared for you. I'm not sure you can simply wave your hand and say bye and expect me to vanish from your life. I've enjoyed us, and I don't believe it's over. What do you think you're going to do now? Crawl into bed with that little sore you're married to? Do you really think that will bring you happiness? Have you forgotten what it's like making love together? Do you really think I'll forget?"

Molly listened, and when he was finished, she looked at him. "You still don't get it, Teddy. It's over." She bent down, picked up the bicycle, and started to walk away.

Teddy walked up to her, grabbed her by the back of the neck, and squeezed harder until she dropped the bike.

"Come on," he said as he dragged her over to a hollow at the base of a nearby sand dune.

There, he threw her to the ground and ripped her baggy trousers down to her ankles. She knew he was out of control and offered little resistance. Instead, she lay there and let him have his way. When he was finished, she got up and pulled her clothing together as best she could.

She looked at him with bitter hatred in her violet eyes. "I never want to see you near me ever again." With that, she picked up the bike and began the ride home.

"Oh, Molly, thanks. I'll let you know when I need you again," Teddy called as she rode away.

❧

Molly cried as she peddled home. She usually felt so much in control, but now she was afraid. Was it really over and the rape just a parting shot manifesting Teddy's own loss of control? Or was this just the beginning of a sick crusade by Teddy, haunting her, stalking her forever? *What can I do*? she thought. If he killed the good doctor, why wouldn't he go a step further and kill her? What was he capable of, if she pointed a finger at him? Would anybody believe her, if she did say something?

The more she thought about it, the more afraid she became.

CHAPTER 31

September 20, 1938:

The morning of September 20, 1938 turned out overcast, with winds from the southeast and powerful bands of rain marching through Connecticut and Rhode Island. Everyone knew of the possible weather anomalies buried within the relative complacency of September and October. These odd occurrences spawned surprisingly violent storms, sometimes springing out of the Atlantic Ocean. Weather fronts like these were defined then, much as today, as tropical storms or, in severe cases, hurricanes.

In 1938, there were no satellite surveillance agencies, no Doppler radar facilities, and no computer modeling of weather systems. Forecasters predicted weather fronts moving west to east in the traditional fashion with some degree of accuracy. At times, they estimated paths of Canadian troughs as they pushed southward. However, storm systems festering in the mid-Atlantic or born off the coast of Africa were as isolated from American forecasters as quarantined patients from an infected population.

Hurricanes running north along the continental shelf had some chance of being reported in time to prepare areas directly in a northerly path. But an Atlantic hurricane, racing hundreds of miles off-shore, bound for a penetrating hit at New England, had little or no chance of being detected.

The day before such an event in 1938 found people looking skyward with wonder. Those people whose livelihood depended on weather, like fishermen, construction workers, and farmers, fretted about going outside and conducting their business. Most asked themselves, could they wait and shake it off, go out tomorrow and make up for a day already lost?

Menhaden boats, clamers, and lobstermen struck off early enough in the day, but by noon, wind gusts topped thirty-five miles per hour and seas became progressively worse. Wave heights in Long Island Sound ran five to six feet and offshore at Montauk Point, seas tumbled at eight to ten feet. As conditions worsened, most everyone working the waters, from Long Island Sound to Cuttyhunk, turned homeward to escape the spiraling squall fronts.

The morning of September twenty-first was decidedly worse. By eleven a.m., winds gusted to one hundred and twenty miles an hour and changed direction from southeast to southwest. People, who yesterday believed it was a mere passing storm, now faced a chilling reality. They were stuck in the middle of hurricane force winds, and they would be there for an undetermined length of time.

At one hundred and twenty miles an hour, whole trees toppled, root balls weighing thousands of pounds plucked from the ground as if they were weeds pulled by the hand of God. Tree limbs were tom away and hurdled through the air like lances. Traffic lights, road signs, and power lines were ripped from their moorings and tossed about with killing force. Shingles torn from roofs spun about like a sharp edged, lethal discus. Poorly constructed buildings lost entire roofs, but it wasn't enough.

By five p.m., wind speeds reached one hundred and eighty miles an hour and now came out of the northeast. A human being couldn't walk about in such a maelstrom. Anyone caught in the open was lifted from his feet and hurtled like a rag doll.

Still, this wasn't enough.

There was an outrageous wind and all of its collateral damage. As the storm system pressed hard toward Point Judith, Rhode Island, the tide rushed westward to Long Island Sound and northward into Narragansett Bay. The forward path of the storm pushed an unrelenting wall of water fifteen to twenty feet above normal into the coasts of Connecticut and Rhode Island. The deadly surge was on its way and nothing could stop it.

The rising water penetrated breakwaters and seawalls as though they didn't exist. Every estuary emptying to the sea became a point of entry. Dark water quickly overwhelmed bays, rivers, and creeks as it rushed ten miles past ordinary flood plains.

Homes, barns, and cars gave way to the force of wind and water. Some bobbed about for a few minutes, while others simply broke up, leaving sections of construction flaying about on the surface ready to smash into more man made construction. People, livestock, trees, orchards, and remaining crops all disappeared in a matter of hours, some never to be found. The terrible storm ravaged New England for over thirty hours, and when it had passed, residual high water remained for an entire week.

When the storm was over, there was little discretionary time available to most of the residents of the Connecticut shoreline. The hurricane left behind a terrible wake of carnage. Six hundred people were dead or missing, countless more were injured or homeless. Record high winds exceeding one hundred and eighty three miles per hour were recorded.

The storm struck at high tide, and what people later described as a tidal wave was actually a storm surge that was twenty feet above mean high water. The first land mass struck was Long Island. By the time people living there realized what was happening, the phone and power lines were down. In a matter of minutes, there was no communication of any type.

Residents had no way to alert the rest of the world to the peril they were about to face. The storm raged inland toward central Massachusetts before losing strength over land. When it was over, devastation was everywhere. The swath of flattened debris was one hundred miles wide and one hundred and fifty miles long. All that remained was the task of rebuilding an entire region.

The cleanup seemed like it would go on forever. Many of the towns along the shoreline suffered extensive damage. Cellars were flooded, power lines were down, and roofs were missing or severely compromised. Whole trees and large branches were strewn about everywhere.

The little state of Rhode Island was the most oppressively hit. The wall of water preceding the storm pushed up Narragansett Bay like a great Pacific tsunami and purged everything in its path. The Providence River overwhelmed the city of Providence, flooding everything from College Hill to Federal Hill.

Teddy Flanders worked a lot of overtime and was unable to get a good night's sleep during the weeks following the storm. In many ways, he enjoyed the aftermath, for it not only provided him with more income but it also offered a break from routine. If there was one thing he disliked in his job, it was anything resembling routine. The storm proffered opportunities for minor heroic acts, challenging his vanity and testing his skills.

He experienced casual dangers that became important measures of his resourcefulness. For the next several weeks, he encountered live power lines, desperate people, occasional looting, and even dead bodies. Most everything he did won him praise and commendations. The time was good for him and the storm proved to be a windfall for his career.

A month after the storm passed found Teddy gradually returning to a pace more typical of his work. He had not forgotten Molly Drew, and as time permitted, he found ways to track her down and observe what she was doing. Everything happening in the aftermath of the storm was a tribute to his ego. As his workload began to subside, he felt good about himself. He decided to try, once again, to rekindle the relationship with Molly.

☙❧☙❧

Clinton was hit more severely than the towns farther to the west. Allen Drew and Uncle Ray decided to take residence at the store after the storm. They stayed there to make repairs and protect the still salable inventory. Besides, there was so much to do in the area, that having extended hours proved to be a boon to both the store and the people in need.

Allen's leg was still in a cast and he was unable to drive, so he focused on running the register, tracking inventory, and keeping the books. That left Uncle Ray as the most mobile worker always available. This situation required Molly's help, and she participated however and whenever she could. She often drove the truck, running supplies and merchandise back and forth from New Haven to Clinton on a regular basis.

New Haven, fortunately so far west, was not struck as hard as more easterly towns and recovered rapidly from the effects of the storm. The hardware business prospered as Uncle Ray, Allen, and Molly worked as a team to keep the shelves full and the necessary supplies available.

When Molly ran her errands, she went out of her way to avoid the stretch of road though the center of Madison. She knew Teddy Flanders followed her whenever he could, and the notion frightened her.

Today, she had to go to New Haven and she decided to use a complex route taking her north of the shoreline towns and bypassing all of Teddy Flanders's haunts. As she drove, she worried about what she'd got into. She was thinking about the huge mistake the whole Flanders thing had turned into. There was a darkness about Teddy that went beyond scary. And why didn't she see it in the beginning, how could she be so foolish? Maybe he'd get tired and eventually leave her alone but, so far, it didn't seem to go away. She knew he sometimes stalked her, so even changing her route didn't negate the possibility of him following from some other starting point.

As she thought this through, she had no idea that Teddy had already planned his day with her as a centered event. As she left the store, she was unaware of Teddy's concealed Ford coupe hidden nearby. He had been there for nearly two hours before the brown pickup truck pulled away from the store. Once on Route 1, the truck made its way to Horse Hill Road and Teddy's black Ford followed some distance behind. Molly turned onto a country road and sped up, still not realizing the Ford was following.

On a straightaway, there wasn't a soul around and Ford accelerated until it was directly behind the truck. It was then Molly realized it was there. The truck sped up with a blast of blue smoke spewing from the exhaust pipe. The driver may not have intended to frighten her but the result was just that. She knew it was Teddy Flanders. He went faster still and pulled alongside her. He mouthed the words, "I need to talk to you," several times, and then he waved his arm and pointed to the roadside.

Molly kept driving.

Teddy sped up until he was ahead of her. Then he slowly applied his brakes, trying to slow her down.

Molly was frightened, but she didn't want to get hurt. She wasn't too sure of the consequences of her stopping. She knew his car was more powerful. He seemed very determined.

As she thought it through, maybe she could control the situation if she did stop. If she didn't, there was a risk she might lose control and perhaps even be injured. Reluctantly, she slowed down and swerved to the side of the road.

Teddy stopped too. He got out, walked to the truck, and climbed into the passenger seat.

"What do you want, Teddy?" There was a weary tone in her voice.

"I just want to talk to you. Things have been so crazy since the storm. I wanted to know how you're doing. That's all."

"Well, I'm doing fine. If that's all, I've got things to do," she said.

"I'm sure you do, but I'd like to be included in those things," he said.

"I thought we've been through this. I don't want to have anything to do with you. Isn't that clear?"

"Molly, I still think about you."

"I don't care. If you don't leave me alone, I will report you to the department."

"That would be just terrific. Even if anyone believed you, how are you going to face ole Allen when everything comes out? Who do you think you're kidding? Actually, I have you in a good place. You have as much to lose as I do, and there's a chance they wouldn't believe you even if you tried some cockamamie story. Why don't you settle down and occasionally put out for me? I can live with that."

"You son-of-bitch, all I want is for you to leave me alone. If I do go to someone, I'll be telling them more than you're fucking me up. What about Sam Stemford? He didn't show up like you said he would. He didn't show up because he couldn't. He's dead, and you know it. You know where he is. If the right people ask the right questions, you're going to come apart like a cheap sweater. I may lose my marriage, but you'll fry in the electric chair. Now leave me alone."

Molly realized she was taking a risk but she was desperate, and she'd had enough. This was her final position. If she didn't have a bigger stick than he did, she might spend the rest of her life under his threat.

❧

Teddy glowered at Molly for a long moment. He didn't say a word. He knew she already suspected too much and he didn't want to risk feeding her anything else until he decided what to do. Instead, he shrugged his shoulders. "Okay, I didn't have anything to do with Stemford, but you're way too upset. Let's forget about the whole thing. I'll leave you alone from now on. I thought there had been so much between us you'd consider getting together, that's all. Don't think badly of me."

"Teddy, just stay out of my life. Now let me go," she said.

"Okay, it's done. See you around," he said as he opened the door and climbed out of the truck.

Teddy followed her at a comfortable distance for the rest of the afternoon. All the while he thought about what to do next. There was only one clear solution to the problem. If he couldn't have her, and she threatened to disclose her notions about the good doctor, she had no right to live. The clarity of what he had to do was reward in itself. He could deal with his frustration if he were the instrument of her destruction.

Molly drove the reverse of the same route home and by the time she reached the long stretch of Horse Hill Road it was dark. Teddy had called in sick from a pay phone while she was making her rounds. Now was a good time to show himself. He sped up to reduce the distance between him and the pickup truck. This time, when he was right behind her, he tapped the back of the pickup truck at thirty-five miles an hour.

∾∾∾

Molly saw the fast approaching headlights in her rear view mirror just before the contact.

When she felt the bump, she knew it was Teddy, and fear like a wretched cancer, permeated her soul. *Oh, shit!* she thought.

She drove as hard and as well as she could. But the pickup truck was no match for a trained cop in a souped-up Ford coupe. At fifty miles an hour, Teddy grazed her left front fender. Molly found herself skidding out of control toward the woods along the roadside. She braced herself against the steering wheel as she careened though a stand of young oak trees. In the shadows, they seemed like slender gray ghosts dancing as the bounding headlights invaded their domain. The truck sped on until it struck a tree that was too large to be mowed over. The force of the impact lifted Molly out of the seat, pushed her into the steering wheel, and out through the windshield.

She wasn't sure how much time had passed, but when

she came to, she found herself draped over the hood of the truck. She smelled the odor of coolant and hot motor oil all around her. She tried to raise her head and discovered that her neck bones still worked. She looked up and saw the front end of the truck neatly wrapped around a large oak tree.

Her head was only inches from what would have been instant death if she had struck the tree. She tried to get up, but she realized her left arm was broken from the support it had provided while bracing her against the steering wheel. She moved her right arm and found it hurt too much to use it. She checked to see if she could move her legs and found they painfully worked.

Molly knew she had to get away from the truck, so she tried to prop herself up, using the painful right arm. As she tried to rise, there in the glow of a single functioning headlamp was the face of Teddy Flanders.

Teddy looked at Molly Drew. "Jesus, what a mess you are," he said with a smile.

"Teddy, help me," she moaned. She ran her tongue around her mouth. Her eyes widened with terror. Most of her front teeth were broken and she had bitten deeply into her tongue.

ⒺⓈⒺⓈ

Teddy looked her up and down, assessing the nature of her condition. Her face was a bloody pulp, but she had been spared the return trip back into the cab. It could have been worse. Broken glass from the windshield sparkled in her matted hair. He saw the compound fracture at her forearm and knew she wouldn't be using it to get up right now.

Then he said, "You know, bitch, you can keep your sorry ass all to yourself."

"For God's sake, help me," Molly sputtered through her broken teeth and swollen tongue.

"Help you? Of course, I'll help you. I'll help you all the way to hell." As he spoke, he picked up a can containing gasoline and poured it over Molly and the front of the truck.

"G—God, don't do this, Teddy," she sputtered.

"Fuck you and the good doctor, too," he said as he struck a match and tossed it on the glistening, wet fender.

PART III

Outrage

CHAPTER 32

Fall, 1998:

Gordy left the house at six a.m. and began the seventy-five-mile drive to Springfield, Massachusetts. He allowed himself a half-hour cushion to make the eight o'clock start up at the Smith & Wesson Academy. As he drove, he reflected on what he knew of circumstances surrounding his one-week assignment.

The nearest SWAT team to Guilford was based in New Haven. Although the unit could be accessed in the event of a crisis, the shoreline towns were feeling the stress of the time and distance from New Haven. With the increasing number of situations requiring the use of a specially trained team, the need to have access to a more local force was inevitable.

Although there were many skills required to qualify for the new team, one of the most demanding was the certification required from the Tactical Scope-Sighted Rifle Course, in layman's terms, sniper school. Gordy felt good about his assignment and relished in a sense of pride as he drove to Springfield.

He also felt the burden of the added responsibilities as he plunged deeper and deeper into the content of the course. The more he learned about the disciplines of

SWAT activities, the more he wondered whether the benefits out-weighed liabilities for his career. There was little he could do now. He was chosen, and the best outcome, he expected, was he'd learn the course well, and hope he never got called to use it.

Despite the grim image of some future altercation, Gordy looked forward to one positive outcome of the entire program. In compliance with the recommendation that each certified officer own and have exclusive access to their respective rifles, the Guilford Police Department agreed to purchase a Hart modified, Remington Model 700 with a Leupold 4.5-14X tactical scope, custom built just for him. The idea—one man, one gun—ensured a unique relationship between the officer and his weapon.

During the day, Gordy worked hard to exceed the requirements of the course. When it was over, he knew he had to pass both a written exam and a series of practical shooting challenges. There was no room for an incomplete or a missed target. The course demanded one-hundred-percent accuracy. As part of the final exam, he was required to complete ten long distance shots—one hundred yards each. Nine out of ten were simulated head shots. A miss was a failure, and a failure constituted a terrible personal defeat. In spite of the pressure, Gordy kept focus and met each assignment with stoic resolve.

As he was kept busy each day, in the evenings, when the classes were done, he found relaxation in the phone calls to Emily. She listened to him. She listened like no one before and, in the process, relieved the ever-present stress of learning how to function as an efficient killer. *Great knowledge carries great responsibility*, he concluded. At least he had her to share his experience.

She promised to help him practice at home and maybe even learn to shoot herself.

CHAPTER 33

Emily had worked out a schedule that kept her pretty busy during the week Gordy was at the academy. She knew she had to make two trips a day to Clinton to care for the animals, and she was prepared for the change in her routine. When Gordy showed her what to do, they worked out a plan to fit her own work schedule.

She realized her grandfather's investigation would slow down during the week, but she believed they'd make up for it when Gordy was back in town. In the meantime, she decided to do simple follow-up work in order to monitor the progress of the case. In keeping with her plan, on Monday afternoon, she called Detective Barry Lands at his desk in Clinton.

"Hello, Detective Lands, it's Emily Pierce. How are you?"

"I'm fine. How're you doin'?"

"I'm okay, but I wanted to touch base with you and find out if there were any new developments," she said.

"Yes, Emily, it's a good thing you called. I think we've found the bullet we've been looking for. Hartley Shiff and I were going through the remains of the right door and we came up with something looking like a piece of lead embedded in the rusty steel. I've sent it out to the ballistics lab in New Haven for confirmation. It'll take a day or two to get results, but I'm betting we got something here." He spoke like he thought this tidbit of information would impress the hell out of her.

Emily was pleasantly surprised with his discovery and she found herself speechless for a minute. "That's really fantastic. I didn't really expect to hear any more about the bullet. I figured it was lost forever. Do you think it can be matched to a particular gun?"

"Can't say yet. At this point, it's a dirty, obscure bit of metal. I didn't even try to clean it up, because I didn't want to damage any traces of rifling that may still be on it. The ballistics people will be able to give us a whole lot more by the time they're done."

"Have you found anything else," she asked.

"Only things I suspect you already know about. Stuff like the files at the old Madison archives and conversations with some people either you or Gordy Powell have already talked to. Other than that, only the bullet is really new. Maybe we can get together during the week, have lunch or something, and compare notes. Just to make sure we are getting everything right. How about tomorrow, or Wednesday?"

"I'd like to get together, too, but this is a difficult week. My schedule is really packed. I'm busy tomorrow and the day after. Let me call you on Wednesday and see if we can do it later in the week. Is that okay?" she asked.

"Sure, sure, that'll be fine."

"Thanks for the great news, and I'll talk to you on Wednesday. Goodbye."

Emily hung up the phone. Now she was thinking she couldn't wait for the opportunity to tell Gordy about the bullet. This was great news, and maybe it'd be the first piece of hard evidence they'd found.

On Wednesday, Emily kept her promise to call Barry

Lands. The phone rang several times before he picked up.

"Hello, Barry. It's Emily. I hope you remembered I'd call later in the week," she said, "I've got a break tomorrow at noon, can you make it?"

"Yeah, I think that's all right. How about meeting at the SeaTails Restaurant? I think it's about halfway."

"Sure, sounds good," she answered. "By the way, did you get anything on the bullet?"

"Yeah. There's enough to make a match to a gun, if we can find one."

"Great. Let's talk about it at twelve o'clock, okay? See you then."

With that, they exchanged good-byes and hung up.

Emily wheeled her Camry into the parking lot at Sea Tails at exactly twelve noon. Barry Lands was already there, and he got out of his blue Caprice as she pulled in. She greeted him with a cheerful "Hi," and the pair went into the little clam shack. They ordered cafeteria style and carried their plastic trays over to a quiet pine booth in the corner of the room.

"Well, what do you think, can we find a gun?" she asked.

"If we had a lead as to where to look, we might have a chance, but I'm not sure what we can do with what we got. While the pond was empty, we went over the whole thing with metal detectors and came up with nothing. We dug into the mud at every acoustic signal we picked up. I don't think the gun was thrown in the pond. Whatever happened during the killing, the perp took the gun with him when he left the scene. It's possible he disposed of it somewhere else or maybe he even kept the damn thing.

"The good news is, if he kept it, maybe he's still got it, or someone else bought it. Based on the ballistics report, the bullet came from a thirty-eight caliber Smith and Wesson revolver, standard fair for the time. Most of the Shoreline PDs used them for years. It was also a common choice for use as home protection. I'm sure there's a lot of them scattered around the area. We can run a check on how many are licensed and see whose names fall out. There are probably twice as many out there that aren't licensed. But we'll run it through and see where it takes us. If we're really lucky, we might find it with a subsequent owner since 1938. That may give us a way to trace it back."

"Have you found anything else?" Emily asked.

"Not too much more. There were some rayon strands tied to the door handle. Could have been some kind of cloth tied to it. Maybe the car was acting up, causing the doc to pull over, maybe he had tied some cloth to it like a flag or something. At any rate, I don't know what to do with it right now. Otherwise, there's not much more than you already know. Let me ask you something," he went on.

"Go ahead," she replied.

"What was going on with the files over at the Madison Town Hall? I spent a few hours over there, came up with nothing, and a few days later, Gordy Powell comes out with a gold mine of information."

"We figure someone else has taken a personnel interest in the case," Emily explained. "Gordy found out Avery Johnson from the *New Haven Reporter* was in there right after you and he didn't find anything either. When Gordy went in, he found a whole box of files labeled 1938. Our guess is someone else has got an interest. They secretly copied all the information that was there and even added some old newspaper clippings to the files, just to make sure the investigation connected some dots.

"We figured they were going to feed the investigation, if it got bogged down. Whoever it is, they're trying real hard to stay out of the limelight. That's our theory anyway."

"We'll need to find out who this joker is," Barry said.

"Gordy went through the log book used at the archives and wrote down the names of people that have been in and out of there since the discovery of Sam's body. He plans to interview everyone on the list and try to figure out who our friend might be. So far he hasn't come up with anything. We suspect our friend will be someone in the log book."

"Nice work, most of my time's been spent poking around with the Chrysler and other forensics. It sounds like we're both heading in the right direction."

Emily felt better having reviewed her information with Barry, but she was disappointed with his progress in interviewing people contemporary to the crime. "Are you going to follow up with all the people Gordy's been talking to?"

"Of course, but I've been holding up some of the interviews until I got the results back from the doc's appointment book. I needed that to complete the list of folks I wanted to check out. We had to send the book to a lab in Canada for the processing required. They just sent a fax last week with the list of names written in the book the day Stemford disappeared. Allen Drew and his broken leg was the last entry, so it looks like he may have been the last patient on Stemford's rounds. The lab is sending the restored notes back to us next week. Keep in mind the crime is over sixty years old, and I'm just trying to keep the investigation organized."

"Sure, but you need to remember if you delay long enough, those people you're going to check out might just die of old age. You know what I mean," Emily said with a note of sarcasm.

"Okay, Emily. I got your point. I had intended to finish the check-out process next week anyway."

"Good," Emily said. "Gordy and I will look forward to sitting down again and comparing notes as soon as you're ready."

"By the way how's he doing at the sniper school?" Barry asked, "Everyone in the local PD is talking about his being chosen. It's really quite an honor."

"He's doing well," she said. "I've been taking care of his place while he's gone, and he's called every night after classes. Some of the stuff's too technical for me, but he certainly seems to be getting a lot out of it. I guess it's a pretty significant experience. All he could talk about last night was the fact that when he graduated, he was going to have to visit a rifle manufacturer and select some sort of custom-made weapon. He was kind of excited about the prospect. He even offered to show me how to use the rifle. I promised that I'd at least listen. He'll finish his field shooting today and tomorrow he's got a written exam. He'll be coming home tomorrow night."

"Give him my best when you see him," Barry said. Then he apologized, saying that he had to leave. He picked up the check, told her lunch was on the town of Clinton, and thanked her for the information.

CHAPTER 34

The phone rang four times and the announcement message began the usual request when Harlan shouted into the receiver, "Hello, Dad. Pick up. It's me!"

It took a minute and then Teddy Flanders said, "Yeah, Harlan, I've got it." There was a click as Teddy pushed the reset button. "What do you want, boy?"

"Just thought I'd let you know Barry Lands gave you good grades for your help in describing the events of 1938 around the Stemford murder. He says you have a great memory."

"Well, I'm glad he thinks I was able to help," Teddy said.

"By the way there's more news about the case," Harlan went on, "Barry and Hartley Shiff found a bullet fragment in the door of that old Chrysler. It looks as though they may make some progress after all."

"When did they find it?" Teddy asked.

"Friday afternoon."

"Where is it now?"

"At the Lab in New Haven."

"Is that all they got so far?" Teddy asked.

"That's it. How are you doing?"

"I'm okay, but I'll need to have you come over one

night late in the week. Probably Thursday would be good. Let's try for Thursday night, okay?"

Teddy hung up the phone and stared into space for a moment or two. He realized the discovery of the bullet meant serious trouble. He had kept his old thirty-eight caliber service revolver for all these years, and now he knew he had to get rid of it. The gun, coupled with any bit of the old ballistics evidence extracted from his police records, could provide a link to him, especially with the new technology available to the police.

Shit, he thought, *so much time has gone by, and all of a sudden they come up with this—a corpse and then a friggin' bullet. What next?*

He'd believed he was in control of the consequences of his actions for his entire life. And now, for the first time in his memory, his life appeared to be spinning out of control.

Teddy realized whatever he did next affected how he spent the rest of his life. Shame and/or prison at his age seemed like the worst fate imaginable. If he did nothing and waited, there was a chance someone would muster a search warrant and tear his place apart looking for his old weapon. Of course, by then, he would have disposed of the gun permanently. But if the seed were planted, the harvest that could follow might be the discovery of one of several bullets used as evidence in other cases involving his service revolver.

Such evidence, in either original or photographic form, could be used to tie him and his old gun to the bullet found at the Doc Stemford site. It really depended on how motivated the current investigation was. If they were able to match a bullet from a different case to the Stemford bullet, they'd have something stronger than circumstantial evidence, and they could press for an indictment.

If things got that far, it would definitely mess up the

rest of his life, however long or short that may be.

If he went to Harlan and asked his help to slow the pace of the investigation, he'd eventually have to tell him why and make him an accessory and certainly test his loyalty. *Hell of a thing to do to your own son,* he thought.

Teddy reflected for a moment, recalling Harlan as a small boy.

He was a good boy. A chip off the ole' man's block, but he had a lot of his mother in him. Often Teddy thought there was too much. Teddy recognized Harlan as a good politician but sometimes he sorely lacked balls. Harlan always played it safe, much too safe for Teddy's liking. But his son was successful enough as a large fish in a small pond. They reached an accord over the years, and although there was little emotion expressed between them, there was a basis for mutual respect. Harlan wouldn't like it but, when push came to shove, he would knuckle down and do what was asked of him.

Faced with options, and assuming Harlan would help, Teddy knew he still had to deal with the Stemford's granddaughter and Gordy Powell. There was no doubt in his mind, if he pressured Harlan, he also had to pressure Emily Pierce. At that point, her friend, the cop, would try to come to her rescue. What then?

The first step has to be damage control. Do I do nothing, or do I try to change the course of events to follow? Do the risks outweigh the benefits?

The more Teddy thought about the situation, the more he realized he must do whatever was necessary to help the investigation slip into oblivion. He decided to wait for more information. The next decision point would be contingent on the ballistics report from the recently discovered bullet fragment. If there were enough rifling marks to identify the gun, he must try to slow the investigation by whatever means possible.

CHAPTER 35

On Thursday evening, Harlan Flanders drove to his father's place in Durham. He checked his watch as he pulled into the driveway and noted it was just seven o'clock. He parked the Toyota SUV under a stand of maple trees and shut the engine down.

Two Rottweilers trotted over quietly and paced in circles as he climbed out of the vehicle.

"How are you guys doing?" he asked as though they were human enough to answer. There was no surprise when they whined in response.

They fell in behind Harlan and trotted in step as he headed across the yard toward the house. As he crossed the wooden floor of the front porch, he saw Teddy standing behind the screen door.

"Hello, Dad."

"Come on in," Teddy said as he held the door open with one hand.

The two men went through the front hall and made their way to the kitchen. The odor of dog permeated the air. The interior was dimly lit by stray sunlight penetrating the dirty windows. Teddy reached over and tripped the light switch on the wall. The fluorescent bulbs clicked on and crackled as they reluctantly flashed and poured white light everywhere. The kitchen was a mess.

Dishes were stacked in the sink and the counter tops were strewn with cereal boxes, sugar, coffee grounds, dried puddles of milk, and other not so easily identified foods. Harlan was worried. Teddy had always been so neat. His father was slipping.

"Sit down, Harlan," the old man said. "Wanna beer or something?"

"How about some coffee, instead?"

"Is instant all right?"

Harlan nodded. "Sure, that'll be just fine. So why did you want me to come out tonight?"

The old man went about preparing two cups of instant coffee while he talked. He seemingly ignored Harlan's question. "So tell me what's been happening with the Stemford case."

"Chris Forhey's made some progress. Barry Lands spent some time with the Pierce woman today going over the case. I guess she's been on her own all week since Powell's been away in Massachusetts. She's been taking care of his place while he's gone."

"Yeah," the old man said. "I heard he was selected for the Scoped Rifle Course at Smith and Wesson. Have they got any ballistics info on the bullet fragment that was found in the old car?"

"From what I was told today, they've got enough to identify a gun if they can find one."

"Well, son, this is where rubber meets road, kind of our moment of truth. I want you to slow down the investigation."

"What do you mean slow down the investigation?"

"Just what I said. Slow down the investigation. Frankly, I don't care how, and you shouldn't ask why. Just slow things down. Make the damn case go away."

"Dad, I can't simply make a dead body go away. There's a thirty-five hundred pound rusted car and all the other items that go on an evidence list. Plus, there's too many people involved."

"Let me say this one more time. Forget about the investigation. Sit down with Chris Forhey and let him know he's got other things that take priority. Make a list, go through it with him, item by item. Convince him the Stemford case is old, and there's nothing to pursue. I want this thing to slow down and eventually disappear."

"Dad, you know this is obstructing justice."

"Yeah, so what? I'm not telling you to suddenly shut down the investigation. I'm simply asking you to influence the priorities of your limited-resources police department. Review some of the cases that are pending and tell Forhey you need to see more results, faster. Ask him what the Stemford investigation is doing to his budget. Don't do anything outrageous. Just redirect things a little bit."

Harlan paused for a moment and tried to decide whether or not to ask the next question. And then he decided he wanted to know. "Why?"

"If I tell you, you'll become involved. If you become involved, you may not find it a good place to be later on. I'd rather you just do what I ask and forget about all the questions, at least for the time being."

"Suppose I'm unable to influence the way the case is going?" Harlan asked.

"The consequences could be very unpleasant for everyone, and particularly grim for me."

"What about the Pierce woman?" Harlan asked.

"Don't worry about her. You just concentrate on the Clinton PD."

"I don't like it, Dad, but I'll see what I can do."

The old man looked at his son and smiled. "Good. Now that's settled let's play some gin rummy. By the way, that's why I called you over here in the first place."

While they played cards, the old man traced out a plan of action in his mind. Teddy knew Gordy Powell was away for the week at the sniper school in Massachusetts. He reflected on the comment offered by Harlan about Emily Pierce tending to Powell's small farm while he was away. In his mind, Teddy visualized a series of events that would put the Powell/Pierce relationship into total chaos. He smiled to himself as he pictured the things about to happen.

Harlan noticed the old man's smile across the table and asked, "Are you okay, Dad?"

"Sure, son. I'm just fine."

They played until eleven o'clock and Harlan finally complained it was late and he had to leave and get some sleep. Teddy told him it was okay because he was tired too. He walked Harlan to the SUV and waved to him while he pulled out of the driveway. As soon as the glow of the taillights disappeared into the night, the old man whistled into the darkness. The two Rottweilers pranced to him with their yellow eyes glowing in their black faces. They were both panting like they knew there was something exciting in the air.

Teddy walked to his pickup, lowered the tailgate, and signaled to the dogs to jump in.

They did and continued panting nervously in anticipation. Teddy closed the gate and climbed into the cab behind the wheel.

"Okay, fellas," he said through the cab rear window. "Let's go and have some fun."

Teddy drove slowly over to Gordy Powell's place, and by the time he pulled into the woods by the pond it was nearly midnight. He turned the headlights off and inched the truck into the brush as far as he could without leaving an obvious trail. He got out and used his flashlight to check the ground for tire tracks.

Everything was dry enough not to leave any marks.

From inside the house, Romulus and Remus began to bark. Teddy heard them pounding against the front door, frantically trying to get out. He'd tend to them later.

Teddy quietly lowered the tailgate and walked to the fence that opened into the barn compound. He carried a large pair of bolt cutters. There, he cut off the padlock on the gate and put it in his pocket. He swung the gate open, curled his tongue, and let out a brief whistle. A moment later the Rottweilers trotted nervously by his side. He walked them to the barn and pulled back the sliding bolt on the door. He opened it, and gestured them to go inside.

"Enjoy," he whispered, as they disappeared into the barn.

The old man closed the door, sat down on an overturned feed trough and waited. The sounds coming from the barn were chilling, as the two dogs ripped and tore their way through all the flesh they could sink their teeth into.

CHAPTER 36

The first of the dogs' prey were Heckle and Jeckle. The two dogs had hunted often in the woods of north Guilford and learned to work well as a team. Taking down the two young goats inside the walls of a barn was pretty easy work. One of the dogs took the front legs of the first goat while the other clamped his jaws on the throat of the second animal.

Once the goats were down, the dogs bit into their soft under bellies and shook their heads vigorously until the delicate flesh ripped apart. With their bellies opened and legs flaying, the young goats were disemboweled where they fell. The dogs buried their muzzles inside the steaming body cavities and snapped at the organs remaining. They bit everything, savoring the smorgasbord of flavors but swallowed nothing.

The horse and donkey, confined in stalls, heehawed and whinnied in terror as the two little goats were decimated on the floor nearby.

When the dogs finished with the goats, they jumped over the boards into the piglet pen and tore into Pirate and Penzance. They gutted the two pigs, sat down by the still breathing carcasses, and licked the warm blood off one another.

A few minutes later, they were ready for Ivan, the

horse. During the earlier carnage, Ivan had gone wild and had kicked at both ends of the stall until he was exhausted. Sweat ran from his shoulders and ribs and his face was slick with tears and saliva. He knew the horror wasn't over.

The dogs, as if on signal, leapt over the gate and into the stall. Ivan went berserk and flayed all four legs in frenzied kicking motions that surprised the dogs. They clamped vicious bites on his forelegs, but his great strength prevailed, and he flung them off time after time. Both of his forelegs became bloodied, ragged strips of flesh as he kicked and kicked again. The horse took nearly as much damage from his strikes against the wall as he did from the ferocious bite of the dogs.

The siege went on for several minutes and then the dogs appeared to tire. They stood panting in adjacent corners and then, almost as though connected telepathically, they leaped out of the stall and began sniffing the air. They continued sampling the air while Ivan snorted and bumped about inside. His eyes were still wild with fear and hatred. With his forelocks bleeding and torn, he seemed to wait for the next assault.

The dogs had run deer before, but those animals were considerably smaller, and when hunting outdoors there was room to attack and feint without getting thrown against something hard. Inside tight quarters, they felt the impact of the horse's blows and the force of hitting the walls of the stall was starting to hurt.

They paused, looked around, and noticed the donkey was not so great in height and thought he may make a better target than the larger horse. They looked at one another, and as their yellow eyes met, they sensed they had still another victim. They'd go back for the horse later.

The scent of donkey sweat saturated their canine noses, and they focused their attention toward Sammy. They squatted in preparation for the leap over the gate into Sammy's stall. Then with nostrils flared and teeth exposed, one of the dogs leapt first.

ℰℐℰℐ

Sammy knew he was on their list of things to do. He was waiting when the dog hurdled the gate. The donkey's timing was perfect. As the first dog cleared the top of the gate, he caught a perfectly placed kick square in the face. The blow caught the Rottweiler in midair and thrust his head back against his shoulders, his neck broken in two places. One hundred pounds of dog cartwheeled backward, perfectly retracing the arch of his leap. As his carcass flew, it passed the second dog that was midair, on his way into the stall.

ℰℐℰℐ

At first, the airborne Rottweiler didn't realize what had happened, but as he landed inside the stall he was struck with a barrage of heavy kicks. The first several blows were glancing and the dog danced around the murderous hooves. Then a kick from Ivan's left quarter caught him on his right side and he felt himself smash into the wall of the stall. He lay gasping for air when a second blow struck. This time, he nearly went unconscious. He yelped, struggled to his feet, and managed to jump out of the stall before another kick found its mark.

On the other side of the gate, his companion lay in a pile with his head twisted back unnaturally, its opened eyes seeing nothing. The surviving dog whined and staggered toward the barn door. Once there, he scratched at the wood and managed a muffled bark.

ﻌﻌ

Teddy heard the noise and opened the door. He raised his flashlight, clicked the switch forward, and projected a cone of light into the barn. The scene surprised him. One of his dogs stood on wobbly legs by the door and the other was dead a few feet away.

"Shit," the old man said in a whisper.

He shot the light around the room and did an accounting of what he saw. Blood and entrails were scattered everywhere. He went to Ivan's stall and looked in. He could see the horse's forelegs were badly mauled but it was still standing. The old man noted the animal was bleeding but not heavily.

The donkey appeared untouched, but the carcasses of the gutted goats and pigs were strewn about.

Teddy looked down at the dead dog and tried to figure out what to do next. Certainly, the dog was too heavy to carry. He looked around the barn, found some rope, and tied it around the carcass. Then he dragged it to his truck. He figured the passenger side of the cab was lower than the cargo bed so he lifted and pushed the carcass into the front of the vehicle and finally closed the door. When he finished, he returned to the barn and swept away the path made from dragging the dead animal.

The other dog lay on the ground, still panting when Teddy returned to the barn. He signaled to the dog to get up and follow, and a minute or so later, the Rottweiler struggled to its feet and staggered along beside him as he walked to the truck. Teddy helped the dog onto the cargo bed and closed the tailgate. As the dogs in the house continued to bark and pound Gordy's front door, Teddy decided to pass on killing them. He walked slowly to the truck's cab, got in, and drove home.

CHAPTER 37

At ten o'clock on Friday morning, Teddy Flanders pulled into the parking lot of the Madison Town Library. He climbed from his Dodge pickup truck and went in through the front door. He walked up to the woman at the checkout desk and asked to see Emily Pierce.

A moment or so later, Emily stood in front of him. The old man stretched out his hand in greeting and noted her slight hesitation as he introduced himself.

After he gave his name, he smiled. "Ms. Pierce, I understand you've had this fellow, Gordon Powell, asking questions about the death of your grandfather. I think we should talk. Maybe we can go someplace private?"

"Okay, Mr. Flanders," she said. "We can go to my office."

The pair walked to the rear of the building and Emily ushered him into her office. Inside, she offered Teddy a large chair in front of her desk while she made her way behind it. Teddy eased himself down and waited until Emily sat.

"So tell me why you're here, Mr. Flanders."

"Well, mostly to give you a little background on your grandfather's disappearance, 1938 was a long time ago. I recognize there is some justice in discovering Stemford's remains after all this time. I'm not sure whether you know this or not, but I was the officer at the Madison Police Department who took the missing-person report for your grandmother. That was the day after the doctor disappeared. I actually worked on parts of the investigation. So I was as close as anyone to the case when it was going on.

"I wanted to talk to you about some of my recollections of the situation. You must understand there was a lot going on at the time. Although there was never any hard evidence, I began to suspect perhaps your grandmother and maybe her brother were mixed up in some pretty strange events back then. Now, I'm not accusing anybody, so don't get me wrong. The reason I'm telling you, is because maybe there are things you don't want to know."

Emily stared for a long moment. "You have to give me more than that. Just what do you know?"

"I can't say any more than I just did, but keep in mind if you continue poking into what happened back then, you may open things nobody needs or wants to know. You especially may stumble onto stuff which is best left undisturbed. You may even end up disappointed and perhaps a little ashamed. If I was you, I'd let sleeping dogs lie, and move on."

"Mr. Flanders, I implore you to tell me whatever you know."

"I'm sorry, Ms. Pierce, but I've got to go now. Remember what I said. I'll see you around." With that, the old man got up and left.

⌘

Emily sat at her desk for a moment and pondered the content of the brief meeting. She wasn't sure if she had been advised or threatened. The longer she thought about Teddy Flanders, the more uncomfortable she felt.

At ten minutes to eleven, she got ready to leave for Gordy's place. She reminded Gladys Bower of her temporary schedule and that it was about to end, allowing her more regular hours next week. She left the building, got into the car, and made the drive to Gordy's place in Clinton.

When she pulled into the driveway, the air was still and the surface of the nearby pond reflected the late morning sun like a mirror. As she left the car, she looked around and shaded her eyes from the glare with her hand.

Suddenly, the dogs in the house began to bark wildly and pound at the front door. All three cats sat on windowsills, staring out at her. The frantic dogs had never behaved like that during her former visits, and Emily sensed that something was wrong. She left them in the house and approached the barn.

During her inspection, she noticed the corral gate was open. *That's odd,* she thought, *I know I closed and locked it when I left last night.* She walked through the gate, noticing the padlock was missing. Then she saw the barn door was slightly ajar.

At this point, Emily felt an even more uncomfortable sensation in the pit of her stomach. Something was terribly wrong. Even if she had forgotten to lock the gate, where was the padlock? She couldn't believe she forgot to close the barn door. As she approached the entrance, she felt weak and had to force herself to enter the doorway. At the threshold, the sound of a thousand buzzing flies amplified her sense of trouble.

The inside was aglow with ambient orange light streaming through the windows. She looked around. The sight drew a gasp from her lips and the queasiness in her stomach turned into revulsion then to wretchedness. She pulled back and stumbled outside. Her stomach roiled and she vomited.

God, what's happened? she thought, as she fell to her knees clutching her cramping gut. She made her way back to the car and braced herself on the front fender. *This is horrible.* She had never seen anything like the inside of the barn at any time in her life, and until this moment, she could not have imagined such terrible mutilation. She didn't know what to do. She opened the car door and sat down on the front seat. She waited for the waves of nausea to pass. A few minutes went by before she felt stable enough to rise and try to think about what to do.

Certainly some of the animals in the barn were probably dead, but she couldn't be sure. Although the amount of blood and viscera was conspicuous, suppose there were injured animals that could be cared for? In order to do a thorough assessment of what happened, she had to go back inside. She didn't think she could do that, at least not right now. Maybe whatever did this was still in there.

Finally, Emily went into the house and called Gordy's veterinarian. Maybe the animal specialist would come out and help.

Emily was relieved to finally get hold of Dr. Janice Shroder on the phone. The receptionist was doing too good a job of insulating her boss and the additional delay only served to heighten Emily's aggravation.

"Doctor Shroder," she said. "This is Emily Pierce. I'm at Gordy Powell's place and something awful has happened."

"Calm down, Emily, tell me what's wrong."

"Something's happened in the barn. There's blood and dead animals all over the place," Emily wailed, trying to control her voice as she spoke.

"Are you sure they're dead?" Janice Shroder asked.

"I don't know. Everything is such a mess. I—I couldn't go inside."

"Well, you've got to find out what the situation is."

"I'll try, but I still need your help. Suppose whatever did this, is still in there. Please come right away," Emily pleaded.

"Okay, I'll be there in fifteen minutes, but in the meantime, call the police and get an officer over there.

"Yes, I'll do that, but please hurry." Emily hung up the phone.

Emily sat at the kitchen table and waited. She sat there and tried to think of what Gordy's reaction would be. She went over and over the past night's memory, convincing herself her recall was indeed real. She could not be responsible for such an awful disaster.

Even if she were sure, what would Gordy think, she asked herself. When she left last night, she knew she had left six animals plus some chickens in the barn. A few minutes ago, when she looked in, the goats and pigs appeared to have been slaughtered. Sammy and Ivan were still standing, and she realized she didn't know whether either animal was injured or not. She had to find out.

Oh, God, she thought, *Gordy loves those animals so much*. She composed herself enough to feed Romulus, Remus and the cats, and then let the nervous dogs outside to run.

CHAPTER 38

Doctor Shroder kept her promise. Fifteen minutes later, she pulled into the driveway and parked beside Emily's Camry. She crunched to a stop as the wheels of her Ford truck locked up on the gravel surface.

Emily heard the noise from inside the house and hurried to the door. She wasn't sure whether it was the police or Dr. Shroder arriving first. When she looked down, she was a little disappointed to realize the police still hadn't shown up. She went out the door and rushed down the stairs as quickly as she could without risking a fall.

Once she was on the landing she called out, "Thank goodness, Doctor Shroder."

Janice Shroder climbed down from her Ford F-150 truck carrying a huge, aluminum Louisville Slugger. "You Emily Pierce?"

"Yes, I'm so glad you're here. The police still haven't arrived and I didn't know what to do." Emily burst out crying.

"I guess you haven't been in the barn since we spoke on the phone?" asked the doctor. Janice Shroder was a good-looking woman in her early forties. She had close-cropped brown hair that was just beginning to streak naturally with wisps of silver gray. She wore jeans and a white smock that suggested she had dropped whatever she was doing to hurry to the Powell farm. "Come on." She led the way to the barn.

The two women paused at the doorway. Janice raised the baseball bat over her shoulder and slowly went inside.

Emily stayed behind while the veterinarian went from animal to animal and assessed its condition. Finally, she came back to the door and asked Emily to come in and help.

"I'll need you to give me a hand," Janice said, as she headed toward Ivan's stall. "The horse has been badly bitten around his forelegs and I'll need to sedate him so I can tell how much damage has been done."

"What about the other animals?" Emily asked.

"Not much we can do with the goats and piglets. They're all dead. The donkey looks okay, so they evidently didn't get to him, or he became more than they could handle. Ivan, on the other hand, is in rough shape. His tendons are torn and he may have a fracture. I won't know for sure until I can X-ray. This horse is in serious condition. Very serious, indeed," Janice explained.

As she spoke, they heard the crunch of another vehicle stopping in the driveway. Emily went to the door and looked out. "It's the police."

A minute later Officer Laura Fellows appeared at the barn door. As she entered, she shook her head at the carnage and whistled a single tired note. "What do we have here?" she asked, not really expecting an answer.

Janice stepped in front of Emily. "Looks like a dog pack, or if we were living in the woods, I would have said wolves. Knowing the neighborhood, I'd say it's most likely a dog pack, maybe three or four large animals. From the damage they've done, I'd say they'd had plenty of practice. Probably running deer. Looks like they're good sized animals, maybe as much as seventy or eighty pounds each."

Officer Fellows walked around the barn as the two women knelt beside the injured horse. "So how did they get in?" she asked aloud, not really caring who answered.

ↂↂ

Emily felt obliged to say something, so she did, "I've been taking care of the place while Gordy Powell was away. At around eight-thirty last night, I closed the barn door with the two goats, the donkey, the horse, and piglets inside. There may have been a few chickens in here, too. I closed the door, locked up the gate, and went home. At eleven-fifteen this morning, I came over here to feed the animals and let them out until this evening. When I got here, the gate was open and this was what I found."

"Are you sure everything was secure when you left last night?" Fellows asked.

"Yeah, I'm sure."

Janice sighed. "Wild dogs don't open gates and break into barns."

"Was the house locked up when you got here?" Fellows asked Emily.

"Yes," she answered.

"When's Gordy due back?"

"Sometime this afternoon," she said.

"Well, I suspect he isn't going to be too happy when he gets here," Fellows added with a hint of sarcasm.

While Officer Fellows tried to understand Emily's version of what happened, Janice managed to get a syringe into Ivan. And soon the wild look in the animal's eyes faded into a glassy stare. Now she was able to get a close look at the wounds on his legs and make some determination as to what needed to be done.

Emily looked at her watch and noted it was nearly one o'clock. Gladys Bower was still expecting her back at the library. She realized she needed to call in and make preparations to take off the rest of the day. She figured she had better stay until Gordy got home. His return would be bad enough, and without her there to offer some explanation, it would be even worse for him.

Officer Fellows walked around the barn one more time, and then asked Emily to accompany her to the gate.

"Show me where the padlock was and tell me why you're sure it was secure when you left last night," she said.

Emily felt her face flush as she followed Fellows to the gate. *Goddamn it,* she thought, *I know I locked the gate.*

"Just what words do you want me to use to describe what I just told you inside? This is the gate," she said, pointing as she spoke, "and when I left last night there was a padlock on that hasp. Now there isn't."

"Look Ms. I understand you've suffered some trauma, but it's not going to help at all if you start to lose it. Getting hostile isn't going to help the dead animals, it's not going to help you, and it isn't going to help Gordy Powell when he gets home. There's going to be a period of uncertainty until we can find out exactly what happened. Even if we can find the animals responsible, the only satisfaction Gordy may get is restitution by the dogs' owners. That's it. Forget about the emotional attachments and forget about whatever the disposal costs might be. Getting rid of a horse carcass could cost some money."

Emily listened carefully. She knew Laura Fellows was right. "I'm sorry," she said. "I've not had anything like this happen before. And I'm obviously not handling it well."

"Okay, let's take it from the top." Then Officer Fellows posed all the same questions one more time. Emily answered all the questions with the same answers. Fellows took copious notes. She examined the gate and pointed out tool marks on the lock chain. Then she excused herself and went back to the barn for a talk with the veterinarian. Inside the barn, she knelt beside Janice. "Okay, Doc, what do you think?"

"Laura, this was a pretty heavy attack. It's been a while since there's been any organized dog packs in the area. But it has happened before. If these guys are just beginning to get together, they are very effective, and one thing's for certain, they will strike again."

"How do you think they got in?" Fellows asked, not mentioning the tool marks.

"In my mind, there are only two ways for that to have happened. One, is our Ms. Pierce wasn't entirely as thorough as she says she was last night, and the dogs found enough of an opportunity to take the advantage, and they simply had their way. They can be very clever, if motivated by an easy kill. That means she left the padlock off the gate hasp and the barn door ajar. Two, is someone came back after she left and opened everything up and left it that way because of sheer stupidity, or left it that way for the express purpose of what ultimately happened. That's a little farfetched, but I suppose it's possible."

Fellows narrowed her eyes in reflection, and then asked one more question, "What do you figure the odds to be for either of the two scenarios?"

"Hell, I don't know, Laura, but in my mind it's more likely the gate was left open than the idea of someone running around with a killer dog pack, waiting to wreak this kind of havoc just for a night's entertainment. There is one more consideration," Shroder went on. "If the animals belonged to somebody who would do such a thing, there is considerable risk to the dogs themselves during this kind of attack. Poor old Sammy wasn't touched at all. Why did the attack stop when it did?"

"Maybe some of the dogs were injured," Fellows said. "You might alert the other veterinarians in the area to let me know if any dogs with blunt trauma are treated during the next several days."

"Good idea," Janice said and thanked her for her thoughts.

∾∾

When Emily came back into the barn, Fellows was just finishing her conversation with the veterinarian. Emily felt more than a little paranoid at this point. And she wasn't sure what went on between the two before she came in. She sensed they had been talking about her, but on reflection, she consoled herself with a whispered, "So what?"

"Will Ivan be okay?" Emily asked Janice.

"It's too early to tell. I can stitch, disinfect, and wrap, but if we can't get him on his feet soon, he will die. I may have to put him down before we can let that happen. I know that Gordy has a harness, so we'll get a crew out here and lift Ivan. I should know whether there's a chance, or not, by tomorrow. In the meantime, all we can do now is pray for him. I'm going to have to get back to the clinic to get the crew. I probably won't be here when Gordy gets home."

At five-fifteen, Emily found herself alone in Gordy Powell's house. She had left a message at the Smith & Wesson Academy just about the time Janice Shroder got ready to leave. But Gordy hadn't returned the call. She supposed by the time the message got to wherever he was, he may have already left. If that were the case he was probably en route and might show up at any moment. With the veterinarian and the police gone, there was nothing to do but wait.

She was sitting on the living room sofa with the cats when she heard the crunching sound of a vehicle. She got up, went to the door, and looked down to the driveway. It was Gordy. She hesitated as he climbed out of the truck, and instead of heading for the house, he started toward the corral gate. Then she rushed to the deck railing and called to him.

"Gordy, hold up for a minute, I'll be right down," she called.

He looked up, smiled. "Sure, Emily"

At the bottom of the stairs, she said, "Gordy something's happened."

He could tell it was bad by the tone of her voice, and this realization dissolved the smile. "What's happened?"

"Some dogs got into the barn last night," she told him.

"What's happened in there?" he asked.

"Ivan's seriously injured and the goats and piglets are dead," she explained. *There, you did it,* she thought. *The hardest part is over.*

Gordy's relaxed look twisted into a worrisome frown, as his eyes opened wide in preparation for more unpleasant news.

"Do we need Doc Shroder over here?" he asked.

"She was here most of the afternoon. And so was Laura Fellows. Doc Shroder left about a half-hour ago. She's not sure about Ivan. She's gone to get a crew to lift him. We need to get a harness ready. She says she won't know if she can save him until tomorrow. In the meantime, she's got him sedated. She thinks a dog pack of maybe three to five dogs got into the barn.

Gordy hurried toward the building. Emily tried to keep up with him as she followed behind, still talking.

Gordy threw open the door and rushed inside. "Holy

Christ," he moaned, as he looked around. The number of flies in the stalls had doubled, and the exposed viscera smelled terrible.

Once he satisfied himself the dead animals were indeed dead, he went to Ivan's stall. The speckled horse still lay on its side. His eyes were dull with the sedative circulating through his brain. Both his forelegs were wrapped with bandages up past the knees. His great rib cage heaved with long labored breaths. Gordy looked around and noticed the quantity of dried blood in the stall. Small bits of tissue and hair were mixed with the hay on the floor. Emily stood at the stall gate and gazed at Gordy while he did his assessment.

"How did they get in?" he asked.

"I don't know. I closed the barn door with all six animals in here on Thursday. I padlocked the gate when I left for the night. When I came over here at eleven this morning, this is what I found. The corral gate was opened and barn door was ajar. Laura Fellows found tool marks on the gate chain. I think someone used a bolt cutter."

Gordy walked over to Sammy's stall, went inside, and examined the donkey. As he inspected the animal, Sammy's skin rippled in an attempt to discourage the buzzing flies. When Gordy finished, he left the stall, walked to Emily, and looked into her eyes. She noticed his face was pale and his eyes floated in tears.

"How can you be sure everything was sealed up when you left on Thursday?"

"Because I remembered what I did, and that's the statement I gave the police when they asked. Gordy, this is not my fault," she said emphatically. "There were tool marks, Gordy."

"I didn't say it was. I'm just trying to imagine what happened."

"Well, imagine whatever you want, the padlock was

missing from the gate when I got here." Emily tensed. She knew the obvious question would come from Gordy just as with Laura Fellows. It still angered her, and she couldn't hide the fact.

CHAPTER 39

Gordy didn't need any more stress, and Emily seemed too defensive for productive conversation.

He turned away from her, went to the tool array hanging on the far wall, and pulled down a rake. Next he removed a box containing plastic bags from a nearby shelf and walked past her. Using the rake and a set of pruning shears, he removed the rest of the internal organs from the dead animals.

He raked up the organs already on the floor and piled everything into the plastic bag.

When he finished, he shrugged his shoulders. "I don't know what you can do. After I get all the loose stuff in plastic, I'll have to bag the carcasses and bury them. Then I need to go in and call Janice Shroder and talk to her about Ivan. If we've got to put him down, I'm going to have to make some preparations. At the very least, I'll need a medium sized truck with a jib crane or a small bucket loader to dispose of him. Maybe he'll be okay. Then all I'll have to do is put him in a sling and get him some rehab."

"Look, Gordy, I've fed Sammy and the birds. The dogs and cats are fed, so you don't have to worry about them tonight. I'd like to go home and take care of Isabel.

Let me do that, and I'll call you after to check on Ivan. If you want, I'll come back later tonight. Okay?"

"Sure, that's fine," Gordy replied, still distracted by the situation around him.

Emily walked toward the door. At the threshold she paused, turned around, and looked at Gordy. Tears welled in her hazel eyes, and her voice trembled. "Gordy, I'm so sorry," she cried. Then she disappeared outside.

❧❧❧

Gordy woke up at four a.m. on Saturday morning. He dreamt there were wolves in the barn and they ripped and slashed everything alive. The dream was the kind in which the dreamer was impotent, he could only watch in anger, as the mutilations took place a few feet away. He couldn't move or call out, and as he woke, he realized he was covered in sweat. Knowing the dream mirrored reality, Gordy realized the day ahead was bound to bring him more sadness.

He lay there awhile trying to lose the feeling of despair. His thoughts went to the day ahead, and he began counting off the things he had to do this morning. It was then that he realized that he wouldn't get any more sleep.

Gordy stumbled out of bed and made his way to the bathroom. He brushed, washed, and tried to prepare himself for events of the up-coming day. Hauling Ivan into his sling had been physically challenging, despite the muscle-bound crew Doc Shroder had provided the night before.

The doc was due at seven a.m. to examine Ivan. At that point, she'd determine a prognosis. Gordy had to make arrangements to either put the horse on some kind of care regiment or dispose of his massive body. Either of these outcomes required the proper mental attitude to initiate. And so far this morning, his attitude was far from clear and methodical.

Even when Emily called last night, Gordy found himself distracted and unable to concentrate on what she said. He hoped his lack of attention on the phone didn't upset her. In his heart, he didn't hold her responsible. Still, he felt detached from her, and he found it difficult to ignore the shadow of her participation in what happened. He also knew when he called the police department to talk about the dog attack, they would have a difficult time getting excited about the damage done. This knowledge added more frustration to Gordy's state of mind.

PART IV

Revelations

CHAPTER 40

Several weeks passed and the colors of late October were evident throughout the countryside. Allen Drew raked leaves from around his front walk until pains in his chest became too uncomfortable to continue. He let the rake fall to the ground and went inside to find his small bottle of nitroglycerin pills. He'd suffered occasional attacks of angina for the past two years but turned down the suggestion of another by-pass operation. Allen figured at his age, the results of the procedure favored an unhappy outcome.

He resigned himself to using the pills to manage his condition. He opened the bottle and placed one of the tiny tablets under his tongue. He sat in a bedroom chair and felt the rush of his blood vessels rapidly dilating and then the brief headache that usually followed.

Once again, Allen was reminded of his mortality and vowed to hire someone to finish the leaf raking. As he sat there, he reflected on the fact he had much to do in life. He'd better pay close attention to the requirements of his body. If he didn't, he risked not completing the tasks.

A few minutes passed and the pressure in his chest subsided. *There,* he thought, *that's better.* The idea of those important things to do rose to the surface of his mind, and he realized he had had no further contact from anyone regarding the Sam Stemford matter. A month had passed and no one even called for a follow-up series of questions.

The more he thought about the delay, the more concerned he became.

Allen rested for a while in the chair and then made up his mind to drive to the Clinton Police Department and get some kind of up-date on the investigation.

The drive only took him twenty minutes. He parked the old station wagon in the lot and walked slowly to the entrance. He asked to see Chief of Police, Chris Forhey, and stood by the front desk while the young officer called the chief's office.

A few minutes later, Chris Forhey greeted him with a friendly, "Hello, Allen."

Allen had been active in the Clinton Rotary Club until a year ago. That was when he began to slow down on his list of commitments. Although he still maintained a membership, his attendance during the past year had put him below the specified requirements. During his active years, he had worked with the chief on a number of club related projects.

"It's good to see you, Chris," he said sincerely.

"What brings you down to my place?" Forhey asked.

"Well, I want to talk privately, if I may?"

"Sure, we can arrange that. Let's go to my office," Forhey said, as he led the way toward the back of the building. In the office, the chief sat down behind his desk, and Allen sat in a chrome-upholstered chair across from him. "Well, what's on your mind?"

"A few months ago you fellas discovered Sam Stemford's body in the pond over on Nod Road."

"Yeah, we sure did."

"Right around the time of the discovery, a young police officer, name of Gordon Powell, stopped by and asked me some questions about Sam and about what I remembered was going on back in 1938. For a while after, there were a few articles in the newspaper talking about a murder investigation. Now it's more than three months later, and I haven't seen anything more about the case. I'm kind of curious about what's going on. I was hoping you could fill me in."

"Well, Allen, I'd like to be able to help you out, but there's not much I can tell you. The murder happened a long time ago, and any trail leading back there is pretty cold. We may have had something going for a little while, but there's a whole lot of crime happening right now with real victims who also have needs. I've got limited resources and there are priorities imposed by the town."

"Are you telling me you've shut down the investigation?" Allen asked.

"Let's say, slowed down, more than shut down," Forhey replied.

"Does that mean you are still working on the case or not?" Allen was agitated.

"It means when there is time available with my detectives, they look at the case."

"You mean, when there is nothing else to do, they try to pick up where they left off and then try to add new information," Allen said.

"It's not that bad, Allen," Forhey said. "Right now isn't a good time to try to deal with the kind of resources this case requires. As soon as we get caught up with cases involving current victims and real time situations, we'll be able to catch up with the old items like the Stemford thing."

"Frankly, Chris, I'm not sure what you're thinking. Murder has no statute of limitation and just because justice is overdue, nothing should influence the need for it to prevail." Allen was getting angry, and he felt his chest tighten. He sensed he could work himself into a dangerous attack if he continued.

"Look, Allen, this is a small town, and so far I haven't found a way to get outside help. I've talked to the state police and the FBI. No one else seems to have the time either. If you want to sit in with the board of selectmen, maybe you can influence how this is going to play out. Otherwise, we'll do what we can, when we can. By the way, Allen, what's your interest in the case anyway?"

The question came too late and the chief had already lost his audience. Allen was tuned out and, in his mind, he was ready to leave. He rose from his chair. "Maybe I'll do that." He turned and started for the door.

Forhey shook his head. "Do what?"

Allen paused and looked at him for a long moment. Finally, he said, "Maybe I will attend the next selectmen's meeting."

With the remark, Allen Drew left the chief's office and returned to his station wagon. He thought the turn of events must have something to do with Teddy Flanders. He wasn't sure how, but Allen was certain Teddy was manipulating the situation behind the scenes.

When he arrived home, he sat down and looked up the phone number of Emily Pierce. He punched in the number and listened as the line clicked and rang through several repeats.

Finally there was a brief click and a woman's voice said, "Hello" at the other end.

"Hello, Emily Pierce," he said. "My name is Allen Drew. A few months ago, Gordon Powell visited with me to discuss the murder of Dr. Sam Stemford. I believe the Doctor was your grandfather?"

"Yes, Mr. Drew, Gordon Powell spoke to me about the interview. What can I do for you?"

"I was wondering how you've been doing with your own inquiries into the matter."

"Well, Mr. Drew, I don't know what to tell you, except my investigation has slowed considerably. Recently, I've not been able to accomplish anything with the local police. It's been over a month since I've learned anything new."

∽∽∽

As Emily spoke, she realized she had better proceed with caution. After all, Gordy mentioned he felt Allen was hiding something during the interview. If Drew were involved with the Stemford murder, it was possible he was just fishing. She didn't need to give him anything that put him on a trail to her, even if he was in his eighties.

"Well, Ms. Pierce, I feel an obligation to advise you the entire investigation is being sabotaged. I believe it's no coincidence that nothing new has been found and things seem to be slowing down."

"What information do you have that brings you to such a conclusion?" she asked.

"If you and Officer Powell can visit me at my home, I can share what I believe are some very important concerns."

"I'll be delighted to meet with you," she replied. "There is one thing, though, I'm not sure I can bring Officer Powell with me. He seems to be terribly busy lately, and I've not seen him for the past couple of weeks."

"Well, Ms. Pierce, you better call him and tell him it's extremely important I meet with both of you as quickly as possible. Don't spare a sense of urgency."

Allen knew he would feel a lot more comfortable if somebody like Powell were involved as he began to open

up his perspective of Teddy Flanders. His story was going to expose new aspects of the events sixty years ago. It
may even tie together more recent events.

CHAPTER 41

After Allen hung up, Emily Pierce dialed Gordy Powell's number. She tried to be cheerful as she greeted his voice with a warm hello.

"How you doing, Emily?" he asked politely.

"Okay, how about you?" she replied.

"Good. Good. Ivan's going to make it," he said.

"Oh, that's wonderful. I was terribly sad about the others," she added.

"Yeah, it's too bad. But Ivan's a great horse. Doc Shroder did her best, and it paid off, even though he was really injured. One of his forelegs is fractured and there was some tendon damage. He'll be in a sling for a long time. Saving him was the right decision, and Janice was sure it was the right thing to do. It's still going to be pretty hard. Ivan will need a lot of rehab."

Emily could tell from the stress in his voice that the trauma Gordy suffered wasn't over. She yearned to comfort him, but since his return from Springfield there seemed to be a barrier between them. They were no longer able to communicate at any level. Emily tried to meet with him several times, and he canceled each occasion just before it was to happen. Their fledgling relationship had quite literally disintegrated after the attack at the barn. She sensed his distraction on the phone, and she felt there was little chance of bringing them back together. The only thing new was Allen Drew's phone call.

"I received a phone call from Allen Drew a while ago," she said.

"That's interesting," Gordy said, trying to sound like it was important. "What did he have to say?"

"He wants us to meet him at his home. He said the investigation into my grandfather's death is being sabotaged. He also said he needs to talk to both of us right away. I told him you've been very busy, but he insists he needs to speak to both of us. I told him I'd talk to you and try to arrange something."

"I'm pretty busy this weekend. I don't know when would be a good time."

"Look, Gordy, I don't want to impose on you, but I've a feeling this is important. If you'll agree to meet just one time, I promise, I'll leave you alone from then on. No obligation implied or otherwise required."

"Oh, come on, Emily. What do you take me for? My whole life isn't tied to what you and I were doing for your grandfather. It's not like that at all. And I'm not looking for a contract that guarantees our perpetual separation. I'm just trying to rebuild my farm, that's all. When I've put things right at home, I'll have time for you and your grandfather." Gordy paused for a moment, as if realizing the harshness of his tone may sound like over-reacting. Before she could respond, he offered, "Call the old man back and tell him we can meet tomorrow afternoon at his place. Tell him two o'clock, and I'll pick you up at your place at one-thirty. Okay?"

"Are you sure it's okay?" she asked one more time.

"Yes, I'm sure. I'll see you then. Bye."

After Gordy hung up, he went back to the business of restoring the farm and managing rehab for Ivan.

He kept his promise and arrived at the Pierce house on

time. He turned into the driveway, and instead of shutting the motor off, he bumped the horn a couple of times with the palm of his hand. The barks from the horn drew a brief appearance from Emily inside the window. A moment or two later, she rushed out through the front door and made her way to Gordy's truck.

When she climbed into the passenger side she was breathless.

"I thought that you'd come in for some coffee or something," she said.

"Maybe later. Let's just get this meeting over with."

"I hope you're not upset," she said.

"No, not at all. I'd like to be done with it, that's all," he said.

"Maybe we can get something to eat, when we're finished?"

"Sure, we can do that," he said.

The drive only took a few minutes and it was just two o'clock when they turned into Allen Drew's driveway. They went to the door and Gordy pressed the glowing white button for the bell. Allen appeared and greeted them. He showed them into the living room and asked them to sit down. Once they were seated, Allen paused for a while, staring at Emily.

Finally he said, "Please forgive me, but I noticed a striking resemblance to your grandfather."

The comment startled her. No one had ever said that before. It took a moment for her to grasp the scope of what he said. "Thank you, Mr. Drew. I do believe I'm quite flattered."

"Please, call me Allen," he said to the both of them.

They nodded in agreement.

"Well, Allen, your phone call was quite a surprise. I called Gordy right away and persuaded him to come," Emily said.

"Good, dear," he said. "I've been having a difficult time since the discovery of Sam Stemford's remains. For the first time in sixty years, things became very clear, and I wasn't sure what to do with them. The last thing I felt comfortable doing was running off at the mouth when I didn't know who to trust."

"You mean you have direct information regarding the murder?" Gordy asked.

"Yes, you could say that," the old man said. As he spoke, he scratched at a red crusty patch of skin on the side of his neck.

Both Emily and Gordy sat in their chairs with their eyes wide. For a moment neither one of them knew what to say next.

Then Gordy couldn't deny his professional curiosity any longer. "Do you know who killed Sam Stemford?"

"Yes, I believe I do," he answered. "Before I go into it, I must tell you about what I knew was going on at the time. You see there was more to the killing of Sam Stemford than a bullet in the head."

"Please, go on," Emily said.

"Yes, my dear," Allen replied. "My wife died a little while after Sam Stemford disappeared. I believe the same person who killed the doctor killed Molly. That year was an awful year, so much happened. Molly and I had been married for nearly five years when we moved to Clinton. I accepted a job with my uncle at the Clinton Hardware Store. Business was beginning to pick up at the time, and it seemed like The Great Depression, which began with the crash of 1929, was finally going to end. Up until then, there were very few jobs available in New England, and what jobs were available paid poor wages. My last job had me working as a supervisor for a government work camp outside of Middletown. I earned eight dollars a week.

"When I started with my uncle, he paid me fifteen dollars a week, and he gave me pretty much free reign to help manage the store. He even let Molly work part-time when possible. Molly was only twenty-five and she was pretty and full of life. She was energetic and never complained, even when things weren't going very well. As I got involved with the store, I became obsessed with improving the business. I guess there was a time I became so passionate with the store that I stopped paying attention to Molly. Once again, she didn't complain, she just found other ways to occupy her interests. I think that's when she became involved with Teddy Flanders."

The old man twisted in his chair, reached into his pocket, and removed a handkerchief. He slowly mopped his forehead and moistened his lips with the tip of his tongue. "You'll have to bear with me, I've never spoken of this before, to anyone," Allen said before going on.

Emily used the pause to release some of the tension. She looked toward Gordy to see how he reacted. He stared at Allen with an intense expression on his face. His eyes were still wide and his policeman's mind seemed busy working. Although she wanted to say something, anything, to ease the stress in the room, she decided on the path of silence. She'd let Allen Drew continue without interruption.

"At any rate, their relationship went on throughout most of the winter and into spring. In April, Molly got sick with the flu, and Doc Stemford helped with her treatment and stayed close during her recovery. It was during her recovery that she seduced Doc Stemford. I don't think the relationship went on for very long, and it probably ended as soon as it began. As you might expect, I was very upset when I found out about it. For a while, my way of dealing with the situation was to put more hours into the store and keep my mind occupied there.

Besides, whatever else was going on, I believed Molly loved me. When she did something like that, it was out of vanity or boredom. She wasn't a malicious woman. As a matter of fact, she was insightful and full of life. She was intelligent and caring, and there wasn't a moment I doubted she loved me." Allen hesitated for a moment and rose from his chair. "Would you like some coffee or something? I didn't realize this would take so long and there is quite a lot left to say."

Both Emily and Gordy recognized the invitation as an opportunity to regroup and perhaps discuss Allen's story among themselves, so they welcomed the offer of coffee and let the old man retire to the kitchen.

When he left, Gordy turned to Emily. "Allen's been sitting on this information for a very long time."

"It sure seems that way," Emily said. "Why do think he hasn't come forward till now?"

"I suppose there are a lot of reasons. Not the least of which is the fact Teddy Flanders is still around. He can be a very formidable character," Gordy said.

"Yeah, he left that impression when he visited me at the library."

"Oh, when did he do that?" Gordy asked, quite surprised.

"Friday morning just before I was getting ready to go over to your place to take care of the animals," she answered.

"What a weird coincidence, what did he want?"

"It was a strange visit. All he said was he had worked on my grandfather's disappearance and suspected something about my mother and Uncle Bert. He wasn't specific, but he implied that if I continued to dig into the case, I'd find something that could hurt my relatives. It wasn't a threat exactly, but after he left, I remember feeling like I was threatened."

Allen returned to the room. He carried a small tray with coffee, condiments, and a bowl of cookies. He passed it around and Gordy and Emily each took a cup. Then he placed the tray on the table and returned to his chair, holding a cup of his own. "You see back in those days, divorce wasn't as common as it is today. That's not to say we didn't hurt one another. The time I spent with my new responsibilities at the store caused Molly to feel alone and, to some extent, rejected. She didn't complain, but she sought other ways to find the attention her personality craved. In my old age, I can only try to remember what it was like to crave, because I no longer crave anything, and I can assure you the memory is not nearly as gratifying as the experience itself.

"Had Molly complained about my interest in the business, perhaps our relationship may have disintegrated because of the stress of her complaints. One transgression may appear more serious than another, but who's to say that prolonged or chronic complaining wouldn't have taken a greater toll than her sexual indiscretions. Whatever the tribulation in a marriage, I believe you must care more for the relationship than the grievances that emerge from it. At any rate, just before her death, Molly explained she was afraid of Teddy Flanders. She told me what had been going on during the year, and what her suspicions were regarding the disappearance of Sam Stemford. She asked me to forgive her, and I did.

"When she died, it was a terrible blow for me. Several years passed before I could deal with other people." Allen paused and once again blotted his face with a handkerchief. This time he wiped his eyes. He took several deep breaths and continued. "Before Molly died, we talked about going to the police with the story about her relationship with Teddy Flanders. But then, there was the big storm of 'thirty-eight and the awful clean up afterward. With everything else going on, we still had no proof connecting Flanders to the Doc Stemford matter. So we just waited, in the hope that perhaps Stemford's body would be found or some other compelling evidence turned up.

"Nothing we hoped for happened. Instead, Molly was killed mysteriously in October. And then I didn't know where to turn. If I accused Flanders directly without evidence, I was sure he would go unprosecuted. After all, he was a policeman and I was just an ordinary fellow working in a hardware store. I had no proof, only hints of events around me. And if Flanders were half as evil as I thought he was, I knew he was capable of hurting someone else. Instead of taking a stand then, I decided to wait and strike with better information. I've waited years, and until now, there's been no better situation. Time may be running out, and whatever the outcome, I must not wait any longer. After I buried Molly, I tried to keep track of Teddy and the Stemford matter as best I could, just in case something changed. As you know, Teddy went on to become chief of police in Madison. No new evidence turned up until September this year, when Sam Stemford's remains were found. Poor Annie Martin and her little girls, their deaths may have solved a murder."

Gordy looked at the old man and all of a sudden he needed to ask an important question. "Excuse me, Allen, but did you tamper with the records at the Madison Town Hall?"

"Why yes, I did. As soon as I saw the first article in the paper, I went to the old archives and took everything out of the files. I brought the material home and made copies of the entire package. I was thinking Teddy might show up there sooner or later and destroy anything he found. It occurred to me he might have even gotten to them before the police investigation.

"When I finished duplicating the paperwork, I added some items from my own scrapbook and returned everything a few days later. My idea was to inspire a connection to the death of Molly. I chose a time when the receptionist, Miss Kampers, was away from her desk and I slipped into the cellar without logging in. I figured there was a chance the police would get there and discover the files before Teddy. If they didn't, I was ready to turn over the duplicate file to the police and/or the press."

At seeing the distress on his audience's faces, he continued, "Please understand, I was still trying to avoid a direct confrontation with Teddy Flanders. It was my hope the combination of interviews, the old file information, and the car containing his remains would produce enough evidence to put someone on a trail to Teddy Flanders. I believed if the police were reasonably motivated, the leap of faith required to connect the dots to Flanders wasn't terribly complicated. I was especially gratified when you stopped by and asked a great many questions about the murder."

Then it was Emily's turn. "Tell us why you've decided to bring us into this now, instead of going to the police."

"Last week, I did go to the police," Allen replied. "I met with Chief Forhey and tried to get information on the status of the case. Basically, they're dragging their heels. I was told the investigation's slowed significantly, perhaps, even stopped. Forhey said the list of current crimes is taking up his resources and he didn't have time to spend on the case. I suspect Teddy Flanders is somehow behind this, but there's little I can do about it. Even if I risked telling Forhey what 1 knew about the case, I still don't have any hard evidence. I thought before I tried to resurrect his interest, I'd talk to the both of you. I believe there's risk associated with telling anyone. It's likely

Teddy's killed at least two people and perhaps there are others we may never learn about."

"You think the man is that dangerous?" Gordy asked.

"Oh yes," the old man answered. "He's older now, but I think he's still a very dangerous man. You don't know what he did to my Molly. Her charred body was found draped over the hood of our Ford pickup. The fire destroyed most of the truck, but there were several inconsistencies. During the investigation, there were serious questions as to why the fire only burned portions of the truck and didn't set off the tank. Questions I believed were never answered to my satisfaction. Molly died a horrible death, burned alive, while she lay helpless over the top of the motor. Yes, Teddy Flanders is a very dangerous man."

Gordy's face suddenly paled as it occurred to him that Teddy did have those two Rottweilers. He looked at Emily. "When I interviewed Teddy, there were two very big dogs at his place. You don't think he had anything to do with the attack at the farm, do you?" As he asked the question, he knew the answer. Gordy looked at Allen. "Six weeks ago, while I was away, my farm was decimated by what appeared to be a dog pack. Emily was watching my place until I finished a training program up in Springfield. In the attack, I almost lost my horse, and did lose two pigs and two prized Nubian goats. The place was wide open when the mess was discovered, and we never did figure out how they got in. Do you think Teddy Flanders could have done such a thing? If so, what the hell possessed him to do it?"

Allen appeared to think over the question for a moment. Then he replied, "I'm sure he's capable, but the real question is why. Maybe we can back into the answer. What's happened since the attack at your place?"

"I can answer that," Emily joined in. "The first thing

that's happened, is this terrible barrier between Gordy and me. That's one obvious outcome. The second thing is the energy we had been putting into my grandfather's murder has evaporated. Neither one of us is working the way we were before the barn incident."

"Do you really believe the man is that diabolical?" Gordy asked to no one in particular.

Emily looked at Allen across the room and slowly nodded her head. The old man nodded in agreement.

Then Gordy placed his head in his hands. "Shit."

Finally, he looked up and asked Allen if he had a video camera or a tape recorder. The old man looked puzzled and shook his head, "No."

Emily reached for her purse, shuffled around inside, and pulled out a small tape recorder. "I've got mine," she offered.

"Good, it's important we record this information," Gordy said, as he took control. "Allen, start from the beginning and run through the entire story one more time. We need to have all of this on tape. When it's convenient, we should video tape the entire story too."

CHAPTER 42

Gordy and Emily said goodbye to Allen Drew and climbed into the pick-up truck. Gordy backed out of the driveway and turned to speak to Emily.

"It's going to get interesting as we decide what to do next," he said. "Teddy Flanders seems like an opponent in a chess game, everything we've done has met with some kind of counter move, and we didn't even realize it. Here we are, living in a world of chaos, trying to create order, and he's out there shaping things around us. We muddle along feeling like victims in a sea of coincidence, and that son-of-a-bitch has been in control ever since he killed your grandfather."

"What do you think we should do now?" Emily asked.

"I'm not entirely sure. I guess the first thing we need to do is go back to where we were two months ago and try to pick up where we left off"

"There is still the matter of the bullet," Emily said. "That's as hard a piece of evidence as anything we've got."

"You're right about that. On Monday, I'll call Barry Lands, talk to him about the bullet, and get his side of what's going on. I have a hunch if Chief Forhey put the brakes on the investigation, Barry will be a little pissed off. If that's true, he'll be real happy to have someone to talk to right about now. I should also call Chief Deering at the Madison PD. There are two more questions worth having answers to. One is, what weapon was used by the cops back in 'thirty-eight, and the other is, whether there have ever been any trial cases using ballistics information from Teddy Flanders's service pistol. Any information we may find there could provide a link to Teddy and give us grounds for a search warrant at Teddy's home. Something like that would, at least, put pressure on the old man."

Gordy was wound up tight. "I also want to look at ways to connect him with the attack at the farm. The idea he may be responsible changes everything. If I had thought of him at the time, maybe I'd have taken samples to verify the DNA of the animals involved in the attack. DNA evidence taken from my place could have tied us to his dogs—irrefutable evidence connecting him to a crime. It could have been hard evidence putting even more pressure on him. Now it's too late to do anything about it. Damn it."

"Even if it's too late, Teddy doesn't know it."

"What a great idea," Gordy replied with a grin. "This kind of situation calls for some creative lying. There's nothing to stop me from letting it be known I've got DNA testing in progress."

"See, now we've fixed one problem, how about we celebrate and get something to eat?" Emily said.

Gordy nodded in agreement and smiled.

They drove a few miles up Route 1 and pulled into the parking of a local restaurant called Francie's. The building was painted pale blue and there were large porthole windows in front, facing the road.

Two huge mahogany doors protected the entrance. They were heavily varnished and decorated with small oars that served as handles. Alongside the road was an a-frame sign advertising *PRIME RIB SPECIAL* in large red letters.

They parked the truck and went inside where they were greeted by the owner, Francie "Mama" Carnelli. The woman curved her mouth into a big toothy smile and gave Emily a warm hug. "It's a about a time, 'Oney," she said, using her most favorite greeting. Although, Mama Carnelli was casually dressed, there was still something about her that presented an over-statement. Her white blouse was open wide enough to show several inches of cleavage. Her skintight blue jeans suggested surgery would be required to remove them. Although she had recently turned fifty, she was an attractive woman and didn't need the thick application of make-up painted on her face. "Well, it's been a long time since I've seen you two together," she said as she greeted them.

The couple nodded, and Emily felt her cheeks flush pink in embarrassment. Mama showed them to a quiet booth near a window in the back of the dining room. They sat down, and Emily picked up her menu. While she scanned through it, Gordy gazed out the window.

The view swept to a vast sea of bulrushes stretching all the way to Long Island Sound. In the distance, over the top of the rushes, perhaps a mile or so away, were the tops of a hundred masts; all belonging to a fleet of sailboats docked in a local Marina. Gordy noted that the gray November sky colored the background for what could have been a Winslow Homer painting.

Wind blew across the tops of the bulrushes, creating waves of undulating light and dark green colors. The bristling, tumultuous stalks resembled the rippling coat of some great beast about to plunge into the sea, a strange beast all too eager to abandon the security of dry land in favor of the chilly seclusion of open water.

Gordy's perception of the shoreline had changed. Until recently, this was a relatively tranquil place. Now the little collection of towns seemed more like the depths of Long Island Sound where the drama of life and death played repeatedly with no one to care or even chronicle the sordid details, a place possessing no recall, no revenge, no justice. A place where creatures having a nature like Teddy Flanders preyed and left ache in the souls of residents like Emily Pierce, Allen Drew, and Gordy Powell. Flanders, the old bastard, had even crippled Ivan.

While Gordy brooded over the loss at his farm, he had forgotten about the loss to others around him. The tragic circumstances surrounding the deaths of his animals had temporarily robbed him of the simplest vision of compassion.

The notion of Teddy Flanders's involvement offered some relief to the mystery of the event. If nothing else, it absolved Emily from any carelessness. Teddy had made the situation very personal. The good part was Gordy felt some sense of clarity. The awful weight of despair was lifting, and what appeared muddled was coming sharply into focus. For the first time in two months, he felt there was life beyond loss. He smiled, thinking maybe there was a way to get a piece of Teddy Flanders.

Emily looked at Gordy across the table and asked the silly old question. "A penny for your thoughts?"

Gordy took his eyes from the window and looked at Emily. "Oh, I was admiring the view toward the sound, and then I thought there must be a way to get a grip on Mr. Teddy Flanders. All the while there's the undeniable fact that it feels so good having dinner with you. I just realized it's been nearly two months since we've done anything together. I'm sorry for being such an asshole."

"Apology accepted," she replied. "What did you think about Allen's story?"

"A pretty tragic tale," Gordy answered. "After all this

time, there's probably no way to tie Teddy to the murder of Molly Drew. I guess that's one crime he'll get away with."

"What did you think about Allen's description of their marriage?"

"I don't know," he said. "There is a lot to be said about trying to value a relationship, and how did he put it, not the grievances that result from it. He must have been very much in love with Molly."

Emily thought for a moment. "One thing you and I have in common is a condition I would describe as 'relationship challenged.' We both seem to work hard to avoid them, almost unnaturally hard. And here is an old man who is entirely consumed with a marriage that ended sixty years ago. This guy was willing to forgive Molly for what she did."

"Wow! I don't think I could go that far. He appears almost saintly in how he values the interactions between two people."

"He seemed to believe grievances between two people should have equal weight, that no perceived crime is worse than another. Maybe he was saying all perceived grievances were equally severe and any small grievance could be the core of a situation that ruins the relationship." Emily was on a roll, and found it hard to stop. "Gordy, the old man can't be that philosophic. When my ex, Charlie, was sleeping around, I was really pissed off. If I were to take Allen Drew's view of what was going on, I would have tried to find out why Charlie was doing what he was doing and then made some investment in dealing with the why, in contrast to dealing with my personal feeling of betrayal. Maybe that would have been a different forum for fixing things."

Gordy listened and appeared to understand what she was saying, but he leapt ahead. "What you're saying has merit, but keep two things in mind. One, whatever Molly Drew did to keep her marriage with Allen was apparently successful, but she was probably murdered as a result of what she was involved in. And two, if you had valued your relationship differently with Charlie, would you be better off today? Think about it, if you were still with Charlie, you probably wouldn't be having dinner with me."

Emily smiled at him across the table. "Stop by my place after dinner."

Gordy smiled back. "I thought you'd never ask."

CHAPTER 43

When Gordy telephoned Barry Lands, he was pleased to learn the detective was in the frame of mind he had expected. Barry grumbled that he had been told to back off the Stemford case.

"So what's going on with the bullet?" Gordy asked.

"I requested a computer search of all the licensed Smith and Wesson thirty-eight revolvers in the state. No sooner had the paperwork been submitted when I was told we had new priorities in the department. Everything on the Stemford deal was put on hold."

"What do you think is goin' on?"

"It's hard to tell. The caseload is high but most of it is bush league crap. The chief seems to be reacting to complaints from the town, but, I figured we were just getting some teeth in the Stemford affair. Took the whole thing as a surprise."

"Do you think you'd be willing to work on the case on your own time? I've new info that might shed some light," Gordy offered.

"I might be interested. What ya got?"

"Let's meet over pizza and I'll go through the whole thing. How's tomorrow for lunch? I'll introduce you to the Pizza Palace and I'll buy"

"Sure, I can do that. See you then."

෧෧෧

Barry entered the Pizza Palace and strolled over to the table where Gordy was sitting. "How's the food?" he asked.

"You won't be disappointed," Gordy said.

Barry sat at the table, and the bentwood chair creaked under the load of his large frame. He wore a leather coat and corduroy trousers. He grinned as he loosened his coat in the warmth radiating from the large pizza ovens.

"Damn, it's freezing out there, and it's hot as hell in here. Looks like we may be in for a long cold winter," he said. His brown eyes twinkled as he removed his coat and hung it on the back of the chair. "So what's going on?" he asked.

"I should be asking you the same thing," Gordy answered. "I get distracted for a couple of months and the next thing I know, the Stemford investigation is dying a slow agonizing death. And you're busy busting kids smoking marijuana. Tell me what you think is going on."

"Not much to tell, everything seemed to be moving right along and one day the chief sits us all down in the same room and tells how it's gonna be from now on. He says he has got to run the department to budget and he's putting a cap on overtime and other expenses. Then he says we got to do the same thing. So I asked about the Stemford case and he tells me to talk to him privately after the meeting. After the meeting, he tells me he's got a list of fresh cases he needs to be put to bed, and these cases come in front of Doc Stemford. That's how it was."

"Barry, keep what I'm about to tell you very quiet, at least for the time being," Gordy said. He told the story Allen Drew had told him. While he spoke, he watched the expression on Barry's face. As Barry's jaw dropped and his eyes opened wide, it was clear he had no prior knowledge of what Gordy was telling him. "You can see why I wanted to talk to you privately," Gordy said. "I believe Allen is pretty scared of Teddy Flanders and has been that way ever since his wife died back in 1938. I've got his testimony on audio and video tape, so he may not be in as much danger as he would be without the tapes, but who's to say what a guy like Teddy might do next. He seems to write his own agenda."

Barry leaned back on the chair, which protested with more creaking noises. "You know I'll have to bring Chief Forhey in on this thing before I can do anything else."

"Yeah, I know. While you're doing that, I think Emily should go to Avery Johnson at the *New Haven Reporter*. The one thing Chris Forhey will always respond to will be the press. When something like that happens, the doorway back into the investigation should reopen."

Barry seemed interested enough to say, "I think you've got something there. The more I think about it, the more I like the idea. If Avery writes an updated article, Chief Forhey will be pressured to do something. If the slow-down came from Harlan Flanders, he may have no choice but to let the chief do his job. Then I can go to the chief with a copy of Allen Drew's tape after Avery writes his piece. That should save face all the way around and still end up with a reopened investigation."

Gordy considered what Barry said. "That sounds good. The next thing we need to do is find some old ballistics evidence collected anytime during Teddy's thirty-year police career. Chances are, the old man hung on to his original thirty-eight revolver while he was a cop. It would have been easier for him to keep it, rather than trying to explain losing it. The combination of Allen's statement along with old ballistics data may be enough grounds for a search warrant. That'll put some pressure on Teddy. By the time we get the warrant, Teddy will no doubt have gotten rid of the gun, but at least we can squeeze him a little."

Barry liked the idea. "I might be able to tell where Chief Forhey's coming from, by the way he deals with the request for the warrant. The slowdown has got to be coming from either Harlan Flanders or the chief himself. "At this point, Teddy's been sitting there, thinking he's got everybody fooled. To him, nobody's in a position to invade the sanctuary of his old house in Durham. Even if we only requested a warrant, he'd know somebody's finally on to him."

As Gordy listened, he decided to add a little white lie to the conversation. "It would also be good to let him know I've got tissue samples from the dog attack in my barn and DNA tests are in progress. It would be neat to see his reaction to a request for DNA samples from his dogs. He would've never thought about DNA. It didn't exist when he was cop."

"That may be the biggest bluff of the century," Barry said.

"Maybe," Gordy said. "But I've got a meeting scheduled with Chief Deering in Madison, after work. I want to see how much ballistics information Teddy's got out there. I think it's pretty unlikely for a man like him to go thirty years without having his gun involved in some kind of court case. I'll call and let you know what I've found out. In the meantime, let's try to keep what we're doing quiet. As soon as the old man knows he's at the top of a suspect list, he'll try to sweep away any trail that might lead to him. Certainly he'll get rid of the gun if he still has it. He may even try to get into the county and state archives to tamper with any old ballistics information. He's a pretty clever old guy, and he's managed to stay ahead of a lot of people for a lot of years. We must be very careful how we go from here. At some point, it'll be good to stir the pot and let him know what we're doing, but not just yet."

Barry listened, and added, "If what I'm thinking is right, Harlan will feed everything he can get from Chief Forhey directly to Teddy. If that's true we can probably count on him to be our link to Teddy. Maybe we can use it to our advantage."

CHAPTER 44

Harlan Flanders sat on his regular stool at the counter of the Holiday Diner in downtown Clinton. It was seven-thirty in the morning, and he had just ordered up his usual breakfast of a bran muffin and coffee. He had carried the morning paper under his arm and now it was spread out on the laminated surface in front of him. In his customary manner, he scanned the front page and then flipped through to the Shoreline section. There at the top of the page was an article entitled "Dead Doctor's Murder Buried by Clinton PD."

Harlan's temples pulsed as he felt the reaction to a sudden increase in blood pressure. *Damn,* he thought as he read through the entire article. *Damn it to hell.* The piece went on to say the Clinton PD was dragging their heels on the case. And even though there was new and compelling evidence available, no effort was being made to pursue the circumstances surrounding the death of Doctor Sam Stemford.

Harlan picked up the newspaper, walked out to his car, and picked up his cell phone. As he stood in the parking lot, he dialed the number to his dad's home. He waited while the message machine went through the regular announcement and then shouted, "Dad, pick up!"

"Yes, Harlan," was the gruff response on the other

end.

"Did you read the morning paper?"

"Yup."

"Well, what do you think we should do?" Harlan asked.

"Nothin'," the old man replied.

"Dad, I need a serious answer."

"This is a serious answer. They seem intent on making trouble. And I'm getting pretty tired of it. Can you get out here sometime early today?"

"I'm tied up till nine thirty, but I think I can make it for ten o'clock."

"Okay, then I'll see you at ten."

With that, the old man hung up without saying good-bye.

Harlan pushed the stop button on the phone, got in the car, and drove to his office at the Clinton Town Hall.

CHAPTER 45

Gordy Powell's visit with the Madison Chief of Police, Terry Deering, turned out to be more productive than he anticipated. There were records of three shooting cases involving Teddy Flanders during his career. All three made it through the district courts and one actually went to the State Supreme Court in 1961. The case involved a hot pursuit incident following a gas station hold-up in the center of town. The robbery took place in 1959, and Teddy shot one of the perps soon after the chase began.

The record showed the fellow who was wounded claimed he was forced into the getaway car during the robbery. He tried to prove he was an unwilling participant in the crime and was therefore unlawfully shot by Teddy Flanders. He was later found guilty and Teddy was exonerated of any wrongdoing.

There were three policemen at the scene and several shots were fired. Ballistics data was used to identify the thirty-eight Police Special revolver owned by Teddy Flanders as the weapon firing the wounding bullet.

With Terry Deering's help, Gordy confirmed the thirty-eight special was the weapon issued to members of the police department as early as 1935. Ironically, the court case of 1961 might be the evidence that put an end to

Teddy Flanders tranquil retirement. It would be only fitting, if facts from the past were the means to a conviction for his deeds in the past. Justice had its irony.

As Gordy read through the files, he wondered whether the conviction of a sixty-year-old murder could be grounds for the cessation of Teddy's retirement benefits. *After what the son-of-a-bitch did to my animals, Doc Stemford, probably Molly Drew, and whoever else pissed him off, he's got a lot to answer for. Whatever the courts decide won't be enough.* And then there was the prospect of an eighty-year-old, ex-cop throwing himself at the mercy of a sympathetic jury. *What if he ends up walking away after everything is said and done? It's happened before.*

Gordy would have to persuade Barry Lands to go to Hartford quickly and retrieve all the evidence records associated with the old court case. Hopefully, Barry would get his end done before Teddy Flanders tried to corrupt whatever information was there. One good thing was if Teddy did try to get access to the old evidence, he may inadvertently leave some kind of trail. That meant he risked exposure just by his inquiry.

Principally, they needed to secure copies of the photographs that were attached to the original ballistics report, and to do it as soon as possible. As this notion surfaced in Gordy's mind, he knew he must hurry. Gordy called Barry and briefed him on what he had discovered. He urged Barry to get some kind of authorization to drive to Hartford and secure any evidence on file.

CHAPTER 46

Teddy Flanders wasn't accustomed to having his life go in a direction he didn't like, and this most recent turn of events definitely wasn't something he liked. The newspaper article written by Avery Johnson was a bolt out of the blue. And now he found himself fretting about the situation.

For all of his eighty years, he took pride in his profound sense of control. For the most part, whenever circumstances and/or people didn't conform to his expectations, he took action. In this style, he was usually able to turn events around.

Sometimes the circumstances were so strange that a casual observer might consider them bizarre. Things just happened, one day someone simply disappeared, or changed their point of view. Often, there was no conspicuous reason. But when conflict appeared inevitable, suddenly there was a curious harmony.

As a young man, Teddy realized he was different from most people his age. High perception, combined with an extraordinary IQ, set the stage for his latest chapter in self-proclaimed, superior human beings. Sometimes Teddy's actions suggested he was telepathic. Of course he wasn't, but there were instances when he was so empathetic he actually felt he sensed what was in another person's mind. Maybe he detected changes in a person's body chemistry, like the pheromone molecules that played a role in insect behavior. Perhaps he sensed the inner workings of a person's mind through their expressions or body language. Maybe it was a combination of all of these things. Maybe he was simply demonic.

But whatever the mechanism, there was no doubt he had a gift not often found in the average citizen. Whenever he was with other people, he let himself anticipate their thoughts and then he created esoteric, interactive games through which he gauged his impact and accuracy. He delighted in his success.

In one situation, he might choose passion associated with sex; in another, the idea of petty jealously; and in still another, a powerful feeling of greed.

During the course of routine police investigations the opportunities were endless. He soon discovered the importance of fear. Its application almost always provided the most predictable results. In time, Teddy enjoyed the use of fear most of all. Through fear, he propelled himself to new levels of fulfillment in the pursuit of his self-conceived notion of greatness. The ability to create and administer fear during the course of what might have been an otherwise mindless lifetime kept him focused.

By the time Teddy was twenty and had met Molly Drew, he had practiced his skills casually, but it wasn't until the death of Sam Stemford that he really appreciated the power of his abilities. He engaged in a complex game of acting as policeman in one situation, and as executioner in another, and the extremes provided endless variety for his fertile imagination.

This bold system of behaviors set the stage for the many things he did before he retired as the chief of police of Clinton. Now, after nearly a lifetime of having his own way and playing his own game, he sensed he teetered on the edge of a precipice, looking into the dark chasm of exposure.

This November morning, he sat in a rocker on his front porch and swayed back and forth slowly and pondered his dilemma.

"What to do? What to do?" he mumbled, as he rolled the question over and over in his head.

During his lifetime, whenever he sensed an impasse in a particular situation, the best practical outcome always revealed itself to him. He considered this perception and overview as part of his gift. It was a product of genetic hybridization and contributed to his obvious superiority. At some point, he visualized the best possible outcome and acted things out accordingly, regardless of the consequence to those involved.

In this particular situation, the answer was less clear. Until the recent newspaper article, everything was heading in the right direction. Somehow he missed something. Using Harlan to control the Clinton PD had worked out well. And breaking up the team represented by the granddaughter and the meddling Guilford cop also seemed to work well.

"So, what the hell was going on that suddenly resurrected the news reporter Avery Johnson and most everyone else originally involved with the investigation?" he said out loud. "Even the nipple-head detective, Barry Lands, has somehow become reactivated." The old man rocked and thought and rocked and continued the dialogue with himself. "If no one had interfered, the whole matter would have died a natural death in a year or so. And now, everything is suddenly different."

The more the old man thought about it, the more convinced he became there was something or someone out there guiding events along. It was like there was a cloaked opponent on the other side of life's chessboard, playing directly against him. Someone knew his rules. Someone knew the game. Someone knew Teddy Flanders and understood how he operated. As his mind expanded this idea, he experienced a sudden rush of insight and then everything became crystal clear. It was as though a brilliant diamond pierced his brain and lit up the inside of his head.

In a single fraction of a second, he knew someone else was out there, and that someone was working hard against him. As the idea blossomed, there was a second flood of insight, and then he realized who it was. He clutched his head in his hands and rocked faster in the chair. A terrible, bitter hatred rose in his chest. The image of his enemy materialized in his head.

"That fucking little worm, that crusty skinned little creep. He's trying to take me down and he's not going to make it. Not after he's dead."

Usually rage sealed the fate of disagreeable folks opposing Teddy. It started with rage, but after the rage passed, he was quite the methodical player. He reflected on people much like a baseball aficionado pulls out the highlights of a particular game.

"The power lies in the moment," he said. "The moment, chosen by me, and no one else. Stemford wasn't the first to die and it looks like I'm being called out of retirement."

Teddy, like politicians in ancient cultures, learned dead people, properly contained, get you your best outcome. Teddy realized dead people tell no tales. If there were a problem with the situation today, it was only because he'd not killed anyone in ten or so years. Now he needed to recreate himself, just as he had many times before. If he were to kill again, it would be wise to do it well.

Planning the murder of Allen Drew had its challenges.

Not so tidy as killing a nobody in a dark alley in New Haven, or contriving accidents like Molly Drew. "Too bad, that had to go the way it did," he said. "I liked Molly." But remorse wasn't one of his strong suits and there was no doubt she had to go. "In a way, this was a good thing," he said.

He would not only be an instrument of fate, he'd do it with a touch of poetic irony.

Sixty years later he'd kill the woman's husband, too. "Probably should have done it back then and saved myself all this aggravation."

The exercise in reflection took Teddy to places in his mind unvisited for a very long time. Images of Clara Olson Flanders flashed through his head. "Even Clara had to go. Too bad she became such a pain in the ass."

Teddy married her in 1947, nearly ten years after the events of 1938. After five years married, she took to drinking too much. Teddy was never quite sure why, but he watched while she became more and more combative. It was like she discovered something in her life was rotten, so rotten there was little good coming from anything she did. Little good, except for Harlan, she adored him and did everything possible to widen the gap between him and his father. Often, when he returned home from work, she was already a few drinks down and the same repetitive arguments flew around the table. At some point, Teddy suspected she sensed his true nature and this was somehow the source of the trouble. At any rate, he believed he tried to conduct a normal household. He tried for six years, surviving situations that exceeded his limitations by a great deal.

When Harlan was born, he was even more determined to settle down and create a life of forced complacency. But that turned out to be an illusion.

"Clara was no better than the rest of the women I've

known. Another car wreck, another tragic highway death, another thorn removed from my side."

And when Clara was gone he was free to raise Harlan the way he wanted. Not only raise Harlan, but now Teddy could live the life he wanted. Besides, there was another bonus. Clara had a fifty thousand dollar life insurance policy. The final result paved the way for a widowed chief of police in small town America to enjoy a modicum of privilege.

CHAPTER 47

Emily opened her eyes and realized the yellow light shining in through the curtains was telling her it was much later in the morning than she was accustomed to waking. She lay on her side, fetus-like, facing the window. The gray cat, Isabel, was curled in the hollow between her stomach and knees. Isabel yawned and pressed her front paws, kneading against Emily's breasts. Time to get up.

Behind her, Gordy Powell's breathing was long and rasping. She could tell he was still asleep. Emily felt a kind of ambivalence that struck her as odd, considering she hadn't engaged in any cooperative sexual activities in about a year. She wondered what she was supposed to do next.

How would Gordy behave when he woke up? How was she supposed to behave? She smiled as she wondered if he'd still respect her in the morning.

Emily slowly stretched one of her slender legs from under the blanket and decided to slip quietly to the bathroom. This encounter was a kind of commitment that neither had anticipated.

She reviewed the decision a second time in her head, and surprisingly, she felt nearly as comfortable as she did the night before. Emily believed she trusted Gordon

Powell and knew he trusted her. If nothing else, perhaps that served as a suitable foundation for a lasting relationship.

When Emily finished in the bathroom, she went to the kitchen and started a pot of coffee. Isabel ran ahead, anticipating her breakfast as the first item on her owner's list of to-dos.

Emily's concern for how to behave evaporated as the smell of brewing coffee filled the room. The more awake she became, the less trepidation she felt. By the time she gathered up eggs, sausage, and toast and started heating a frying pan, the notion of uncertainty had all but disappeared.

Hell, she knew what to do, and if he were half the man she thought he was, he'd behave perfectly. This revelation gave Emily comfort and confidence. She felt good about herself.

A few minutes later Gordy, wearing a blanket wrapped like a toga, strolled into the kitchen.

"Good morning," he said in his most polite manner.

"Good morning, Officer Powell," Emily replied. "How were the accommodations?"

"The best since I can remember," he said.

"Well, not to be outdone by what you can't remember, the house is offering a breakfast special this morning. How do you like your eggs?"

"Damn, this gets better and better. I'll have them up, if you please," Gordy answered.

When everything was ready, they sat at the table across from one another and fiddled with the food on plates in front of them. Gordy looked at Emily and decided to take a risk. "I really enjoyed last night. I'd begun to think we were on different wavelengths and would never make a connection. You've been on my mind for months, but I didn't think this could happen. Last night was the first time in a long time that I've felt comfortable with a woman."

"Well you got about as comfortable as anyone could get," she said.

He smiled a response across the table and took a long sip from his coffee cup.

After they finished breakfast, Gordy said, "No matter how much I'd like to stay, I've got to get going. I've still critters to feed."

"I know, don't worry. Get your stuff done. But I would like to sit with you later. How about an early dinner at Francie's? My treat," Emily said.

"Great idea, how about four o'clock?"

"Okay, I'll drive to your place and we can leave from there."

When Gordy left, Emily stacked the dishes on the table and moved everything to the kitchen sink. As she cleaned up, she thought about Charlie Pierce, the ex-husband she had left only two years before. Had there been any reason to continue the marriage?

It's strange how things change. When she married Charlie, she believed they would be together for a lifetime. She had no doubts. In her mind, this knowledge was like a form of faith. An assumption she believed to be fact, and now, the cold truth was there was no connection to Charlie and the lost relationship she had had so much confidence in. In a sense, this was a mystery. The knowledge and review of an experience was the only reality, and there were no absolutes regarding the future.

How could she apply this experience to Gordy Powell? Did the events of last night require she even worry over the situation? Would she again feel faith in a partnership with him? She reflected on an old Billy Graham sermon she had heard regarding the substance of faith in religion. In the sermon, the Reverend Billy reached for a simplistic analogy comparing a person's faith in Jesus to a belief in the conclusion that a common chair will hold the sitter's weight as he was about lower himself. She recalled the eloquent drawl of the preacher in precise detail.

"Of cor—urse, you know that the cha—air will hold you," the reverend declared. "Does it not look like a cha—air. Have you not sat upon countless cha—airs before? The builder of the cha—air certainly knew how to construct it to support your we—ight. Fa—ith in Je—sus is like knowing the cha—air will hold you."

"In fact, the average person's mind doesn't even rattle through such a complex process," Emily said out loud. "They see the chair, and sit in it. Probably, ninety-nine-point-nine percent of the time, the chair will sustain their weight and will not collapse. When I married Charlie Pierce, I had faith in our relationship. I believed the chair wouldn't collapse. Eight years later, not only had the chair collapsed but all the wood incinerated in the crucible of disappointment. Am I ready to sit down again in a relationship with Gordy Powell?"

Isabel began to weave in and out of Emily's legs in an attempt to gain some attention. Emily reached down and picked her up. As the cat lay cradled in Emily's arms, she started the secret little motor signaling feline euphoria. She purred, and purred, and purred.

Emily, still musing, carried Isabel to the living room and lowered herself into her mother's great wingback chair. The chair wrapped itself around the two ladies, and Emily reflected on whether she was ready to try again. Her mother's old chair was sturdy and reassuring. She eased her head back and allowed herself to think about the joy she felt last night.

⁂

As Gordy drove back to his place, he thought about Teddy Flanders. *It seems odd this old man was responsible for bringing Emily and me together.* Without Teddy's participation in the past, it was likely they could have lived out their lives with only a few miles between them, never connecting.

As Gordy puzzled over the irony of the situation, his thoughts brought him full circle to the list of victims involved.

He cautioned himself, "Don't become too grateful. The body count is out there, and whatever this old man's been doing has been pretty sorry for an undisclosed number of people, not withstanding what he may have done to my farm."

CHAPTER 48

Teddy Flanders's biggest problem was how to get near Allen Drew. He certainly didn't need any conspicuous visits connecting him to his victim. Furthermore, how could he make getting rid of Drew something that would give the situation some kind of boost?

"Once I kill the little creep, there should be some kind of benefit to the course of events. That way I can get the biggest bang for the effort."

But what exactly was hard to see. Even after the old man was dead, there wasn't an easy way to slow down everyone else who had been drawn back into the case. Something as profound as killing Drew should be used as a kind of example, but leaving any form of message was going to be difficult to do without revealing himself.

The more Teddy thought about killing Allen, the more convinced he became that he would have to be very creative in order to get the job done at all. Never mind adding in the burden of making a dramatic statement. It seemed unlikely Teddy would be able to persuade the man to meet him at some isolated location.

If Teddy tried to stalk Allen, there was the risk someone would notice him. The easiest way to accomplish the job was probably the most direct.

The more Teddy thought about Allen Drew, the more impatient he became.

Soon, he concluded, "Enough time spent thinking, time to act." The plan materialized in his mind. The lowest risk possible would take him to the top.

A week later, Teddy drove into New Haven and rented a green Buick La Saber at a local Hertz Agency, using one of myriad fake IDs he'd had fashioned in the past. He drove the car back to Clinton and exchanged the license plate with one he stole from a car parked in long term parking at the airport. Then he drove the car up and down a muddy back road in the Haddam woods.

When he finished covering the car with splattered mud, he veered off the road and put on a woman's cotton dress. He paused momentarily, admiring himself in the door mirror. Age had hardly dulled the fierce handsomeness he enjoyed in his youth. Then he carefully placed a long, straight salt and pepper wig over his nearly bald head. He donned a woman's long coat and oversized pumps.

Back in the car, he applied lipstick, rouge, and several strokes of eyeliner. He spent a moment, looking at himself one more time in the rearview mirror, and then he was ready. He took out a Ruger Blackhawk revolver and screwed on a fitted silencer that he had made back when he was still police chief. It was his preferred weapon for termination. Although the gun was out of production, it offered wonderful flexibility. It was a single action revolver; so there was no risk of jams and no shell casings ejected all over the scene. It was manufactured with interchangeable cylinders, so it could be loaded with either three fifty-seven magnums or quieter nine millimeter ammo. There could be no better certainty for death than a Winchester nine millimeter 115 grain Silvertip bullet fired at close range.

He turned out the pocket on the right side of the coat and used a pocket knife to cut a hole large enough for the silencer to penetrate. He placed the gun in the pocket and checked it for fit. The tailoring was perfect and Teddy was pleased with his work.

The night before, he had loaded the revolver from an unopened box of ammo. The Silvertip were the most deadly he knew of, boasting ballistics endorsements that claimed any hit as a lethal hit. The bullet was designed to fragment on impact, and even if the intended target received quick medical attention, there was little hope of recovery. The combination of fragmentation and tissue damage was almost always beyond repair.

The sun was sinking behind the trees in the west as Teddy drove to Allen Drew's home. He knew he must arrive after dark, so he drove slowly in order to maintain his self-imposed schedule. He pulled up, parked in front of the house, and noted there were only two lights on inside one room. He walked up the driveway, went to the front door, and pressed the doorbell.

❧❧

The old man was sleeping in a chair when the persistent chimes dragged him reluctantly from a shimmering dream.

"Bells," said Allen Drew. "The bells from our wedding day, Molly," as oxygen again starved his brain. He raised his head, alert. "No, it's the doorbell."

Allen stumbled to the door and flashed on the outside lamp. The front stoop was bathed in yellow light. He swished open the door and stood facing a pudgy older woman with graying dark hair and a peculiar thin smile. She seemed to recognize him through the screen for a moment.

Then Allen opened the screen and held it open with one arm.

"Molly?"

Without saying a word, Teddy Flanders fired one round low at groin level.

Allen reeled from the bullet's impact. He staggered forward crashing into Teddy. Blood splattered on the open screen as his hands reached out and tore at the dress. Then he fell backward, across the threshold, striking the wall behind him. The tortured expression on the old man's face revealed his confusion and awful trauma. He stumbled, grabbed his groin, and finally fell to the floor. Teddy entered the house and closed the main door behind him. He stood in the light of the living room and smiled down at the crumpled, gasping figure of Allen Drew.

"By the way, Allen, I was in the neighborhood and I thought I'd drop by to see how you were doing. And if you don't mind my saying, you don't look so good at all. Oh dear, you still don't recognize me do you? Well, here's a hint. There are some people you shouldn't mess with. And you crossed the line, my old friend. It's Theodore Flanders. And guess what, I'm still alive and you're not. With that remark, Teddy fired another round into Allen.

Teddy got to work staging the house to look like a home invasion. As he left the house, he never noticed the piece of cloth Allen Drew had torn from the dress.

PART V

Gauntlet

CHAPTER 49

Gordy was in his patrol car when the call came in from dispatch telling of the death of Allen Drew. He sensed right away that Teddy Flanders was involved. He picked up his cell phone and beeped Detective Barry Lands. Ten minutes later, the cell phone rang and Barry was on the other end.

"What's happened?" Gordy asked.

"Allen Drew was shot and killed in his home last night."

"Jesus Christ!" Gordy whispered through clenched teeth. After a few seconds of silence, he asked, "Any leads?"

"Not much. The place is all torn up. Looks like a robbery. The back door is jimmied and the inside's been trashed. It's going to be very hard to tell what's missing."

"Are you thinking what I'm thinking?" Gordy asked.

"Yeah, of course, but so far the only evidence is a torn piece of cloth in Allen's hand. It's from a woman's dress and this crime wasn't done by no woman. Other than that, there's no evidence to connect anybody. I'm still at the Drew place. Doc Steiner and his motley crew just left with the old man's body. Drew took two big ones, both in very bad places. Whoever did it, didn't want any recovery."

After Gordy hung up, he called dispatch and asked for the beeper number of Doctor Merle Steiner. He dialed and entered his cell-phone number. A little while later, the phone rang and Doctor Steiner was on the line.

"Doc, it's Gordy Powell, I talked with Barry Lands, and he told me what happened to Allen Drew. Can you tell me anything about the killing?"

"Gordy, I can't say too much. But whoever shot Mr. Drew wasn't fooling around. This is one of the most brutal executions I've ever seen. The old man didn't have a chance. Even though the scene looks like a break-in, I don't think it was the motive."

"What caliber weapon was used?" Gordy asked.

"Don't know yet, but so far I haven't found any exit wounds. That, in itself, seems pretty strange. I'm gonna be very busy here. Is there anything else I can do for you?"

"No, Doc. Thanks for your help," Gordy pushed the end button on his phone and sat in the cruiser silently. His temples pulsed as anger deep inside overwhelmed him. "The man has gone too far," he growled. "He's gone way too far." Gordy raised a clenched fist and slammed it down on the clipboard beside him on the front seat. The Formica board broke in half under the blow. "Oh, shit." he growled. "That bastard has got to be stopped." He tried to calm himself. "For heaven's sake, don't go off half-cocked. You can't be absolutely certain Teddy Flanders is involved."

Gordy finished his shift and drove to his farm to tend to the animals. When he thought it was late enough for Barry Lands to have made it home, he got in his truck and drove directly to the detective's place. He parked the truck and walked the path to the front door. He knocked, and a moment later Barry's wife Ethel invited him inside.

Gordy offered a polite hello and Ethel showed him to

a large Lazee-Boy recliner in the living room. Her expression showed she knew something was wrong but seemed to dismiss the idea of trying to find out more. Instead, she offered him a choice of iced tea or Pepsi. Gordy realized his effort to conceal his state of mind was not very effective and tried to apologize. She told him to sit down and relax while she went to find Barry.

Ethel left the room, and soon Barry Lands entered and sat across from Gordy. He looked drawn and pale, an appearance Gordy hadn't seen before. No matter how grim events were, Barry usually took them in stride. Often, he had a wisecrack or a twisted, comic view of the darkest situation. Tonight, he appeared distant and cold as he greeted Gordy.

"Sometimes I think I've been in this business too long," he said.

"What have you got so far?" Gordy asked.

"The scene's been corrupted and it's difficult to figure out anything for sure. First of all, we weren't able to lift any prints, so the perp had enough experience to wear gloves. Then the body had been moved around the living room. Looks like he tried to hide it in a closet but gave up when he realized that all he doing was smearing blood all over the place.

"At this point, it's hard to know just where in the room Allen was shot. The place was trashed so badly we couldn't figure out if there is anything missing. We're trying to find a relative who can help us with an inventory of the place. We interviewed everybody in the neighborhood and didn't come up with much. The couple across the street noticed a woman at Drew's door between seven-thirty and eight. She pulled up in a muddy greenish sedan. She left around nine, and that's all anybody knows. We got an anonymous call at eight-thirty this morning telling us that a man was shot during a burglary, and we had best check to see if we could save his life. Milt Cory took the call from dispatch and discovered the mess. The rest is history." He paused. "We're mystified about the piece of cloth. We doubt it belongs to the earlier visitor, and we're convinced no woman did this."

The whisper of a notion floated through Gordy's mind, but the thought was lost. "Well, one thing's for sure," he said, "if Allen was moved around the house, the shooter certainly knew he was dead. That negates the idea of anybody providing meaningful help. The whole deal smells of deliberate confusion, or should I say chaos."

"There's one more peculiar thing," Barry said. "The lower portion of the mesh in the screen door is missing. It looks like somebody cut it out. We're trying to find out how long it's been like that. So far, no one in the neighborhood was able to help."

"After you called, I spoke to Doc Steiner," Gordy said. "From the description of the wounds, it sounds like an execution. For a moment, I got so pissed I almost drove to the Flanders place and beat the shit out of the man."

Gordy hoped, by saying what he felt, he exposed himself to what would have happened if he had acted out his rage. Certainly, he would have lost his job, and perhaps his entire future.

"Just keep a lid on it," Barry counseled. "All the old man needs is for one of us to lose his cool and do something stupid. It would really make him happy. He'd come out looking like a victim and the good guys would look stupid."

"I know, but in the meantime, what are we going to do?" Gordy countered.

"We, my friend, are going to sit tight and gather enough evidence to build a case. That's what we are going to do. As a matter of fact, before this happened, I finally made it to Hartford and secured copies of the ballistics photos from the 1961 Flanders shooting. The lab is still in the process in comparing the bullet fragment from the Chrysler, but the first look indicates that it's a match. I should have the formal report sometime during the week. If you want satisfaction, wait 'til I have a chance to run the results by Chief Forhey. We'll see the shit hit the fan if the match is confirmed."

"Then what?" Gordy asked.

"At that point, we'll get a search warrant approved. Then we'll get into his life big time. That'll be a great opportunity to tear up the old bastard's house. Then we'll see how well he does under some real pressure. We have a case without the gun, but we'd like to seal the deal for good on this guy."

"I'm glad we've got the Allen Drew testimony on tape, at least there is a first-hand account that implicates Teddy in the Stemford murder," Gordy said.

"I don't want to bust your bubble, but having the tape available is a long way from using it as evidence during a trial. I'm sure the lawyers will have a field day arguing the validity of the tape; they might even have it disqualified. Maybe the pressure of exposure will be enough to induce a freaking heart attack. Maybe Teddy will simply drop dead, end of story."

Gordy thought for a moment. "I still want it leaked that a lab is working on DNA samples taken at my barn, even if I have to submit false samples. If we're going to put pressure on him, let's hit him with a blitzkrieg. I want the bastard on his knees."

Barry listened attentively. "Why not?" he said. "The damn test is expensive and I'll have to justify it with the chief, but it'll certainly help to weigh Teddy down."

CHAPTER 50

Harlan Flanders spun the Toyota into the gravel driveway of his father's home. Dust rose in a cloud around the vehicle as the wheels locked up on the stony surface. Harlan threw the door open and climbed down to the ground. He was angry and he could feel his cheeks burn with surplus blood. A lone Rottweiler appeared out of nowhere, ambled toward him, and whined in recognition. Harlan brushed the dog aside and took several great strides across the grounds. He made his way up the porch stairs and over to the front door. He banged on the wooden surface with the back of his fist until the door squeaked open.

Teddy Flanders stood in the threshold and seemed puzzled at his son's hasty arrival.

"Dad, we've got to talk," Harlan said, without even saying hello.

"What the hell's wrong?" the old man asked.

"Chief Forhey spoke to me this morning. He says he's got evidence linking you to the death of Sam Stemford. He also implied he may be able to connect you with the death of Allen Drew."

"That's bullshit, Harlan. There's no way anybody can connect me with anything," the old man said.

"Bullshit or not, Barry Lands is getting a search warrant, right now. And then he's heading out here." Harlan spoke with a sense of urgency in his voice.

"Just what the hell is he expecting to find," Teddy asked.

"Something about a gun. Somehow, they think they have a match between the bullet found in the Chrysler and your old service revolver."

"They're not going to find no old police revolver out here. Besides, even if they did, it wouldn't prove nothin'. If my gun was used, it don't prove I fired it."

"There's more Dad." Harlan swallowed. "The Guilford cop, Gordy Powell, gave samples to Barry Lands. They're supposed to be hair and blood from his barn after the break-in a month ago. They're going to demand tissue samples from your dog to do DNA testing. Chief Forhey thinks you were involved there, too. And that's not all. Forhey claims he has videotape of Allen Drew doing an interview with Powell and the Pierce woman. On the tape, Drew says he believes you killed Sam Stemford and, get this, you even killed Drew's wife."

Teddy's face flushed white, as Harlan revealed more and more secrets he had delighted in hiding for such a long time.

"Dad, you've got to tell me what the hell is going on," Harlan pleaded.

The old man frowned. He realized he had to say something to his son. He always placed great expectations on the boy. After all, Harlan should become his successor.

The younger man, although in his fifties, was not as gifted as his father, so Teddy settled for raising more of a politician than a shrewd, calculating force like himself. The poor lad didn't have the cold detachment required to make things happen. Even Harlan didn't know some of the things Teddy had done on his behalf. Nonetheless, Harlan was his only genetic offspring, and he was entitled to the respect of his father. Teddy decided to give him give him a fragment of truth, just enough to show remorse, but no more.

"Harlan, these folks are going to make trouble for me, and I may need your help," the old man said.

"Tell me," Harlan pleaded.

"Harlan, I killed Sam Stemford," the old man admitted in a quiet tone. "I shot and killed him one night when he was alone."

"Dad, what are you saying? Have you gone senile? Why would you do such a thing?"

"It was a long time ago. Things were different then, and I did what I felt I had to do." Teddy's voice was somber. "There were circumstances I couldn't walk away from. That's why I asked you to quiet the investigation. I wanted to tell you back when Stemford was found, but I didn't want you implicated. I wanted to keep you at a safe distance. Now, there's too much going on. I may need more help."

"What about the other things? Are you responsible for the attack on Gordy Powell's animals? Allen Drew's wife? What about Allen Drew?" Harlan asked, his voice rising with each question.

"Look Harlan, I killed Sam Stemford sixty years ago. What's done is done, and I can't undo it. But that's all I've done, and you should believe it. I didn't do nothin' else. Either it's a strange set of coincidences, or someone is trying to frame me. The more I think about it, the more I believe someone is trying to set me up. What better way to attack an old man and drag him through the mud? Since there's no real evidence in the Stemford case, who-ever's out there is trying to make things happen. If you ask me, I'd say it's that woman from Madison and maybe her cop boyfriend, Powell. They're doing this, just to get to me."

"Dad, I've known Gordon Powell for eight years, and I can't believe he'd mess up his own place in an attempt to get at you. That just doesn't make sense." Harlan paced, raising his hands, and then lowering them. "Maybe you're right about him, and if you are, that leaves only one person left to benefit. Emily Pierce. Wasn't she taking care of the Powell farm when shit happened over there?"

Teddy believed he was truly the king of the spin masters. With his help, chaos would once again rule the day. He felt like he was back in control. He could actually persuade his son to consider the merit of his invented scenario.

☙❧☙

Without realizing the subliminal implant, Harlan found himself thinking perhaps this small-town woman was so consumed with the mystery of her grandfather's death she was willing to go out on a limb to focus attention on his father. Just maybe she was that vengeful and clever.

As Harlan considered the idea Teddy had thrown out, he caught himself and nearly choked on the question that next came to mind. He wrinkled his forehead and wanted to dismiss the idea, but still, he was compelled to ask. "What about the death of Allen Drew?" he blurted out.

"Now what the hell are you trying to say, Harlan? Are you suggestin' I killed ole Allen too?"

"I'm not trying to say anything. I'm simply asking a question. Don't you think it's an odd coincidence?" Harlan continue to pace.

"I suppose it seems odd, but I can assure you I had nothin' to do with it," the old man said.

Harlan studied his father's face for a moment, trying

to read his eyes. His choices were simple, but the implications carried tremendous weight. If he believed Teddy, at the very least, he had just become involved in a sixty-year-old murder. At the worst, he may become involved in another, more recent, murder. Perhaps there were even more.

"What are you going to do now?" he asked his father.

"I'm not sure, boy. I'd like to know how far this Pierce woman is willing to go to implicate me."

"Sure. Dad, it would be nice, but you know you've got to stay away from her."

"Yeah, I know. But I was thinking maybe you could talk to her. Feel her out, get some idea about what's on her mind. Try to figure out where she's coming from. What do you think?" Teddy asked. "Underneath all that fluff, I know you're a charming guy. Just use some of your natural mojo on her."

Harlan hesitated for a minute trying to figure out where such a meeting would take him. Finally with reluctance, he agreed, "I suppose 1 can try and talk to her. But you know Chief Forhey's back on the case and Barry Lands' comin' out here with a search warrant. There's nothing I can do about that."

"Let him come. There's nothin' here to be found," Teddy said, his voice low and husky.

"What do you want from me? Should I stay here with you, or do you want me to leave?" Harlan asked.

"It's probably best if you leave. They probably suspect you're going to tell me all you know is going on. There's no point in rubbing their noses in it. I can handle these fellas on my own. So, go on. Get out of here. Figure out how you're going to deal with the Pierce woman. I'll call you later," the old man said.

Harlan shook his head. "Okay, if you're going to be all right, I'll talk with you later."

CHAPTER 51

As Harlan spoke, he was already heading for the door. Teddy followed him, wondering if he should change his mind and ask his son to stay. Instead, he remained silent and watched Harlan climb into the Toyota and wheel out of the driveway.

The old man had second thoughts a few minutes later, when Barry Lands's big, blue Caprice crunched into the yard. Close behind him, a green and white Guilford patrol car pulled in carrying three uniformed police officers. Behind the patrol car, a green and white Chevy Blazer, bearing sheriff's department markings on the doors, slid to a stop only inches away from the police car.

The big Rottweiler left the barn and barked in rapid throaty reports. As he stood there, the dust began to settle, and he found himself thinking aloud.

"Well, well, I guess the gang's all here," he muttered through clenched teeth.

Five men made their way from the vehicles toward the house. All the while, the big Rottweiler stalked them openly, with its head down, still barking. The men climbed the porch stairs, the uniformed officers with their hands near their holstered weapons. The dog followed them closer to the house.

Teddy watched the scene play out through the window. If the dog hadn't been injured during the attack at the Powell farm, he probably would have gone for the men when they reached the porch, but he was still sore from the broken ribs he suffered nearly four months ago. Teddy figured the dog would make a fuss, but in his present condition would stop short of an attack on four grown men. However, the policemen didn't know that, so it was still good sport to watch them sweat.

They kept nervous eyes on the big dog as they approached the front door: The man from the sheriff's department led the group and banged on the door. Teddy waited a few minutes and finally opened it.

"What can I do for you fellas today?" he asked pretending he had no idea of why they were there.

The man from the sheriff's department spoke. "Theodore Flanders?"

"Yeah, that's me, all right," the old man said.

"We have a warrant to search these premises," the younger man said.

"Can I ask what you're looking for?" Teddy asked.

"We can tell you we're looking for evidence concerning the deaths of Dr. Sam Stemford and Allen Drew," the sheriff's man replied.

Teddy looked past the group and caught Barry Lands's eye. "What about you, Barry, are you going to tell me some more about what's going on?"

Barry's face revealed no emotion as he replied, "Sorry, Teddy. I can't add much more."

"Well, guess there's no point in holdin' you fellas up, then. Come on in," Teddy offered, while pulling the door open wide.

The four men entered the house, split up, and each went a different direction.

Teddy called the dog inside. He sat down on the couch and watched as the men went from to room, methodically picking through all his personal belongings. The Rottweiler lay sprawled out on the floor near Ted's feet and growled softly.

Teddy thought that he was in the proper frame of mind for the search before it began. But as drawers were removed, furniture pushed around, and the ringing sound of shuffling coat hangers echoed from the closets, he found himself becoming more annoyed. How dare these sons-of-bitches invade the sanctity of this place? *Fellow policemen are at work, peeking and poking into my private things. It's none of their friggin' business what's in this house.*

For a moment, Teddy wanted to take his shotgun and blast them all to kingdom come. He let his mind visualize what it would be like. In reality, he had to bear his frustration. There was little he could do in retaliation. For the moment anyway, his only option was to sit there and let them have their way.

Perhaps there was some kind of irony at play. Maybe a spirit of justice watched nearby and smiled as the old man squirmed.

Then one of the uniformed cops suddenly called out, "In here!"

Barry Lands flashed through the living room and joined the young officer.

"Watcha got?"

"We've got an opened box of nine millimeter Silvertips. Looks like twenty-one bullets missing," the uniformed cop said.

A few minutes later, the three cops gathered around Teddy and held the box of nine millimeter bullets in front of him.

Barry Lands spoke first, "Teddy, what are you doin' with these?"

"Self-defense," Teddy replied. "I keep a Beretta nine

in the house for protection. There's no law against that, is there?"

"Did you know that Allen Drew was killed with nine millimeter Silvertips?" Barry asked.

"How would I know that?" the old man fired back cryptically.

"So, where's your nine, now?" Barry pressed.

"It's under my pillow," the old man answered.

Barry motioned to a uniformed officer to retrieve the gun. The young cop left the room and returned a moment later dangling a Beretta semi auto-pistol from a pencil clenched between his thumb and forefinger.

"Well, well. What do we have here?" Barry said, as he removed a pair of latex gloves from his pocket and pulled them over his hands.

He pulled back the receiver, ejected a cartridge, and left the breech open. He then pressed the clip release button, and dropped the clip into his other hand. The clip was filled with Silvertip bullets. He then took the gun and sniffed at the barrel and opened breech. There was a momentary look of disappointment, as he concluded the weapon hadn't been recently fired.

Barry looked at the old man. "Don't you think it's a little curious this Beretta holds fifteen rounds and there are just six other rounds missing from the box. Seems like the right amount to fill a revolver, doesn't it? You wouldn't happen to have a nine millimeter revolver too, would you?"

Teddy still tried to play dumb. "Look. Barry Lands, you're turning into a real shit head. No, I don't own a nine millimeter revolver. There ain't too many made, is there? Besides," he continued, "if you put one in the chamber you can really get sixteen rounds in the Beretta. That only leaves five left over for a six shooter. In truth, I usually keep fifteen in the gun. I used the other six rounds doing some target shooting. There ain't nothing wrong with that either. Why don't you guys just leave me alone?"

"Where were you last Wednesday night, Teddy?" Barry finally asked the question.

"It's about time you asked the hard questions. What happened last Wednesday?" Teddy replied.

"Allen Drew was shot in his home. Did you know Allen Drew?"

"Yes, Barry, I knew who Drew was, but you can hardly say I knew the man. I don't think I've spoken to him in forty or fifty years. I read about the killing, but I didn't have nothin' to do with it. What makes you think it's something I'd know about?"

"Teddy, did you know Sam Stemford?" Barry was moving right along.

"Hell. I knew of the man, over sixty years ago. Hadn't even thought about him, until he was pulled from that pond in Clinton a few months back. Don't tell me you're trying to pin that on me, too. It seems pretty strange you're asking me these questions. When I was a cop, I usually got my ducks in a row before I went off half-cocked, trying to get information from someone. I'd really like to know what you've got that connects me to the murders of both these fellas. Maybe you guys are on some kind of witch-hunt, and just because I'm old, you think I'm easy pickins. With all the press goin' on, you guys are likely to frame anyone just to get out of the news.

"Well, I'm not sittin' here and let my name get dragged through whatever you've got up your sleeve. Now if you boys are done, either charge me with something or get the hell off my place."

Barry gestured to the other cops to head toward the door. He told one of the policemen to bag the box of Silvertip bullets and take them along. After they left, he stayed behind, and when he was sure they were out of earshot, he leaned over and supported himself with his arms on top of the sofa. He looked directly into Teddy's face. The acrid smell of the old man's sweat surrounded the pair like an odorous halo.

Barry narrowed his eyes and spoke in a low tone that sounded more like a growl than a human voice, "Look, old man, it was your service revolver that took care of Sam Stemford. I don't know what you've been doing for the past lifetime, but it's over. If I can't put you away just yet, you better understand it won't be long. I know what you are and what you're capable of and believe me, there is nothing else you're going to get away with. If you so much as appear in my town, I'm going to put your decrepit, sorry ass in a cell. I don't much care whether or not you're a senior citizen, an ex-cop, or your son is on the board of selectmen, you're mine, gramps. Take my advice, pray you have a heart attack before I can get to you."

Teddy admired the intensity of the younger man's glare. Even though the old man was agitated, he simply looked back and managed a casual half smile. After all, this nitwit detective had only an inkling of who he was talking to. And even though the experienced detective believed he knew his man, he really had no idea of what he could do.

CHAPTER 52

Emily had just placed a bowl of cat food on the floor for Isabel when the phone rang. She hurried to the kitchen wall unit and picked up in time to prevent the intercept of the answering machine. She said hello and noticed the voice on the other end was unfamiliar.

"Hello, Emily Pierce?" the strange voice said.

"Yes, speaking," she replied.

"Miss Pierce, my name is Harlan Flanders. I'm on the board of selectmen over here in Clinton and I'm aware of your interest in the murder investigation involving Sam Stemford. I was wondering if I could arrange to meet with you to discuss the case."

Emily was surprised. She knew Teddy Flanders had a son who was in town government in Clinton, but she had never met the man. She never expected to. *Why does he want to meet with me?*

"What's the nature of this discussion?" she found herself asking.

"Well, Ms. Pierce, I thought we might talk and exchange more about what really could have happened that night in 1938."

Emily sensed this inquiry was peculiar, and although she had a genuine interest in talking to Harlan Flanders, there was a caution flag waving in her head. Perhaps, he was sincere, and he did have real information regarding her grandfather and/or the case. More likely, he was acting in some way on behalf of his father.

There was still something wrong, something wrong with what he had just said to her. Then it occurred to her; he had just said, "What could have happened that night in 1938?" How was he so sure the murder happened at night? Was he messing with her, or did he slip, and say something he shouldn't have? She was momentarily confused and wasn't quite sure what to say. She realized this conversation could become a crucial slice of information to add to the case, and decided to play it out.

"Mr. Flanders, are you related to Teddy Flanders?"

"Yes, I am, Ms. Pierce, he is my father," he replied.

"Do you know he may be implicated in the death of my grandfather?"

"I thought we might talk about that," he said.

"Do you think it's a good idea to meet? We probably have a severe conflict of interest running between us," she said.

"I think that's all the more reason to meet, perhaps we may even have some common interests," he countered.

"Well, sir, before I agree to such a meeting, I will need to give it some thought. Give me your number, and I'll take some time to think it over."

Harlan agreed to wait for her consideration and rattled off his phone number.

When he had hung up, Emily immediately dialed Gordy and explained what had just happened. "What do you think, Gordy?" she asked.

"I think that you should meet with the man. But, we're going to add a twist. I'm not sure what he's up to, but you'll have to wear a wire. I truly hope Harlan isn't involved in whatever his father's been doing, but who can say? If you wear a wire, we'll have a good record of everything that's said. Maybe we can use it as evidence later."

Gordy wrestled with idea of bringing Barry and the Clinton PD into the plan, but thought better of it. If the Clinton Chief of Police were involved with slowing activity on the investigation in the first place, his link to Harlan may be closer than imagined. If so, he might blow the whole deal. *No*, he decided, *let's keep out all the non-essentials and see where this is going.*

A few days later, Emily sat in Gordy's kitchen. She was topless on a straight-back chair while Gordy taped a thin transmitter to her lower stomach. He tried to stay very business-like, when she smiled and asked, "Are you sure you don't mind doing this?"

He glanced up, his nose a mere ten inches from her nipples. He cleared his throat. "You're making this unnecessarily hard."

Emily nervously laughed off the comment, thinking if their activity weren't so damn serious, she'd follow his pun with something really provocative. But the situation was serious and she dropped the idea.

In half an hour, she was going to have lunch with Harlan at the Clinton Holiday Diner. She knew this was risky business and the weight of the intended meeting had her less than relaxed. Gordy finished installing the borrowed equipment, and, after a few checks of various fittings, Emily stood up and dressed.

"Remember," Gordy said, "I'll be in the truck right nearby, say as much as you can to learn as much as you can. Keep in mind, maybe he knows nothing, and the whole deal is little more than a fishing expedition. On the other hand, maybe he's been part of everything since the beginning."

CHAPTER 53

Emily drove behind the diner and looked around the parking lot for signs of someone waiting for her. Her eyes finally caught a silver Toyota SUV, with a man seated behind the wheel. She pretended to straighten her hair in the visor mirror, as she spoke into the microphone buried low in her cleavage.

"Gordy, he's here," she whispered.

As she watched, the man opened the door and climbed out. He was thickly built, gray haired with deep set dark eyes, pretty much matching the description given to her by Gordy. He wore khaki trousers and a blue bomber jacket with some type of emblem embroidered on the upper left side. She got out of the car and walked toward him. As she drew nearer, she noticed the embroidered emblem spelled *First Selectman* above the symbol of the town of Clinton, Connecticut.

I guess I've got the right guy, she thought, *but I don't believe the jacket.* She resisted the temptation to shake her head in bewilderment.

The man with the emblem extended his hand like he knew exactly who she was. But just in case she had any doubts, he said, "Ms. Pierce, I'm Harlan Flanders."

Emily took his hand limply. "Hello, Mr. Flanders."

He flashed a phony smile. "Let's grab a bite and talk."

They entered the diner and made their way to an empty booth at the back of the room. As they passed, the owner standing behind the counter acknowledged Harlan with a nod of his head.

The rest of the dining room was filled with people, leading Emily to conclude the booth was held just for their arrival.

As they sat, a middle-aged woman in a white outfit approached the table and dropped two menus. "How ya doin, Harley?"

Harlan grinned. "I'm fine, Trudy, nice of you to ask. Give us a minute and we'll be ready to order."

"I'm not all that hungry. Just bring me some coffee and cream," Emily said before the waitress could leave the table.

"Okay," Harlan chimed in, "I'll have a chicken club and a cup of coffee."

Emily drew back from the table and started, "So what's this all about?"

"Like I said on the phone, I want to become more familiar with the Stemford affair. At least from your perspective," Harlan said matter-of-factly.

"Well, Mr. Flanders, I'm not quite sure why you're asking me, you probably have complete access to the police investigation. After all, doesn't the chief of police work for you?" Although she tried to keep her remarks benign, she realized she might have crossed the line.

Harlan smiled. He was not to be provoked. "Ms. Pierce, I can assure you, Chris Forhey works for the town of Clinton. There is no reporting relationship between his job and mine. That's part of the reason why I asked you to meet with me. I'm curious about what's going on."

"What specifically do you want to know?"

"I guess I'm trying to get a handle on what's happening. I'm not a very good observer. Consider this a kind of interview. For obvious reasons, I need to know the details of how and why my father is implicated in this mess. What do you know that isn't already public record? I need to find out if you're for real."

Emily listened, hesitated for a moment, then added, "You can bet everything you've been told is real. The curious part is your father's success. He's been getting away with incredible feats of mayhem for most of his life. We have information suggesting your father murdered at least two people, and with Allen Drew's death, probably three. Who knows, there may be more. Please understand we were conducting interviews right after my grandfather's discovery. Even then, people like Allen Drew were cautious about what they said. Your father has a long reach back in time. We believe there will be an indictment soon and your father is going down."

"Well, we'll just have to wait and see," Harlan said in a relaxed way.

"Maybe I'm not being specific enough for you," Emily tried a different course. Instead of random allegations, she decided to focus on Teddy's style, "You may know your father better than anyone. Think back, and you'll see the patterns we've identified. Notice when a plan wasn't going right for your dad, something happened that somehow put things back in his favor. For example, he had an affair with Molly Drew just before she died. We have Allen Drew's account of that and what else went on during Doc Stemford's disappearance in 1938. A key thread tying everyone together is your father. Think about other events you alone may know about. Who suddenly died, changed their mind, or simply disappeared while involved with him? Then ask yourself, was he to blame?"

⌒⌒⌒

Harlan glared at Emily. He was getting too much input, and he didn't like it. The idea of shifting from non-specifics to a more comprehensive description of Teddy's style was indeed more discomforting. There were so many events in his life that seemed incredibly lucky. Maybe there was something to what she said, but after all, he was who he was, and in a way he was entitled to a certain amount of good fortune. At any rate, he figured he'd had enough input for one day. "Okay, Ms. Pierce, you've given me enough background, or at least a strong opinion of background, but the proof will come if there is some kind of indictment. If there isn't, I guess the whole business will remain an unsolved mystery."

Emily picked up her coffee cup and drained the contents. "Well then, I guess there's nothing left to say. I've got to go now, but you take care of yourself. Please take my advice. Watch out for your dad and good luck." With that, Emily rose from the chair. "Goodbye, Harlan."

"Goodbye, Miss Pierce."

Harlan sat at the table alone for a while. He thought about his mother Clara. She died, killed in a car accident, when he was only five. By all accounts, Teddy prospered well after her death. Then there was Archie Ridley. He ran against Harlan for selectman eighteen years ago. He suddenly threw in the towel and quit just before election day, even though he had a substantial lead in the polls. Bob Warner, Chief of Police in Clinton before Teddy, died unexpectedly in a hunting accident. Just how many unfortunate events were out there? Was it possible his father orchestrated so much mayhem? *No*, Harlan thought, *no one person could have brought about so many calamities.*

Unbidden, an image came to him, the ghost of another sibling, no, a cousin. His Aunt Beth, Clara's sister had a little girl, Dory. Harlan remembered a chubby child with red hair. She was born with some kind of sickness and cried all the time. *What happened to her?*

Harlan's scalp prickled as he recalled the story of the abducted child. He was so young at the time, the details were sketchy. "This calls for a look at the newspaper archives," he said, as he left bills on the table and hurried away.

❧❧❧

Emily spoke into the wire as she drove back to Gordy's place. "Well, what do you think?" she asked. She realized he couldn't answer, so she stopped, waiting to continue after they were together. She noticed his truck in the rear view mirror and relaxed until she pulled into his driveway. He drove in behind her.

The pair left their vehicles and climbed the stairs together.

Gordy spoke first, "I guess that was a waste of time."

"I suppose you're right," Emily agreed.

"Was there anything in his eyes that didn't come out in what he said?" Gordy was reaching when he asked.

"Maybe," she replied, "For a minute, he looked thoughtful. Kind of like a light bulb went off in his head. It only lasted for a second, but I think he drew some connection to too many coincidences. Maybe even beyond what I told him. I gotta say the jacket he wore was a little much. Kinda gave me the creeps."

"What about the jacket?"

"He was wearing a jacket with a town emblem and his title embroidered on the front. Pretty cool, but way too presumptuous."

Gordy laughed. "When you're 'the man,' I guess you've got to look the part. Maybe we did do something. Let's wait and see what he does next."

CHAPTER 54

The Connecticut shoreline was blessed with mild temperatures, often prevailing well into December. Most likely, the warming effect was caused by the proximity of Long Island Sound. As winter approached, this large reservoir of seawater radiated warm air into the region. Despite the warming effect of the water, there was nothing to be done about the shortened daylight hours of winter.

It was just such a mild winter's day when Barry Lands left the Clinton Police Station in his three-year-old Nissan Maxima and headed home. He had stayed late that day, and he was anxious to leave his desk and languish in front of his own fireplace. As he pulled onto Route 1, he glanced at the digital clock in the dashboard and noticed the time was six thirty. He had been working on the Teddy Flanders case all day and was becoming increasingly more frustrated.

So far, the county prosecutor was reluctant to bring an indictment against Flanders. Even though there was a great deal of circumstantial evidence, the kind of hard, crisp evidence prosecutors like was still elusive. There was no doubt in Barry's mind regarding the old man's guilt, but building a case he could prove in court was still a great leap of faith. At the speed the legal system moved, it seemed Teddy Flanders could just "keep on going."

Barry smiled to himself as he imagined the sleazy old man in a pink bunny suit speeding down the highway with a caravan of SUV's in hot pursuit. In his mind, he pictured a close-up of the driver in the lead vehicle shouting some kind of slogan about the long lasting Teddy batteries.

"That crazy old bastard," Barry said to the windshield. He allowed his mind to jump from the bitter-sweet comic notion of a mechanized Teddy Flanders to the more satisfying idea of spending a quiet night by the fire with his wife.

A few miles went by, and he realized he needed cigarettes for tomorrow. He pulled into a dimly lit convenience store on the right hand side of the road, parked, and nearly got out of the car with the engine still running. He shook his head, turned the key off, and put it in his pocket.

He said, "Just my luck to have the car stolen while I'm getting cigarettes." He went inside and bought a pack of Marlboros.

A few minutes later, he left the store and started to re-enter the car, when he noticed a rather stocky woman at the dark end of the parking lot. She stood in front of a Ford Taurus with the hood up and a confused, helpless look on her face. Barry wanted to go home, but the gray haired woman looked so pathetic. She gestured to him to come to where she was. Barry shook his head and walked to her.

"What's the trouble, ma' am?" he asked.

She pointed under the hood. "It won't start."

Barry bent down and looked under the hood. He was in this position when he glanced to the side and noticed the tear on the bodice of the woman's dress. Right away he knew who had killed Allen Drew, but he was too late. As he tried to straighten, a man's voice emerged from the woman's mouth.

"It's like this, Barry; I really need to talk to you."

Barry nearly hit his head on the underside of the hood, the sound startled him so. A second or two passed, and he realized the woman was really Teddy Flanders.

"Why, you fucking cockroach," Barry uttered as he reached behind his back for the revolver clipped in his waistband. While he reached, there was a sharp whistling sound as a muffled nine millimeter round ricocheted off the macadam near Barry's feet.

"Please don't try that again," Teddy cautioned in his regular voice. "Like I said, I just need to talk to you. Turn around." The old man patted the detective down and re-moved a snub nosed three fifty-seven magnum from the waistband under his jacket. "Now get in the car," he or-dered, gesturing toward the driver's side of the Taurus.

Barry shrugged his shoulders and got in the car. Once in the car, Teddy said, "Start the motor, we're goin' to my place."

CHAPTER 55

Barry put the Taurus in gear and pulled onto the main road. As he drove, his mind raced along on the limited number of possibilities the old man may have had mind when he set up this situation. He supposed Teddy really had something worth discussing and he was taking extraordinary precautions to meet in secret. That didn't make a lot of sense, but given he was an old man, maybe his thought process wasn't easy to follow. The troubling part was that the dress and disguise made sense.

Barry felt new respect for the people who lived across the street from Allen Drew. They had reported seeing an older woman approach Allen's front door the night he was killed. It didn't mean much when he wrote it down, but now the back of his neck began to prickle and a nagging sense of dread filled the core of his stomach.

"What the hell is so damn secret?" Barry asked. "Why the getup? Are you lookin' for some kind of an award as an antique drag queen?"

"Just keep driving. And don't even think about doing nothin' crazy. I don't want to get hurt, and you don't want to get hurt. Just keep in mind you could become terminally injured just before anything happened to me. Like I said, I need to talk with you. And I want to show you something at my place. Just relax, and get us there in one piece."

Barry reached into his shirt pocket for his pack of cigarettes and felt the hard muzzle of Teddy's silenced pistol poke into his thigh.

"Take it easy," Barry said.

"Don't care much for smoking," Teddy said. "Gave it up forty years ago and never regretted the decision. As a matter of fact, I don't even like the smell of it, but you can go ahead if you want. Just don't make quick moves like that."

As they drove along, Barry felt his cell phone vibrate on the side of his belt. He had called Ethel before he left his desk and now he was overdue.

She was probably checking up on him or simply trying to get his attention to stop for something she needed. He let the cell vibrate and showed no indication of the signal.

A half-hour later, Barry wheeled the Ford into Teddy Flanders's driveway.

"What do you think you're doing?" Barry asked. Now he was clearly agitated.

"Like I said, I need to talk with you. And I want you to see something that will help clear this mess up. Get out and walk over to the barn."

Barry climbed from the Taurus and Teddy urged him over to the side of the barn.

"For Christ sakes, Flanders, don't you think this has gone far enough?" the detective asked.

"Well, it would have been far enough, if you didn't take everything so damn personal," Teddy answered. "When you told me you knew what I was capable of, you were dead wrong. You see, if you really knew what I was capable of, you wouldn't have said that. As a matter of fact, you would have been smart enough to try real hard not to piss me off. It was your choice to make this thing personal."

Barry had been trying to force himself to think Teddy was serious about just wanting to talk, but now he realized the old man was probably going to kill him. He gauged just how far behind him the old man was, and then he convinced himself to make a move. He ducked his head, and spun his body around to his right, thinking if he was fast enough, he could take Teddy down at the knees and maybe get the gun deflected. If he was quick enough, he might just disarm the creep.

Teddy expected Barry's move on him and fired the first round just as the younger man turned around. The Silvertip bullet caught Barry Lands high in the left side of his chest, right under the collarbone. The impact threw him to the ground where he lay on his back gazing up. His body felt as though a hand grenade had exploded inside him. He coughed warm blood and it splattered over his face and on the ground. While he gasped for air through his mouth and nose, a large ragged hole in his chest gurgled still another fountain of blood. Unmercifully, he was still conscious and he knew he was dying.

As he lay there, he thought, did he leave enough behind? Surely his fingerprints were on the car, and his DNA could be obtained from the cigarette butt in the ashtray, was it enough? As the old man looked down into his face, he smiled. His dark eyes seemed demonic in the glare of a nearby flood lamp.

There was an instant, perhaps a nanosecond or two, when Teddy Flanders stood exposed, and his true nature was revealed in the night, a grizzled old mate suitable for the she-beast, Grendel. An ancient monster unshackled by the common chains of compassion or pity. He was an entity who survived, and perhaps even prospered in the total disregard of surrounding life forms. Barry's pain became a mere drop in the ocean of fear that followed.

The old man looked down at him and cocked his head in curiosity, as though he were trying to feel the debilitating force of the bullet. As Teddy focused on his face, the detective slipped his hand under the back of his jacket and pushed the button to switch his cell from vibration to sound.

Teddy looked down at the detective and frowned. "Well, Barry, now you know what I can do."

Teddy pointed the silenced revolver at Barry's face and pulled the trigger one more time.

A little while later, the hi-pitched roar of Teddy Flanders's chain saw shattered the stillness of the December night.

CHAPTER 56

While Teddy was busy behind his barn, Gordy Powell and Emily Pierce were having dinner at Francie's Restaurant in Westbrook. There, they enjoyed a relaxing meal and good conversation. It was nine o'clock when they finally left and headed back to Gordy's place for the night.

They pulled into the driveway at Nod Road. Gordy turned the key off and doused the headlights.

As they left the truck, Emily felt the chill of the night air on her face. The night was clear, with a striking canopy of stars filling the sky overhead. Emily paused, looked up, and savored the beauty of the near infinite view of the heavens. Suddenly, she felt a shiver, and then a sense of dread rippled down her spine. She reached for Gordy's arm and wrapped both her hands around it. She wasn't sure whether it was the cold or some mysterious omen hidden in the darkness. Gordy gazed at her and smiled a reassuring smile. A moment later, the motion-sensing outside floodlights exploded away the darkness. The couple climbed the wooden stairs to the front door of the over-sized raised ranch. At the top of the stairs, Gordy unlocked the door and reached in to snap on the front hallway light. He pushed the door open and ushered Emily in. Romulus and Remus greeted her with nuzzles and drools. The cats were perched on the back of the couch.

Emily removed her coat and threw it over the back of a nearby chair.

Gordy went to the closet and began to mount his jacket on a plastic hanger. He stood there, half in, half out, of the closet when the phone chirped.

Emily was nearest to a phone on the kitchen wall, so she picked up the receiver. A moment later, she called to Gordy, telling him Ethel Lands was on the line and she sounded very upset.

"Hello," Gordy said into the hand set.

"Gordy, have you seen Barry? He was supposed to leave the PD at six, and he's still not home." Ethel's voice was high pitched and stressed.

"No. Ethel, I haven't seen or heard from him. Did you call the station?"

"Yes. And I've been ringing him since seven, with still no response. I don't know what's going on, but I know something's wrong. He called me just before he left, and I know he was tired and heading straight home. That was three hours ago and he's not here, and he's not answering his messages. Something's terribly wrong Gordy." Her voice sped up. "I don't know what to do. I've been thinking all kinds of things. You know how frustrated he's become with this Teddy Flanders thing. I was thinking the old bastard is trying to get even. You don't think he would try anything, do you?" She was blurting and not making perfect sense.

"I don't know, Ethel. But it is more likely Barry's doing something else, and he'll show up any time now," Gordy said. While he spoke, his mind considered her suggestion. Would the old man really do something bizarre?

"Look Gordy, I can't get anyone at the PD to do anything. Dispatch says they'll keep an eye out for his car but they're saying he's gonna show up. I know something's wrong. I think I'm going to drive out to the Flanders place and see what's going on," Ethel said with determination.

"No, Ethel. You don't want to do that. Just sit tight. Wait a while longer."

As Gordy spoke, he wondered about Teddy Flanders. If the man did kill Allen Drew, Molly Drew, Sam Stemford, the animals in his barn, and who knows who else, would he kill Barry Lands too?

Come on, he thought. *Barry's a big boy, an experienced cop, he can take care of himself.* Then he thought, *I could say the same thing about Teddy Flanders and probably add the idea he is a highly skilled mass killer.*

"Listen, Ethel, here's what we're gonna do. Sit tight by the phone and keep trying Barry's cell. I'll drive to the Flanders place and check it out. If you don't hear from me by twelve, call the state police and tell them what's going on. Ask them to send the resident trooper over there. Okay? In the meantime, just try to relax. Barry will probably show up while I'm on the way. If he does, try my cell phone."

"Okay, Gordy. That makes me feel a lot better. I really appreciate your help. I'll do what you say, but please let me know what you find. Thanks so much." With that, Ethel hung up the phone.

"What's going on?" Emily asked, as Gordy rested the handset back in the cradle on the wall.

"Barry hasn't showed up at home and Ethel's frantic. I'm going to run out to the Flanders place and take a look around. Why don't you put on some coffee? I'll be back in an hour or so and then we can hit the sack."

Emily looked at him for a long moment. "I don't think so. If you're going out tonight, I'm going with you."

"Please, Emily, I think this may be a wild goose

chase, but it's not a good idea for you to come along. Just be cool and wait for me. Okay?"

"I'm coming along," she said again.

"Goddamn it, Emily. I need you to stay here. If you're with me, I'll have too many things to worry about. It's bad enough I'm being drawn away from you tonight, without you making me feel worse. Please, make some coffee and I'll see you in a little while. Please!"

Emily looked at him, shook her head, and went to the cupboards to look for the coffee. She didn't say a word, but Gordy knew she was angry. He turned, went to the bedroom, and strapped a cut-down thirty-eight-caliber revolver, with a holster, to his ankle. He stuck his Smith & Wesson semi-auto in his belt, along with three clips of ammo in his pocket. He removed his Remington sniper rifle from the closet, and headed for the door.

Emily watched him from the kitchen, and shouted to him as he went out the front door. "Looks like a lot of protection for a wild goose chase." Then she said in a voice that was too low for him to hear, "Take care, I love you."

As soon as she knew Gordy's truck had left the driveway, Emily picked up her coat from the back of the chair and went down to her Camry. She followed him at a safe distance.

⌘

Harlan Flanders sat in his darkened living room. "Damn it," he muttered. The old newspapers had confirmed that his four-year-old cousin, Dory Beth Donovan, had been kidnapped when Harlan was five. The cop investigating the disappearance happened to be Teddy Flanders. The child was never found. Strangely, Teddy never spoke of it. The story made headlines for several weeks, then died down to just a paragraph on the inside pages. Aunt Beth and Uncle James had left town and Harlan never saw them again.

"All right," he said. "I gotta go talk to Dad." His heart was full of sadness and dread.

ᘒᘒᘒ

Gordy pulled his truck off the road and parked as far away from the Flanders house as practical. He checked his watch and noted that it was ten-thirty. He sat there for a moment and surveyed the grounds. A single light shone from inside the house and large floodlights blazed around the barn. Gordy expected a hearty welcome from Flanders's dogs but nothing happened.

The air was still and quiet. The kind of quiet often found on cold New England nights. Gordy wasn't sure whether to go directly to the house or to the barn. The inside of the house was lit, but the barn displayed half-open doors and even stronger lighting. He paused for a moment and then decided to head for the house. As he drew near to the building, he kept an ever-watchful eye for the dogs.

Gordy wasn't aware Teddy had set the surviving dog into the woods behind the house. The big animal took off like a bolt, enjoying his freedom. The old man knew the dog would have been a nuisance as he prepared Barry's body for disposal.

While Gordy walked toward the house, Teddy was in his barn laying out a number of large plastic bags on the floor. He wore a great rubber apron as he went about his work, unaware Gordy was outside.

Gordy slowed as he neared the porch, and just before he climbed the stairs he heard a curious sound. Like a cell phone ring tone. The tiny sound of a muffled cell might as well have been the hammers of hell being swung by a dozen demons shattering the silence of the night. The sound, amplified by the still, cold air was deafening to Gordy's ears, as he remembered he had told Ethel to keep trying Barry's cell.

"Holy shit," Gordy muttered to himself, and he released the semi-auto from his belt.

He cocked his head and tried to focus on the direction of the sound. He knew he had a limited amount of time before it stopped. He turned and started walking in the most likely direction, which seemed to come from somewhere near the barn.

As he walked, he hoped to hear the second round of rings that should happen if the first message wasn't retrieved. Sure enough, a minute or so later the ring repeated. This time Gordy homed in on the second round of rings and quickened his steps to the back of the barn.

As he turned the corner, the gaze of Barry Lands's lifeless eyes greeted Gordy. His disembodied head hung from a hook on the barn wall. There was a neat black hole in his forehead. The back of his head was splayed open like some kind of Halloween mask. A great plastic sheet lay on the ground, and like slices of lunchmeat, the remains of Barry Lands lay neatly sectioned.

Gordy gasped and vomited. He struggled to reach inside himself to curb a rush of panic that tugged at the core of his body. Something in his mind told him to run, to run so fast the evil lurking here couldn't catch him.

In the midst of the terrible fear, there was the voice of his training that kept interrupting the idea of flight. Deep inside, something said: "If this moment is lost, evil will prevail, and all innocence will become victim. Babies slain in the night. Mothers, fathers, grandmothers, and grandfathers could forever remain fair game for the slaughter."

The idea of grandfathers brought Gordy full circle, and his mind focused on the image of Emily. He knew if he didn't stop this monster here and now, no one would ever be safe. The idea anchored him for a moment, and slowly Gordy crawled from the mire of panic. With great force of will, he harnessed the fear that permeated his very soul. Gordy opened his cell phone and called for backup.

ᥫᩣ

While Gordy was checking the Flanders place, another drama had already played out on a shoreline highway. Twelve miles away, Betty Atkins and Jamie Sutton were cruising Route 1 in the town of Guilford. Jamie bought a couple of six packs of PBR, and they spent an hour or two drinking in the parking lot of the Cove Marina. It was a pretty safe place and Jamie's dad kept his boat there so the car was equipped with bar-coded sticker. They drank for a while then made out for a while, and when they finally satisfied their primal needs, they decided to drive north to Chubby's, a cool little hamburger joint in Clinton. On the way they never expected to meet Ginger Olson.

Ginger had just acquired a new-fangled cell phone and couldn't wait to use it. She drove south on Route 1, struggling with the little buttons on the tiny phone. "Press red phone icon until musical signal, phone is ready. Done. Dial number, press green phone icon. Wait for ring. Done. Oops! Nope. Oops!"

Ginger Olson's brand new Chrysler Concorde side-swiped Carl Samuelson's vintage Hudson next to her and sent it flying into the northbound lane of Route 1. That car swiped Evan Bonasera's Buick. It careened into Jamie Sutton's dad's brand new Chrysler LHS, sending it into the parking lot of an all-night pharmacy. All told, the Concorde had taken out seven cars, including three in the parking lot. The wrecks covered all four lanes of Route 1.

No one was hurt seriously, but a few folks required ambulances. Those vehicles, state police cars, local police, other motorists' cars, and a hundred rubberneckers jammed Route 1 from Madison to Guilford, CT. Every cop for miles was at the scene—every one except for Barry Lands and Gordy Powell.

"Don't do anything. Do ya hear, Gordy?" dispatch answered. "We'll get there as soon as we can. Back off for now. As long as you're sure no one else is in danger, go sit in your truck and wait for help. We have a monster pileup on Route One. I'll get someone out there ASAP."

CHAPTER 57

Inside the barn, Teddy thought he heard a noise coming from outside. After years of listening to gunfire, his hearing had become unreliable. He considered whether or not he should stop and look around. At times, some sounds went right by him unnoticed, but not tonight.

The old man convinced himself he had heard something, however faint.

After the second repeat of Barry's cell, Teddy removed his single action Ruger pistol from under his apron and unscrewed the silencer. He opened the cylinder and checked the ammo. He counted the unfired rounds. *Only three shots left in the gun, and they're plain old nine millimeter wad cutters*, he observed.

Teddy wasn't aware that Gordy was outside when he muttered, "That damn Barry Lands used up the last of my Silvertips, and the bastard confiscated the box, during his lame search. Well, I guess I showed him."

The old man went to the large front door and eased his body into the yard. He moved slowly around to the corner of the barn and peered down, alongside the wall. There was no one there. He was about to walk down to the next corner, when he noticed a shadow cast by an overhead floodlight, moving across the ground.

"What have we here," the old man asked himself softly.

If someone else had stumbled into the party, they simply couldn't stay very long. He humored himself with the idea of dismissing any unwanted guests. Of course, his concept of dismissal was annihilation.

⋐⋑⋐⋑

Gordy wished the outside lighting wasn't so powerful. This was one of those few times in life, when more darkness would have been appreciated. He could see everything around him, and what was worse, anyone nearby would find him equally easy to see. Besides, Barry's remains were all too clearly visible and the sight was wretched.

Gordy had forced his eyes to search the mess on the plastic tarp in hopes of spotting the cell. If it kept going off, Teddy would eventually hear it. There was no doubt it was somewhere near the body, but he hadn't the stomach to poke around and look for it. Instead, Gordy thought, he'd be better off finding some cover while he waited for the state police. All he had to do was stay alive until then. He left the bloody slices and began to make his way toward the shadows on the other side of the barn.

⋐⋑⋐⋑

Harlan Flanders was anxious. He took a little known shortcut and drove to his father's farm. He could see the place was lit up and hoped all was well. He felt a strange mixture of fear for his father and fear of what his father may have done. Things were adding up, and Harlan didn't like the answers.

He parked on the dark side of the house, intending to

use the back door. By the time he left his car, he found he was breathless. "Dad! Dad?" He called into the kitchen.

No answer.

Harlan ducked outside again and headed for the barn. As he reached the side door, a familiar odor from the two cycle chain saw exhaust wafted to his nostrils, it was combined with the metallic smell of blood. Then he saw the back of his father exiting the opposite side of the long building and he was about to cry out when he noticed the exploded head of Barry Lands hanging on the outside wall. He stopped and, instead of entering the barn, walked toward the mangled face. A wave of nausea swept through him as he recognized the severed head. He clutched his stomach and as his gaze moved downward he saw the bloody slices. Harlan gagged, and tried to fight back the revulsion he felt then silently collapsed to the ground as he fainted.

⌘⌘

Gordy still wasn't sure whether Teddy Flanders was in the house, in the barn, or somewhere on the grounds. Since the dogs weren't close by, and he didn't seem to have been spotted yet, he still figured his best option was to try to get away from the buildings and back to his truck. He'd be safer there, waiting for the State Troopers to arrive.

He walked around the back of the barn, thanking the Almighty for the lack of windows along that particular wall. He surveyed the area and decided his best move was to get past the circle of floodlights and reach the shadows beyond. Once there, he would have a better chance of blending into the night. The trek meant that he must get at least fifty feet from the barn before claiming the natural shadows of the woods.

Finally, he shuffled across the side yard and then decided to make a quiet run for it. He perched himself on the balls of his sneakered feet and raced for the shadows. Gordy had gone about twenty feet from the barn when a round pierced the back of his right thigh and bore right through to exit into the night air.

Gordy felt as though someone had whacked him with a spiked mace. The wad cutter bullet passed though the muscle of his leg, narrowly missing his thighbone and the vulnerable femoral artery residing there. The tissue around the bullet burst as the pressure wave in front of it plowed through him. He spun on his good leg and nearly cartwheeled from the impact. So much for watching and waiting. In his mind, he needed to keep running but no longer had the machinery to do it. He felt frustration, then fear, and finally the searing pain of the bullet.

After the erratic flounce, Gordy's body crumbled. He tried to break his fall with his hands but the tumble was out of control and he felt his face scuff along the ground. Finally, he lay sprawled on the ground like a rag doll. Somehow, the Smith & Wesson he so often relied on was thrown from sight. A blur of consciousness cursed through his head and something inside him cried for any form of escape. The world around him faded in and out of focus, and the bark of a dog sounded in the distance.

∾∾

Teddy waited to be sure the younger policeman was disabled. He wasn't sure whether there were any backup cops around. If there were, they wouldn't stay silent and concealed for long. Finally, the old man called out to the wounded cop.

"That you, Gordy?"

"Yeah. It's me."

"You come alone?"

"Yeah, I'm alone."

"Backup coming?"

"Nope," Gordy lied, hoping the lie would buy more time.

While Gordy spoke, he had no idea Emily had followed him to the Flanders place. She turned off the headlights and coasted to a silent stop behind Gordy's truck. She had a bad feeling about Barry's disappearance. She decided to wait and sat patiently in the car.

Startled by the sound of a gunshot, it took her several seconds to understand the meaning of the noise and the possible consequences. A sick sensation rose in her stomach. *Is Gordy in trouble? What can I do?*

Quietly, Emily opened the car door and closed it. She went to Gordy's truck and eyed the .308-scoped rifle behind the seat. She picked it up and studied the rifle carefully. She had watched Gordy dismantle and clean it several times after a session at the PD range. She never did learn to shoot it.

She dropped the clip and noticed there was but one bullet left. She returned the clip and opened the bolt and the remaining round slid into place. Then she closed the bolt, locked it, and realized the gun was chambered and ready to fire. She inspected the rifle for a trigger safety and tried to determine its position. In the dim light, she couldn't be sure of the symbols or their meaning. But she knew this must be the safety and in one position or the other the gun should fire.

She lifted the lens covers at either end of the scope and shouldered the weapon, pointing at the moon high overhead. She peered through the scope, tucked the rifle hard against her shoulder, and pretended to fire it. She tried to imagine the burst of sound, the flash of the muzzle and finally the mule-like kick of recoil.

There in the moonlight, Emily's shadow cast on the ground resembled the ancient figure of Artemis raising her bow, ready for the hunt.

❦

Teddy emerged from behind the big barn door and slowly walked toward the downed cop.

"What the hell were you thinkin, boy? Did you really believe you could come out here alone, raise hell at my place, and simply walk away? Not gonna happen. By the way, how's the leg doing?" the old man asked. "I bet it hurts like a bitch. I think I'm gonna believe ya. You probably didn't bring anyone with you. If you had, they'd have come out by now. Actually that was a pretty dumb thing you did. Coming out here alone was risky enough all by itself. Coming out here while I'm busy at work is just plain fatal. I'm gonna have to kill you tonight. But that's not so bad, because I was gonna kill you sooner or later, anyway. Might's well be tonight as any other time."

❦

Gordy lay on his back, but he had regained full control of his faculties. The wound hurt, but now he had bigger concerns on his mind. His only hope of survival was to stall the old man long enough for the police to arrive or to somehow get the hideaway gun out of his ankle holster. He tried to move his legs in such a way as to minimize the risk of Teddy seeing the weapon. As he moved, he spoke to the old man, hoping to distract him away from his leg.

Teddy walked closer to Gordy and stood directly over him. He stretched out his arm and pointed the Ruger at Gordy's face. He cocked the hammer and closed one eye, let the other follow a line down the barrel directly to Gordy's forehead. Gordy braced himself for the impact and the idea of painful oblivion sickened him. He closed his eyes and waited.

"You were lucky," Teddy said. "I used up all my deadliest bullets. If I had hit you with one of those babies, you would have bled to death by now. Since you're still alive, how about some conversation?" As he spoke he let the gun drop and smiled. It was as though he were a great old cat and Gordy was his injured mouse. He could take a moment and let Gordy's fear become rekindled by the spark of a small delay. Why kill the man, when he was still in shock from the first hit? Wait a few minutes longer and Teddy knew it would be so much worse for Gordy Powell.

Gordy opened his eyes and looked up at the grizzled old man in the rubber apron. He felt such contempt that he nearly reached for the hideaway gun regardless of the risk. He gathered himself together and managed to achieve a sitting position.

The old man watched and said nothing to hinder Gordy's effort.

"So, tell me, Teddy, when does it end?" Gordy finally said.

"For you, it ends pretty soon. For me, maybe it doesn't end," the old man answered.

"What kind of bullshit is that? Have you been going through life, stealing souls, thinking the more you take will somehow add to your own pathetic longevity? Is that your own demented formula for growing old gracefully?"

"Gordy, my boy, I never looked at it with so much precision, but it may well be just how it works. Silly shitheads like you ordinarily wouldn't have a clue, because you aren't able to do the things I have done. Things, like this."

Once again, Teddy raised the revolver and pointed it at Gordy's head. This time Gordy denied the terrible fear that gripped him earlier. He grinned at the old man, reached for his ankle gun and said, "Fuck you, Teddy Flanders. Fuck you!"

Gordy heard the shot. He winced then suddenly realized he wasn't struck, and Flanders hadn't fired his gun. The evil bastard is playing with me, he thought. And then he noticed the old man's expression change from sardonic smile to contorted grimace. There was a round black hole in the middle of the gray rubber apron. A hole so small it was barely noticeable.

Teddy certainly noticed, and a second or two passed while his body reacted. He let out a growl, a low rumbling wail that seemed to surprise even him. Teddy lowered his arm as though the weight of the revolver had suddenly become a hundred pounds. His face twisted, and his body spun around as if he were controlled by an unseen puppeteer.

The old man wailed again, and Gordy saw a portion of his back and realized what was happening. There was a large hole in Teddy Flanders's back. Gordy knew it was an exit wound and whatever went through the old man's belly had dragged a length of gut from inside his body. Teddy staggered and then he seemed to regain enough strength to raise the revolver again.

Gordy realized the next few microseconds would be the most important of his life. In one precise action, he drew the thirty-eight special from his ankle and fired.

"For Molly—and Sam—and Allen—and Heckle and Jeckle—and Pirate and Penzance—and Ivan."

All six rounds plowed into the flailing torso of Theodore Flanders. When the gun was empty, Gordy held it steady and pulled the trigger two more times to be sure no bullets were left. When he was sure the gun was empty, he let the weight of the revolver drop his hand to the ground.

Exhausted, Gordy sat holding the warm revolver in his hand and waited. Teddy Flanders lay nearby breathing irregularly. He made a raspy, liquid sound as his body drew in air, only to have it leak out through ruptured lungs.

"Die!" Gordy screamed. He pounded the ground beside the old man. "Die! Die!"

Teddy Flanders died.

Gordy rested his face in the crook of his arm and sobbed.

He waited another minute or two and then painfully rose to his feet and looked around for his savior. There was no one near him, and for a moment he couldn't see anything beyond the light cast from the overhead lamps.

Finally, the figure of a woman shuffled from the outlying darkness. The woman glided in, dragging a scope-mounted .308 bull barrel rifle along the ground. Gordy saw Emily and was overwhelmed. Feelings of gratitude and admiration competed for the front row of his emotions. Tears streamed down her face as she wrapped her arms around him.

Emily held Gordy as if he were an apparition who could evaporate into the night if he were left unrestrained. The two gripped one another with more than tender strength, and the icy fear of their experience melted in the warmth of the embrace.

While they stood holding each other, the sound of barking penetrated the night air. The noise came from the direction of the woods and Gordy remembered the barking dog when he was first struck. And then he realized Teddy's dogs were still unaccounted for.

Gordy had no idea that one of Teddy's dogs was already dead, killed by Sammy's hooves during the raid at his barn. As far as he knew, both dogs were still alive and living with Teddy. Gordy swallowed hard, looked deeply into Emily eyes, shook his head, and whispered, "It's not over."

"What do you mean?" she asked

"Get Flanders's gun," he whispered again.

Emily let go, went to Teddy's body, reached down, and picked up the single action Ruger.

Then it started. A growl rumbled somewhere in the darkness outside the pool of light. The growl was so low that they felt the vibration before they actually heard it. Hair on the back of Gordy's neck bristled, and he realized the dog was watching them. *Strange*, he thought, *I hear only one dog*. One dog, two people, what were the odds of a dog actually taking on two grown human beings? He reached to his belt, gestured to Emily, and exchanged his cell phone for the Ruger.

"Make the call," he ordered. "Call nine-one-one. We need to get our backs to a wall until we get some help."

"Oh, God, the line is busy," Emily wailed.

"The pileup on Route One," Gordy said. "Try again in a few minutes."

Emily provided physical support as she and Gordy stumbled toward the barn wall. In the background, somewhere in the darkness the dog howled a long, lonely cry into the night.

CHAPTER 58

Gordy and Emily stood huddled. Gordy, his face blanched white, began to show signs of fatigue and loss of blood. Emily looked at his wound and realized he was still bleeding. In the synthetic light of the overhead halogen bulbs, the wet blood on his trousers looked black, like a strange dark syrup.

She looked at Gordy. "Are you going to die?"

Gordy shook his head. "Everybody's gonna die," he managed to say. "But I don't think I'm gonna die today."

Emily smiled a crooked half smile, "I love it when you're a smart ass." His remark gave her renewed confidence. "What do we do, now?"

"We've got to slow down the bleeding. We've got to get back up, and we've got to get the hell out of here," Gordy answered. All the while, he pointed Teddy Flanders's gun at the surrounding darkness, disguising his pain and growing nausea with a macho pose.

Emily removed her jacket. "You look for the dog, and I'll try to slow the bleeding." As she spoke, she ripped off her blouse, tore off the sleeves, and made two layers of makeshift bandages.

Gordy reached in a pocket, removed a William Henry pocketknife, flipped it open, and passed it to Emily. "Use this," he said.

She crouched, inserted the blade carefully avoiding flesh, and split the entire length of his pant leg. Then she wrapped the strips of sleeves around Gordy's thigh, trying to identify the entrance and exit sides of the wound.

"Ouch," Gordy yelled.

They heard it again, the unmistakable low-pitched growl of the unseen dog. This time the sound seemed closer. Gordy considered firing one of the remaining rounds into the darkness. Perhaps the noise would frighten the animal away, but the cost of such an experiment would result in even less ammo.

Emily wiped Gordy's blood from her hands with the last remnant of her blouse, picked up the cell with one hand, and punched in 9-1-1 with the other. The Durham PD answered the call. Emily explained the situation and demanded an ambulance. The dispatcher said he already got the call and police and ambulance were on the way. The pileup on Route 1 had delayed them, but they assumed Gordy was still waiting patiently in his truck.

"Who made the call?" Emily muttered.

"Anonymous," was the reply.

She ended the call, searched the call index, and punched Send on the phone number of Clinton Chief of Police Chris Forhey. Then she passed the phone to Gordy.

Chris Forhey answered his phone with a gruff, "Hello."

"Chris, it's Gordy. We're at Teddy Flanders's place. I've been shot. Barry's dead, Teddy's dead, and we're being stalked by one of his dogs. You need to get a crew over here pronto. And while you're—"

Gordy stopped in mid-sentence. There was a sound from above. *Something's on the roof.* He looked up in time to catch the shadowy figure of a large Rottweiler crashing down upon him. The dog struck with the force of a hundred-pound sandbag. The force of the blow, although glancing, squeezed all the air from Gordy's lungs, and he collapsed in a pile of arms and legs. Behind the barn were a stack of old crates arranged by the wall and they provided make-shift stairs to the roof. The dog had used them before and used them again tonight to gain a better view of the commotion.

Emily screamed so loud the dog momentarily slowed its onslaught. In that split second of delay, Gordy was able to protect his throat with his forearm. Unfortunately, it was the arm holding the gun. The action bought just enough time, because the dog bit hard on his arm instead of his vulnerable jugular, but the defensive move rendered the gun useless, as it couldn't be pointed at the attacker.

Emily, desperately frightened, shrieked at the animal. "Get away," she yelled "Go, you ugly bastard,"

Anxiously, she looked around the ground and gagged at the sight of Barry Lands's body. Breathing hard and holding a hand to her mouth, she turned her sight to the doorway, and the walls. The only thing resembling a weapon was a shovel Teddy left leaning against wall. She took the shovel and struck the dog about the head and shoulders. She struck as hard as she could, but the dog seemed unstoppable. Gordy regained some of his breath, but the dog shook his arm like it belonged to a rag doll.

He had a choice to make, let go of the gun and hope Emily could pick it up, or try against overwhelming force to get the dog off long enough to get a shot at it. The dog seemed fixated on Gordy's right arm, so much in fact he decided to try to change hands. If he could grip the gun with his left hand he might be able to get a shot directly into the animal's body. If he lost the gun, Emily might be able to pick it up. The danger lay in that she'd be shooting into the thrashing mass encompassed by both Gordy and the dog. Then he heard the scraping of teeth against bone as the dog's jaws clamped tighter. *Not much time,* he thought.

Gordy pushed his left arm against the dog's throat, trying to keep some of the pressure away from his own neck. Now, he grabbed his right hand with his left and tried to release the gun from the sacrificial arm and put it into service. The shaking of the dog's head took a toll and then he heard the terrifying crack as the radius bone in his forearm shattered. The only remaining protection between those teeth and his throat was the ulna. When it broke, there would be a clear path to his throat. Gordy wrestled the gun free. He managed to grip the trigger along with the guard, and then remembered the gun was a single action revolver. He would have to cock the hammer before he could fire it.

Suddenly he felt a hand on his hand. Then someone pried the gun from it.

Somehow, in the chaos, the shrill of Emily's screams, the thwacking sound of her blows with the shovel, the throaty growl of the attacking Rottweiler, there was the sound of a gunshot, quickly followed by the high pitched yelp of an injured dog.

Then the dog relaxed its grip, seemed to cross its eyes, and staggered back from Gordy Powell. The animal spun around and bit its own soft underbelly, snarling and yelping at the same time. Again and again the dog spun away until it disappeared into the darkness.

A man stood in the moonlight.

ᔕᓬᔕᓬ

Harlan Flanders had waited until the last minute to save Gordy's life. He stood quietly for a moment, and then threw the gun to the ground. He was covered with blood and vomit. He managed to make it as far as Emily's car, and, for the second time in his life, he passed out.

Gordy rolled over and collapsed on his back, panting as though there wasn't enough air on the planet to satisfy his need. Emily fell to her knees, cradled Gordy's head in her lap, and sobbed.

"Gordy, tell me you're okay," she finally managed to say.

Gordy Powell was shot and broken, but incredibly alive, and in the arms of a woman who cared deeply for him. He forced a smile and spoke, "Like I said, I'm not gonna die today."

Surprisingly, Chris Forhey's chief of police cruiser arrived at the scene before anyone else. He was met by a mumbling, trembling Harlan Flanders. Both men left the vehicle and hurried toward Gordy and Emily.

"What the hell happened?" Forhey shouted.

"It's like I said on the phone, when I got here Barry was already dead. Teddy was using the chain saw to cut him up. He shot me and was ready to finish me off when Emily stopped him."

"He's telling the truth." Harlan's voice shook with emotion. "I saw Lands behind the barn. My father was a monster."

Gordy hesitated as he watched Harlan look at his father. "One of the Flanders dogs is still out there," he said, "It nearly tore my arm off before Harlan shot it. The sucker's out there somewhere and it's as mean as the old man."

Harlan knelt beside the prone body of his father, his head shaking back and forth in denial. "It's not possible, none of this is possible," he muttered in a tone almost too low to be heard.

In Harlan's mind, the events of the past year spun by

in movie-like scenes. He had connected all the dots from the time Gordy asked to meet with Teddy, right up to the day Emily told him about his father's connection with the Stemford murder. As he knelt beside his father, his face paled with anxiety.

Chris Forhey left Gordy and walked to Harlan who stood over the bullet-riddled body of his father. The blood-soaked ground beneath his feet offered proof enough of Teddy's death. As a formality, Chris Forhey crouched low and placed his fingertips on Teddy's carotid. "Nothing to be done here," he said. "I'm sorry, Harlan." Then, realizing he was in a crime scene outside his jurisdiction, Forhey withdrew from Teddy's body, saying, "Don't touch anything, Harlan. The Durham PD should be here any minute and everything will be locked down tight."

CSCS

Three more patrol cars pulled in close to the barn. The first was a Durham PD car, and the other two were high-performance state police cruisers.

The three men got out of their respective vehicles with their guns drawn. They walked around the scene, huddled together for a moment, then nodded to one another and walked to Gordy.

At that point, they began asking questions. Gordy was in a great deal of pain and, as he went through the details of what just happened, he felt weak and nauseous. Finally, an ambulance arrived, followed immediately by several more state police cars.

Chris Forhey explained his involvement in the case and Harlan Flanders gave his statement.

CSCS

Harlan stood silently nearby as crime scene specialists cordoned off the area. He was angry. He was angry with Teddy. He was angry with Emily Pierce and Gordy Powell. They not only killed his father but also killed the last chance to learn so much about so many things. What happened to his mother? Was there more to her accidental death than was ever reported? He must have killed Clara, too. If Teddy killed Molly Drew, using a car crash, could he have done it again? With Teddy dead, Harlan may never know.

More questions flooded his mind. What happened to the opposition during his first bid for political office? What happened to Allen Drew? What happened at Gordy Powell's farm? Was Teddy the common chain linking all of these events? All he knew was that he'd rushed to the scene to save his father from Gordy and ended up saving Gordy from his father. The carnage behind the barn confirmed that his father was indeed a vicious killer.

There was no doubt in Harlan's mind, all of these questions were going to surface and beg resolution. With Teddy dead, there may not be simple closure to so many open questions.

Three EMTs started intravenous drips on Gordy, placed him on a gurney, and loaded him into the ambulance. When they were done, the combination of bandages and tubing turned him into a candidate for audition in a hospital drama.

As the ambulance lurched out of the Flanders driveway, Ethel Lands arrived chauffeured by another Clinton Police car. She wore a grim expression as two other officers held her back on the sidelines.

CHAPTER 59

By five a.m., the cluster of vehicles and the number of people converged at the Flanders place suggested the look of a Hollywood set. Among those present were Dr. Merle Steiner, New Haven County Medical Examiner; Chief Chris Forhey, Clinton PD; Harlan Flanders, First Selectman, Clinton town government; Chief Terry Deering, Madison PD; Chief Markus Griswald, Guilford PD; Trevor Johnson, Durham PD; Avery Johnson, Senior Staff Writer *The New Haven Reporter*; Ethel Lands, wife of Detective Barry Lands, Clinton PD. In addition there was a complete TV crew from Channel 3 News.

The Rottweiler was never found and its fate remained a mystery. Pending completion of the investigation by the state attorney general's office, no charges were filed against Gordy Powell, Emily Pierce, or Harlan Flanders. Early, during the investigation, Harlan Flanders quietly resigned his position with town of Clinton.

For years to follow, the events gave citizens in the towns of Durham, Branford, Madison, Clinton, and Guilford, Connecticut, fodder for gossip and rumor over coffee and card games and pillow talk. A mass killer had lived and worked in their midst for sixty years, with no one the wiser.

Four days after the initial story died down, Barry Lands was laid to rest. The next day, Harlan Flanders buried his father.

Emily Pierce scattered her grandfather's ashes over the surface of the new pond near Gordon Powell's farm.

Allen Drew was buried next to his beloved Molly.

Given the evidence that authorities turned up on Teddy Flanders, it was decided that a thorough search of his property was in order.

On a gray morning, a day after the last funeral, twenty-year-old Randy Riley stood on the west side of Teddy Flanders' barnyard. The young policeman's so'wester was soaked from an earlier storm and he was cold. The cadaver dogs had been thorough, so he gamely struck his shovel in the mud and began his grim task.

After the first body was discovered, the place took on the look of an archeological dig. Brooms and brushes replaced shovels and a forensic anthropologist was brought in. At the north side of the barn, the scientist gently lifted a metal suitcase from a shallow grave. It contained a juvenile skeleton. She closed her eyes for a moment and then placed the case in a plastic body bag.

Harlan Flanders watched the scientist's aides carefully digging on his father's property. Inside the barn lay eleven bags, holding the remains of other lost souls. There was a beep, beep, beep behind Harlan. A huge coroner's wagon pulled into the yard.

The corpulent driver leaned his head out the window and addressed him, sucking on a sodden cigar. "You in charge of the bone yard?"

CHAPTER 60

Emily sat in the dim light of the library's computer room and stared at the genealogy chart on the screen. Her innate curiosity made her need to know Teddy Flanders's family history. Earlier, she had perused many newspaper articles about the disappearance of several persons in the area.

Emily knew the approaching storm would force her to turn off the machine, but she had made a lot of progress and refused to stop until the storm got worse.

"Gordy's coming home tomorrow," she said. "I won't have much time for this later."

Gordy Powell left the hospital one day early. He'd heard about the finds in the Flanders barnyard, but he didn't go there. A more urgent task awaited him.

෭෩෭

At last light, Gordy turned his truck into his yard. The two young Nubian goats had been lulled to sleep by the truck's movement. Now they were wide-awake and bleating.

Wincing from his still tender arm and leg, Gordy gently lifted the animals and set them down. "There you go, little fellas," he said. "Welcome to your new home. Tomorrow, we'll ask Emily to help us decide on names for you."

The goats skittered about, then bleated as the first glimmer of lightning touched the sky. Romulus and Remus greeted the little critters with whimpers of joy. Gordy opened the barn door amidst rolling thunder and showed the goats their sleeping quarters. Sporting lightning-shaped scars on his legs, Ivan gingerly walked from his open stall and nuzzled the new arrivals.

Gordy led the big horse back to his stall, covered his back with a blanket, and fondly patted the big rump.

He rolled out his winter-weight sleeping bag in the next stall. The dogs settled down beside the bed. Then Gordy addressed the menagerie.

"I'll just keep you company the first night," as he settled his body onto the hay.

The End

About the Author

William (Bill) H. Smith spent his teenage years sailing the waters of Narragansett Bay. He received a bachelor's degree in Business Administration from Western New England College.

While pursuing his career in manufacturing, he developed his experience in boating, becoming an avid sailor, scuba diver, and captain. In the 1990s, he and his wife moved from New England to Florida and took up residence on the St. Johns River.

Smith currently resides in North Florida. And apart from his novel, *The Shoreline Murder(s)*, he has published poetry and has several other written works in progress. Besides his scholastic credits, he has held a United States Coast Guard captain's license and spent years as a certified diver.